MW00780374

# A VICTIM AT VALENTINE'S

ELLIE ALEXANDER

Storm
PUBLISHING

Ebook ISBN: 978-1-80508-776-2
Paperback ISBN: 978-1-80508-778-6

Cover design: Dawn Adams
Cover images: Dawn Adams

Published by Storm Publishing.
For further information, visit:
www.stormpublishing.co

## ALSO BY ELLIE ALEXANDER

*The Body in the Bookstore*
*A Murder at the Movies*
*Death at the Dinner Party*
*A Holiday Homicide*

*This book is dedicated to the real Jekyll and Hyde, two crows who befriended me at my local neighborhood pool, flying over me as I swam and waiting for me to share peanuts with them. In return, they brought me little trinkets—flowers, rocks, stickers, even car keys (DM me if you're missing a set of keys), and endless joy.*

# ONE

Love was in the air at the Secret Bookcase, the Agatha Christie-inspired bookshop where I was soon to be a partial owner. The path to my present career had been meandering and not without setbacks, but, as I hung paper hearts on pretty strings from the ceiling of the Conservatory for today's event, I realized I was happy, content—and eager to put my own spin on my beloved store. I knew better than anyone that the Secret Bookcase was so much more than a bookstore. It was a place to fully immerse yourself in the hallowed halls filled with treasure—from the yellowed pages of long-lost first editions to glossy new reads with pristine spines waiting to be cracked open. But it was also a gathering spot, where people came to find connection and a sense of community, here in the heart of our beloved town of Redwood Grove.

My colleague Fletcher Hughes and I had approached Hal Christie about the possibility of buying him out shortly before Christmas. We'd spent the last two months reviewing numbers and sketching ideas for future events, and working out plans for how we'd combine managing the store with setting up the private detective agency we would run from our office in the bookshop—the Novel Detectives.

It was a full-circle moment for me. I'd always imagined owning a detective agency during my years studying criminology, but when my best friend Scarlet was murdered the day before graduation, that dream died along with her. Now, here I was, Annie Murray, about to fulfill that dream at last, embarking on a grand new adventure. And, this weekend, welcome dozens of readers on a quest to find love.

I adjusted the ladder and adhered a cotton-candy-pink heart string to the base of the chandelier with its dangling, iridescent crystals that dripped light onto the floor like liquid diamonds in a cascade of shimmering beauty. The Conservatory was a former ballroom. Like everything else in the historic English-estate-turned-bookstore, Hal had transformed it into a special event space, retaining the original parquet floors and refurbishing the ornate gilded ceilings. A hand-painted mural depicting gardens and the bucolic countryside gave the spacious room a regal air. Large arched windows framed the far wall, offering scenic views of the grounds.

Every room in the mansion paid homage to the queen of mystery, from the Parlor with its Hercule Poirot art deco design to the Sitting Room, which resembled Miss Marple's cottage in St. Mary Mead. The Library housed our extensive collection of non-fiction titles as well as mystery reference books, while the Study provided a brooding atmosphere for new writers to pound out stories on laptops. Even the extensive grounds and gardens had touches of Agatha Christie in the form of topiaries and pathways with hidden benches tucked between lattices enshrined in wisteria and neat rows of heirloom roses.

I loved the place with all my heart, which made this weekend's event extra special. I had been approached by one of my favorite and our most loyal customers, George Richards. George was in his late seventies. He'd retired from a tech company years ago, amassing a fortune at the height of Silicon Valley's boom in the 1970s and '80s. No one knew exactly how he acquired his wealth, but according to Hal (who had known him for years), the rumor was that George had been one of the first employees of a little start-up named after a red and juicy fruit. Our proximity to San Francisco and Silicon Valley meant we weren't strangers to tech millionaires, but George was in an entirely different category.

He had become Redwood Grove's largest benefactor. His philanthropy knew no bounds. His donations funded a brand-new children's section of the library, school trips to Washington, D.C., and community enrichment programs for seniors and citizens with special needs. Additionally, and lucky for us, George was a preservationist. He worked with the local land trust to secure miles and miles of wild open spaces surrounding Redwood Grove for future generations. His nature trust ensured the extensive network of hiking trails rich with ancient redwoods and endangered species would remain available to everyone.

I bumped into him at the store a few weeks ago while restocking Emily Henry's latest romance in the Mary Westmacott Nook, aptly named for the nom de plume Agatha Christie used for her romance novels. We housed our romances in the cheerful room. It was the ultimate spot to curl up in, with its luscious floral wallpaper, framed love notes from Mr. Darcy on the walls, and jasmine-scented candles.

"Oh, Annie, you're just who I wanted to see," George had said with a low rumble in his voice. You'd never guess he was a millionaire many times over by his attire. He was dressed in a well-worn pair of jeans, a flannel, and a puffy vest. It was the standard uniform of the tech bros, and it made me chuckle that George still embraced the look. He was on the shorter side and stocky with a receding hairline. What he had lost in the way of hair, he made up for with his bushy white mustache that reminded me of a cartoon character.

"What can I do for you?" I asked, arranging the stack on the center table.

George helped me make room for the books by shifting a display of Valentine's cards. "Hal spent the better part of our chess session this week singing your praises. He's like a proud parent when he talks about you and Fletcher and your future plans for the store. I have it on good authority that you're large and in charge of events these days and are the person I should speak with about a potential project."

I gave him a wink. "Large and in charge, that's me." I pointed to my ankle boots, which gave me a much-needed albeit little lift. "Today, I might even be able to pass for five foot five."

Being short was a blessing and a curse. It was great for sneaking into crowds unnoticed but a pain when I had to retrieve a book from the top of the shelves for a customer. I kept Shakespeare's famous quote, "Though she be but little, she is fierce," hanging above my desk as a reminder that I could tackle anything.

"Ah, kid, I have bad news for you. When you hit my age, you're going to start shrinking. Enjoy that extra inch while you can. It's all downhill after about sixty." His pale blue eyes crinkled as he smiled. He gave me an exaggerated wink and tapped his forehead. "I'm just glad the little gray cells, as our friend Hal would say, are still intact. Did he mention I've bested him in the last three out of four chess matches?"

"Interesting. The only thing he's said to me is how much he enjoys your gaming sessions." Hal and George had a standing chess game every Thursday evening, rotating between houses and sharing a late evening aperitif. Their friendly banter flowed as easily as the drinks, each teasing the other about whose strategic brilliance would reign supreme on the board that week.

"Do you have an event in mind?" I asked, circling back to his initial greeting.

"As a matter of fact, I do." He picked up a vintage card and ran his thumb along the edge. "I've invested in a company that specializes in matchmaking and I think there might be an opportunity for a crossover with the store."

"Matchmaking?" I set the top book on the stack with its cover facing out. Although I doubted the inventory would last long. We couldn't keep Emily's books on the shelves, especially during February when even the most cold-blooded mystery readers who lingered in the dark and moody sections of the Parlor filled with our noir and true crime titles, would wander into the Mary Westmacott Nook for a quick "look" and end up leaving with an assortment of sweet and spicy reads.

"Yes, the owner's name is Aaliyah Kingston. She's been happily matching couples for ten years. I've reviewed her financials, business plan, and stats, and I'm extremely impressed. Her success rate is almost unbelievable. She's at a stage where she's ready to expand the business and make matches on a large scale." George smoothed the edge of his mustache like he was trying to figure out how she'd been so successful.

"That's where you come in?" I was surprised George was investing in a matchmaking company, but then again, I probably shouldn't be. His philanthropic endeavors were diverse. There was no reason his investments wouldn't also reflect his varying interests.

He nodded, blushing slightly as if I'd embarrassed him. Despite the fact that George's name was plastered on half of the village square, he was extremely humble. "As someone who has loved and lost, you might say I have a soft spot for romance. In my discussions with Aaliyah, I realized how difficult it is to meet people these days. You must know about swiping right and online dating. It sounds terrible to me. It used to be that if you were interested in someone, you asked them out on a proper date and saw where it led you."

I was impressed George was up to date in the "swipe right" lingo. I chuckled. "Yeah, it's not like that anymore." Although admittedly, I didn't have much experience with online dating. I'd dated on and off during college, but after Scarlet died, I sunk into a depression and holed myself up, terrified of losing someone else. It wasn't just grief from losing a friend. I felt responsible for her death. Everything I thought I believed and knew about my abilities was called into question. Not by anyone else. But by me. That was almost worse. I'd been at the top of my class in my criminology studies and ready to take on the world with Scarlet. After her murder, I was left floundering like a ship drifting on choppy waters without direction or an anchor.

It had taken moving to Redwood Grove and finding my footing at the Secret Bookcase to help me open up and start trusting myself again. In the process, I accidentally stumbled upon what was beginning to feel more and more like love. Liam Donovan, the owner of the Stag Head, and I had been dating since Halloween and things were going well. Really well.

I bit my bottom lip and subtly knocked on the edge of the wooden table, not wanting to jinx anything.

"What's your idea?" I asked George, pushing thoughts of Liam's ruggedly handsome features to the back of my mind temporarily.

"It's not my idea. I can't take the credit." He wagged his finger at me to clarify. "Aaliyah approached me about the possibility of doing some partnerships with bookstores. Her company is Storybook Romances, and she came up with a marketing plan to play off the storybook concept. I told her I knew the perfect store. If you're interested, I can connect the two of you."

"Sure. I'd love to chat with her and hear what she has in mind." I reached into my skirt pocket to see if I happened to have a business card on hand. I didn't. "If you want to follow me to the front, I'll give you my card."

"Wonderful." He pressed his hands together and gave me a half bow. "As long as it's not too much of an imposition."

"Not at all." I waved him off and headed for the hallway. "Valentine's Day is coming up, so maybe we can put our heads together and do something that weekend. I'm already planning a blind date with a book promotion so perhaps Aaliyah can do the real matchmaking and find readers their dream date while I concentrate on helping them fall in love with their next read."

George followed me to the Foyer where I gave him my card and promised to be in touch once I heard from Aaliyah. He didn't have to wait long because she called me later that day, gushing with excitement about the possibility of hosting an event at the Secret Bookcase.

"Annie, this is such good news." Her voice dripped with a sugary sweetness. "George is a peach. I'm so lucky to have him as a business advisor, and I'd simply love to bring Storybook Romances to the bookshop."

I picked up the slightest hint of a Jamaican accent in her tone.

"My vision would be a three-day weekend. I like to have time to get to know my clientele. I have a proprietary assessment and quiz I would need each participant to complete prior to matching them. We could do a get-to-know-you cocktail hour the first night. I find the most successful matches occur when couples have a joint interest, a shared passion, and a connection that binds them together. This is where you come in."

She paused dramatically.

I waited for her to say more, but when she didn't, I nudged her. "Okay, how do we come in?"

"How would you feel about sending pairs on a scavenger hunt through the store?"

"Fun. Yeah. I like it." A scavenger hunt was one of the many ideas on Fletcher's and my shared brainstorming board in our office. We added to it as we mapped out our event schedule for the coming year.

"I would need your book expertise. A list of popular titles in a variety of genres so I can incorporate that into my screening assessment."

"That's easy." I could talk books and book recommendations all day long.

"Excellent. Yes." Her accent came through stronger with her excitement. "I'll be in touch via email with more details. I'm looking forward to meeting you and making some love matches."

I hung up the call and immediately tracked down Fletcher. He was in our office upstairs, searching for an advanced reader copy among the many boxes we regularly received from publishing houses.

Fletcher was tall, wiry, and dressed in his normal bookstore uniform—a pair of tweed slacks and a long-sleeve button-up shirt.

"How do you feel about matchmaking?" I asked, stepping around the tower of boxes.

He dropped the book he was holding and gaped at me, his powder-blue eyes wide open. "Did you and Liam break up?"

"No. No. We're good." I shook my head and looked at him skeptically. "Why would you think that?"

"Uh, matchmaking. Why else would you ask?" The color drained from Fletcher's already pale face. "Oh no. Oh God. Are you setting me up? That's even worse, Annie. I don't know. I don't do well with dates or women in general."

"No. I'm talking about a potential Valentine's Day event," I assured him, scooting around the precarious stack of books teetering on the edge of his desk to check my calendar.

Our shared office reflected our very unique styles. My side of the office was meticulously organized. I preferred my desk bare short of my collection of colorful Sharpies, my notebook, and my desk calendar. The bookshelves adjacent to my desk were neatly arranged with advanced reader copies based on genre and pub date. Recently, I added a picture of Liam and me and snapshots of our entire crew—Pri, Penny, Hal, and Fletcher —from our holiday party. It felt good to be surrounded by my friends.

Fletcher's side of the office was controlled chaos, or maybe structured disorder. In addition to the wobbly stack of books awaiting his approval, papers and sticky notes were strewn across every section of his desk. They framed his computer monitor and spilled over onto the wall next to his Sherlock murder board. He was currently in the process of building a Lego botanical terrarium. Tiny pieces waiting to be added to the impressive framework were piled among half-chewed pencils and a massive rubber band ball.

"Oh, thank God." He exhaled heavily and tried to shift the stack of books closer to the center of the desk, but they fell to the floor in one big heap. "What kind of an event?"

I helped him pick up the books before consulting my calendar to make sure there weren't any conflicts on Valentine's weekend. Children's story time was scheduled for Saturday morning. We would read *Clifford's Valentines* and make Valentine's crafts, but that shouldn't interfere with Aaliyah's vision.

"You know George Richards?" I asked, penciling in the event on the calendar.

"Everyone knows George." Fletcher stuffed a bookmark in between two new highly anticipated rom-coms. "He's an institution in Redwood Grove."

"Exactly." I drew tiny hearts next to February fourteen. "He invested in a matchmaking business—Storybook Romances. Aaliyah, the owner and matchmaker, is expanding her clientele, and George suggested partnering with us. I just got off the phone with her. She's very enthusiastic about a weekend of bookish matchmaking."

I filled Fletcher in on the details.

When I finished, he slunk into his chair and stared out the arched windows that looked out over the gardens. "Annie, you have my full support on store events, but please, please, please promise me I don't have to be part of it?"

"You mean you don't want to be involved with this event?" That wasn't like Fletcher. I didn't want to steamroll the idea if he wasn't on board. We were going to be equal partners moving forward, and he had as much say as I did about how we managed and operated the store.

"No. I don't want to get set up." His voice cracked. "Have I ever told you about the one and only time I went on a blind date?"

"No." His painful wince was enough to tell me it hadn't gone well. "Was it bad?"

"The worst." He brushed an imaginary fleck of dust from his pressed shirt and arched his shoulders like he was trying to shrug off the memory. "We got set up by a mutual friend who knew we were both mystery buffs and figured we'd hit it off." He scoffed and tossed his head back. "I brought her two rare Sherlock and Watson trading pins. It took me a week to track them down. It seemed like a thoughtful gesture. I wore mine so that she could pick me out of the crowd. When she showed up at the restaurant, she laughed in my face and said, 'Only nerds wear trading pins.'"

"That's cruel and untrue." I wanted to give this woman a piece of my mind on Fletcher's behalf.

"Oh, that's not even the worst part." He scooped one of the Lego piles toward the center of his desk. "She took the pins anyway. Can you believe that? Why? That's weird. If she thought they were nerdy, why did she take them?"

"Excellent question," I assured him. "Probably because she was secretly excited about them but trying to act cool."

"Yeah, but for who? It was just the two of us." Fletcher shook his head and inspected a Lego piece. "Anyway, we ordered drinks. Then she excused herself to go to the bathroom, and she never came back. I waited for thirty minutes. I had one of the servers go check on her because I was worried she was sick. She must have snuck out the back. It was mortifying, Annie. The server told me she was gone. I'm such an unappealing date, she couldn't even stick around for a free drink?"

"That's terrible, Fletcher." I met his eyes and put my hand over my heart in a show of solidarity. "I'm so sorry, but it's her loss. She missed out on a gem."

"You're biased. You have to say that." He tossed the piece into the pile and dismissed me with a flick of his thin wrist. "But if you want to keep going, I'm all ears."

I chuckled. "It's true. Fletcher, you're one of my favorite people on the planet. You're so thoughtful, kind, and in tune with everyone's feelings."

"What about my superior Sherlockian knowledge?" He craned his neck and jutted out his angular chin, getting into character.

"I mean, obviously." I grinned, glad to see him pushing past his embarrassment. "That goes without saying."

His face lightened. "The problem is women don't give scrawny guys like me a second look, or in this case, even a first look. It's been true my entire life. It's nothing new. I could tell the minute she saw me she had already written me off. I don't want to go through that embarrassment again."

"Where's your Sherlock reference bible? I'll swear on it. I promise your only role for the weekend will be professional." I raised my hand, ready to swear an oath.

"You don't need to swear, but I appreciate the gesture."

I couldn't stop myself from giving him a pep talk. I hated the thought of him letting one bad date get in his head. "But, Fletcher, don't sell yourself short. You're such a catch, and you're not scrawny. You're lean and lanky. You're intelligent. You have a distinctive angular jawline and those bright, kind blue eyes. Some lucky woman is going to fall hard for you. I guarantee it."

We turned our attention to sketching out ideas for the event and dropped the subject of Fletcher's forlorn love life.

The crooning sounds of Harry Connick Jr. shook me back into the present moment. I climbed off the ladder and moved it to the windows. I had more heart garlands to hang before everyone began arriving.

Our happy hour meet and mingle was due to start in less than an hour.

I was eager to host another new offering at the store. Books were my love language, and sharing them with the community was the main aim of all the events we planned here. If readers ended up finding love at the Secret Bookcase, the holiday would be even more special. I intended to keep my promise to Fletcher and steer him clear of Aaliyah tonight. But it wouldn't do any harm to keep my eye out for potential love matches for him. There had to be someone for him. Could I put my criminology skills to a different use and sleuth out a date for him?

# TWO

I put the finishing touches on the decorations in the Conservatory. Hal came in carrying a tray of chocolate-covered strawberries. He was dressed for the occasion in slacks and a red cardigan. He was tall and thin, with thick white hair and a tightly trimmed beard. One look at his gentle eyes told you everything you needed to know about him—he was kind, calm, big-hearted. Taking a job working at the Secret Bookcase, and for Hal, was the best decision I ever made. Hal recognized my heart was raw in the early years. Instead of piling on tasks, he slowly gave me more and more autonomy as I learned to live with my grief. There was no way I'd be able to repay him for cocooning me in and providing me with a safe place to land.

"It feels like we're about to host a Regency ball. You've outdone yourself once again, Annie. Thanks for taking this project on. I know it means the world to George. He's very enthusiastic about it." He beamed at me and lifted the tray. "I assume you want these on the food table?"

"Yes, thanks, and it's no problem. It's such a unique event. Everyone is excited—love is in the air in Redwood Grove." I gave him a cheeky smile. "I need to take the ladder to the storage closet, and I'll be right back." I hoisted the ladder onto its side and carted it toward the Foyer.

The entryway was adorned with more Valentine's décor. Cling-on candy sweethearts with sayings like BE MINE and CRUSH ON U adhered to the windows. Our tea and coffee station was decked out with chocolate truffles and red velvet cookies, along with raspberry creamer and pink passionfruit tea. Customers could help themselves to a warm drink and a sweet treat to enjoy while they perused the store.

The front display included rose-scented candles, collections of poetry, cards, Jane Austen bookmarks, and journals. The pièce de résistance was our blind date with a book display. We'd wrapped dozens of titles in brown craft paper and tied them with pink gingham ribbons. Each package had handwritten clues about its contents, like: *Mystery/Suspense. The first in a ten-book series. Will keep you turning the pages, but not up all night.*

The display had turned out better than I imagined. We added Valentine's stickers and little doodles on the wrapping and organized the stacks by genre.

Fletcher stood behind the cash register. "Do you need a hand with that?"

"I'm fine." I hoisted the ladder higher and headed downstairs. We kept decorations, folding chairs and tables, and overstock in the basement. I returned the ladder and grabbed a tub of napkins before returning to the Foyer.

"I'm changing out the sandwich board to say we're closed for a private event," Fletcher said, pointing to the chalkboard. "The last customer just left, so bring on the lovesick."

"I hope they're not lovesick." I winced and gestured to the Conservatory. "I'll help Hal finish setting up the appetizers. Flag me down when Aaliyah shows up." I glanced at the typewriter clock on the wall behind the desk. I was surprised she wasn't here yet. She was supposed to arrive an hour ago.

"This is quite the spread," Hal said, pointing to the long tables we'd pushed together and draped with red tablecloths. Bouquets of carnations and miniature roses were intermixed with appetizers. In addition to the chocolate-covered strawberries, there were heart-shaped individual pizzas, pepper jelly and cream cheese bites, antipasto skewers, cannoli, and Linzer cookies.

We would serve Cupid's Punch, champagne, and pomegranate martinis, along with red and white wine.

"I can't take credit for it. The menu came from Aaliyah. She likes to do romantic tasting bites on the first night to break the ice and get guests mingling while they complete their surveys."

"I'm ready to mingle." He winked and did a little dance.

"What would Caroline say about that?" I pretended to be shocked.

"She'll be here soon, so we can ask her." When Hal smiled, the creases around his eyes deepened. "She's probably sick of me by now. She might nudge me to fill out a love match questionnaire."

"Doubtful." I took napkins out of the box and arranged them in a fluted pattern at the end of the table. Hal and Caroline, the owner of a small boutique on the village square, Artifacts, had been dating for a while now. They were planning a trip to Europe soon. I suspected that part of Hal's leaning toward retirement was due to Caroline.

"Where's the star of our show?" Hal looked around expectantly.

"Good question. I'm wondering the same thing. She should be here by now." I didn't want to worry or catastrophize, but without Aaliyah, we had a stack of books to disseminate and some delicious food to share, but not much else.

"How are your matchmaking skills?"

"Terrible. What's worse than terrible?" I laughed and hid the box underneath the skirted table. "I'm trying not to freak out, but what do we do if she doesn't show? I have no idea how to match people unless it's recommending a book."

"How many people RSVP'd?" Hal asked.

"Sixty. Can you believe it?" The response had been nearly immediate when we posted the event. Tickets included tonight's happy hour, tomorrow's scavenger hunt, dinner, a Sunday morning hike, and a closing brunch. It was a packed weekend of romantic activities, again primarily designed by Aaliyah. In our brainstorming conversations, she used the term "love immersion."

"We want couples to have ample time and opportunities to get to know one another," she had said on our call. "How a potential romantic partner behaves during a fun yet potentially competitive scavenger hunt versus a leisurely brunch can be very eye-opening."

"I can believe it," Hal said, slowly inching his hand closer to the tray of chocolate-covered strawberries. "The question is, will you scold me for stealing one of these? Quick, look over there."

I didn't fall for his trick. "I'll allow you one," I replied with my best stern frown.

"Fair enough." He bit into the juicy berry and made a face like a kid getting caught with their hand in the cookie jar.

I handed him a napkin. "For hiding the evidence."

His eyes twinkled with mischief. "If you need advice on where to stash evidence, I'm your guy. I know these walls like the back of my hand."

"You better pass on your secrets. Fletcher and I might need to alter the contract." I grinned.

"Hey, Annie, Aaliyah's here," Fletcher called from the Foyer.

"Thank goodness. Let the matchmaking begin." I patted Hal's sleeve and went to greet her.

Aaliyah swept into the Foyer with a burst of magnetic

energy. She was in her early forties with long dark hair and an infectious smile. "You must be Annie." She caught me up in a hug. "Sorry, I'm late. Traffic getting out of San Francisco was at a dead stop."

She smelled like jasmine and coconut. Her canary yellow dress accentuated her curves and striking features. She moved with precision and grace, making me wonder if she was a model in a previous life.

"No problem. I'm glad you're here, and everyone in town is buzzing about the weekend."

"Aren't you the cutest?" She clasped my hands and studied me. "Like a pixie. You mentioned you were dating someone. It's too bad because I could match you instantly."

I picked up the slightest trace of a Jamaican accent as I had on our initial phone call.

Heat spread up my cheeks. "I'm quite happy for now, but if that should change, I know who to call."

She squeezed my hands and released me. "George did not oversell this place. He's such a fan, and now I understand why. Wow." She picked up one of the vintage Valentine's cards from the front display. "Your decorations are perfection. You met my brief to the letter. Impressive. Impressive."

"Would you like a quick tour before everyone arrives?" I gestured toward the ballroom. "I think everything is ready to go."

"Yes, thank you." She adjusted one of her chunky two-inch teal earrings, which matched perfectly with her stilettos.

I showed her the Conservatory first. "We set the food against the far wall to give guests space to roam. Per your request, the smaller tables each have questionnaires and pencils. Fletcher and I went through your genre suggestions and wrapped each book per your instructions. They're stacked on the table. We set you up in front of the stage if that works." I gestured to the table where stacks of books wrapped in craft brown paper and pink ribbons waited. Aaliyah asked us to hand-select various titles, wrap them, and mark them with special stamps. Romance books had a red heart stamp in the center; cozies had magnifying glasses, while noir and true crime had bloody knives. One of the participants' first tasks was to make a "book match" by finding someone with a title they were eager to read.

"Yes, this will work. This will work just fine." She pointed to the long table at center stage and nodded with approval. "That's me? Well done."

"Yep." I moved toward the table. One of our roles in preparing for the weekend was procuring a book for each guest. Aaliyah sent us general genre recommendations based on participants' initial surveys. She gave us the green light to use our book expertise to pick titles we thought would be a good match. Fletcher and I had fun coming up with reads for everyone.

"Do you need anything else?" I asked. "We'll instruct guests to get food, have a drink, and take their time filling out the questionnaires. Once they're finished, you want them to hand them to you so you can meet each of them individually, correct?"

Aaliyah set her satchel down. "You've got it. I prefer to have a brief chat with all my matches. Body language tells me as much or more than their words."

"I can relate to that. I have a degree in criminology, and we utilize similar techniques when interrogating subjects."

"Excellent. I might recruit you for your insight depending on how quickly guests complete their surveys." Aaliyah leaned slightly toward me as she spoke, her words flowing softly like a gentle ocean breeze with the melodic lilt of her accent.

"I'm not sure matchmaking is my talent, but I'm happy to help with whatever you need."

Before she could reply, we were interrupted by George, who made a grand entrance by nearly slipping on the freshly polished floors. He caught himself on the stage. "Goodness, what a way to kick off the evening. I nearly broke a hip."

"George, be careful. Not again." Aaliyah rushed over to him. "Are you okay?"

"I'm fine. Don't fuss," George huffed. He was a bit short with her. I couldn't tell if he was embarrassed or irritated. Maybe both.

She tried to offer him a hand, but he brushed off his jacket and jeans and ignored her outstretched arm.

"George, how are you?" Hal asked, clapping his old friend on the shoulder. "Still reeling from the fact that I forced you into a position where you couldn't defend your king in our last meetup?"

George composed himself and cracked his knuckles. "I'm ready for a rematch."

"But you're off from one adventure to the next. The Maldives, Dubai, the Amalfi Coast—what's next?" Hal asked.

"Good question." George massaged his hip. "I don't know about you, but I keep praying the hips hold up. I wish I could stop and make Redwood Grove my permanent home, but alas, I can't seem to make myself stop."

"I told him he's overdoing it," Aaliyah added with a scolding shake of her finger. Her brow furrowed as she glanced at him. Then she softened her gaze and placed her hand on his shoulder. "You'll make yourself sick if you don't take it easy. You're overdoing it with the travel and everything else. You need to slow down."

"Have to make sure my investments align with my values," George replied pointedly.

Aaliyah stepped back as if she'd been stung by his words. The loaded comment deflated the joyful spirit in the air like a leaky balloon. She dragged her teeth along her bottom lip like she wanted to say more but didn't.

"How did you two get connected?" I asked, hoping to lighten the mood.

"George hired me for a private consultation," Aaliyah said, smoothing her dress and recovering her composure. "This is when I was still living on the island."

"Enough. Enough. You don't need to go into the gory details." George cut her off and looked at me. "We don't need to bore you with old stories. How can I be of service?"

I started to respond, but Aaliyah cut me off. "Actually, George, if I could steal you away for a minute. I have a few things we need to discuss." Her voice carried the warmth of the sun, but her face was stern and unyielding.

George looked like he'd rather do just about anything else, but he nodded.

"Is there somewhere we can chat privately?" she asked me, keeping her eyes locked on George as if she was concerned he would bolt.

I pointed to the long hallway. "Any of the rooms are up for grabs. The Parlor. The Sitting Room. George knows the way."

She looped her arm through his and waltzed out of the Conservatory as if they were about to lead a procession.

"I wonder what that was about." Hal ran his fingers along his white stubble, sounding concerned.

"Trouble in business paradise?" I watched them walk away. I couldn't quite get a read on their relationship. She almost seemed to be trying to pacify him as if he were a child that required watching.

"Hey, Annie, a package is here for you," Fletcher called from the Foyer, dragging my attention away from George and Aaliyah.

I glanced at the windows. Any trace of daylight had slipped away. Outside, the sky deepened to a dark lavender. The pathway was illuminated with twinkle lights, and tufts of smoke from chimneys in the village puffed into the eggplant sky. It was late for a delivery. I wasn't expecting a new book order, but publishing houses constantly sent us advanced reader copies and marketing materials for titles they were promoting.

I went to grab the package. "Did the mail just come? It's so late."

Fletcher shook his head. "No, this was on the doorstep when I went outside to put out the sandwich board. I have no idea where it came from."

The large manila envelope had my name handwritten across the front with C/O The Secret Bookcase, but there was no return address or postage.

Someone must have dropped it off.

I carefully opened it and pulled out a bundle of paperwork secured with a large blue rubber band. A watercolor card with hummingbirds sipping nectar out of wildflowers was tucked in the front. It also had my name on it.

"What is it?" Fletcher asked. "You have a weird look on your face."

"I don't know." My gut instinct told me there was something odd about the package. It wasn't from a publishing house or an indie author. I scanned the note.

Dear Annie,

I'm sorry it's taken me a while to respond. As I'm sure you'll understand, I needed time to weigh the risks. My silence doesn't secure my safety. Mark informed me of your conversation and filled me in on the details of Scarlet's death. I'm heartbroken she was killed and can't help but feel partially responsible, which is why I'm sharing this with you. I prefer to remain in hiding. Silicon Summit Partners never had my best interest at heart, and I fear if I come forward, I'll follow in Scarlet's footsteps. I was offered a large sum of money in exchange for my silence. I'm not proud of my choices, but I did what I needed to do to survive. I hope you won't judge me too harshly. I assure you, the shame I live with will haunt me for the rest of my life. These documents contain everything I know about Silicon Summit Partners. My guess is Scarlet learned the truth as well.

It's my hope that you will be the one who can finally bring justice.

With my sincere condolences,

Natalie Thompson

I put a hand to my stomach. A cold shiver washed over me as an all-consuming fear threatened to drag me to the ground.

"Annie, what? What is it?" Fletcher's eyes widened with concern.

"It's Natalie. Natalie Thompson." My hands trembled as I clutched the paperwork to my chest. Was I holding tangible proof that could finally convict Scarlet's killer?

# THREE

I tossed the packet to Fletcher and ran outside to see if I could catch whoever had left it. The driveway was deserted. Shadows merged with the soft light from the strings of twinkle lights and the solar stakes flanking the gravel lane, but there was no sign of a delivery van or driver. The long driveway spilled out onto Cedar Avenue, the main street in the village. I hurried down the lane, kicking up bits of pea gravel as I ran as fast as my legs could carry me. When I reached the end of the pathway, the shops and restaurants were bathed in a warm golden glow. Valentine's banners flapped on the streetlamps, and storefronts beckoned with romantic window displays. Otherwise, the village was relatively quiet, short of a handful of locals wandering into the Stag Head and State of Mind Public House for an early dinner.

A murder of crows soared overhead as I retraced my steps, their inky silhouettes cutting across the dusky sky. Their cries echoed into the crisp night air like a warning. It wasn't unusual to hear the crows at this time of day. They congregated in the trees in the garden. Fletcher had even taken to feeding and naming them.

But at the moment, every caw sent a chill down my spine. It was like the birds sensed a danger I couldn't see.

I'm not typically skittish, but I couldn't shake the feeling I was being watched, so I picked up my pace and kept checking behind me as I hurried back to the safety of the bookstore.

My heart pounded furiously in my chest when I returned inside. "They're gone," I said to Fletcher. "No sign of anyone. I ran down the driveway, and there was no one nearby."

"That's weird." He read and re-read the note three times. I paced from the coffee and tea station to the hallway and back. My head spun so fast that it was hard to concentrate on anything else. Ever since December, Dr. Caldwell, my former criminology professor and current lead detective in Redwood Grove, and I had been following up on dozens of leads. I'd had a big breakthrough when I tracked down a former Silicon Summit Partners employee, Mark Vincent.

My mind swirled as I reviewed everything I knew thus far.

Scarlet and I had been assigned Natalie's cold case in college. Silicon Summit Partners was an investment firm with high-profile clients. Natalie had been an executive assistant for the CEO. She was a star employee for her first few years at the company, receiving rave reviews from her coworkers, bonuses, and promotions. But then something changed. She became withdrawn and sullen. Her friends and family reported a marked difference in her personality. They were worried about her mental health and concerned about her personal safety. Natalie had gone to the local police claiming she had proof of a corruption scam involving her boss and dozens of powerful and influential leaders in the community.

The police blew her off, claiming she was on the hunt for revenge after a failed affair with her boss.

Then she went missing and was presumed dead.

When Scarlet and I began reviewing her case files, we'd discovered that there were huge gaps and clear negligence on the part of the police. The day before graduation, Scarlet set up a meeting with a new source, Bob, who she met with in secret and before turning up dead hours later.

For nearly a decade, I assumed Bob killed Natalie, but Mark dropped a bombshell when he told me Natalie was still alive; she had been in hiding all these years.

He also unintentionally (or maybe intentionally—I still wasn't sure whether he was trustworthy) called into question everything I thought I knew about Scarlet when he showed me an employment contract she signed with Silicon Summit Partners the morning she died.

"Annie, what are you thinking?" Fletcher's voice yanked me from my swirling thoughts.

"I don't know. This is huge. This could be the break we've been waiting for. I want to read everything, but there's no time. Guests will be showing up any minute." I stole a glance at the clock. My entire body pulsed with a mix of anxiety and eagerness. I thought I might throw up.

*Pull it together, Annie.*

I closed my eyes and inhaled slowly.

"It's monumental." He tapped the envelope with his index finger twice. "The Novel Detectives will be on the case, but you're right. We should table it for the short term. Especially because you never know who might be watching. It's odd the package magically appeared. How did it get here?"

"Right?" I moved closer and examined the envelope. "There's no return address or even a stamp. Someone must have hand-delivered it, but where did they go? They just vanished."

"Correct. Which is why we play our cards close to our chest. No big moves. There's a slim margin for error."

"And we need to loop Dr. Caldwell in," I said, taking the note from him and returning it to the envelope along with the documents. "I'm going to put this in my desk upstairs. We'll deal with it after we get through round one of The Dating Game."

Fletcher bobbed his head in agreement. "For now, we keep it under wraps."

My heart thudded against my chest as I climbed the stairs. It wouldn't hurt to take a quick look, but then again, it would. I knew I couldn't let it go, and whatever paperwork Natalie had shared needed careful time and attention. I knew myself too well. Once I was on a case, especially anything involving Scarlet, it became like an obsession. I was like a dog digging for a bone. Once I started, I wouldn't be able to stop.

*You've waited this long,* I reminded myself. *A few hours aren't going to matter.*

By the time I'd secured the envelope in my desk and returned downstairs, people were already starting to arrive. The atmosphere was electric. I could feel the eager excitement of readers, hoping tonight might be the night they met their future spouse or partner.

Aaliyah greeted everyone at the door.

I took a few minutes to collect my thoughts by walking through the store. The gas fireplace had been lit in the Sitting Room. Its floral-papered walls and cozy collection of plush chairs with throw pillows provided a perfect spot for couples to chat and get to know each other better. I fluffed up a heart-shaped pillow the color of the wild orchids that bloomed in the English garden outside and readjusted the Tiffany lamp on the antique desk.

Then I moved on to the Parlor with its Poirot-inspired art deco designs—sleek lines, rich jewel tones, and touches of brass and gold. Perched upon one of the dark wooden bookcases were a pair of fake crows. Their glossy black feathers looked unnervingly lifelike in the dim light.

I jumped and threw my hand to my chest.

*Geez, Annie. Jumpy much?*

I let out a long sigh and turned the dial on the fireplace higher. The room had a bit of a chill. Or maybe it was just me.

The crows' beady eyes seemed to follow my every move.

What were they trying to tell me?

Was I in danger?

Was Scarlet's killer nearby?

Normally, I would blow it off as my overactive imagination, but the more I learned about Natalie and the cold case, the more convinced I was that I was closing in on Scarlet's killer.

I shook it off and returned to the Conservatory, which was humming with activity. I ducked behind the food table to help pour drinks.

One of the first people I spotted in line was one of our regulars I hadn't seen for a while, Gertrude Demeyere. Gertrude recently moved to Redwood Grove and "found her people," as she liked to say, at the bookstore. Last month, she'd celebrated her seventieth birthday with a high tea in the Sitting Room. She invited her book club friends and treated them to finger sandwiches, petit fours, and tarts. It was hard to believe she was seventy. Her energy matched that of someone much younger. She was very friendly and always chatting up people in the store, talking about her favorite books and offering her personal recommendations. She reminded me of our very own Miss Marple, with her white curls that could only be achieved with old-school rollers and her tendency to wear hand-knit sweaters and practical shoes.

"Hey, stranger. Where have you been lately?" I asked as she approached the table.

"Annie, I've missed that bright smile of yours. It's wonderful to see you, dear." Her eyes landed on the champagne. "Do I help myself to a glass?"

"Please." I swept my hand in that direction. "And don't be shy. We have appetizers and treats."

"I'll start with the champagne. A little nip to settle the

nerves." She scrunched her curls as she picked up a glass. "I've missed the store, too. I was overseas visiting my sister and niece. It was a nice trip, but it's even better to be home."

"Are you participating in the matchmaking tonight?" I asked with a hopeful smile. Gertrude had often talked about her long-lost love, Walter. They dated in their twenties, but Walter had died in a tragic accident, and Gertrude had been single ever since. I handed her a glass of champagne.

Her lips puckered as she sipped the champagne. "My friends signed me up. Can you believe it? Who is going to want to date this saggy little old lady?"

I let my mouth hang open. "Hey, no. You're a stunner and so jovial. We always say we need to hire you because anytime you suggest a book to a stranger, they buy it. I think you hand-sell more books than Hal, Fletcher, and I combined."

"That's because I'm a book pusher." She raised her eyebrows as she took another drink. "It's the former English teacher in me. I can't stop myself. I try. I say, 'Now, Gertrude, leave that poor, unsuspecting woman alone. She wants to browse in peace.' The next thing I know, I'm piling book after book into her arms."

"On behalf of the Secret Bookcase, let me thank you." I pressed my hands together in gratitude. "I love that you're going to join in the matchmaking fun. You never know, the love of your life could be in this very room tonight."

Her smile faded. She fiddled with the gold ring she wore on a chain around her neck. "I know I've told you this dozens of times, but I'm afraid I lost the love of my life a long, long time ago. My friends insist it's not too late. I don't agree, but I'll give it a shot, mainly to get them off my back. What do I have to lose?"

"That's the spirit." I handed her one of Aaliyah's compatibility tests. "Your first task, after you load up a plate of appetizers, is to complete this form. Then take it over to the woman seated by the stage. She's our professional matchmaker this weekend. She'll give you your next task and a book that will be part of tomorrow's scavenger hunt."

Gertrude looked in that direction. She moved her oversized candy-apple-red glasses to the tip of her nose, leaned forward, and squinted. "Oh dear. Oh my. Am I seeing things? No, no. It can't be. Ghosts? Is that—"

"Is that what?" I glanced at Aaliyah. She was seated behind the table, chatting with a young woman I didn't recognize. George hovered over her shoulder. I got the impression tonight was a performance review. Was he worried he'd made a bad investment in Storybook Romances?

"I'm sorry. I need to use the restroom." Gertrude abandoned her champagne glass and, despite her age, moved briskly out of the ballroom. Her steps were much quicker than I would have imagined. She brushed past a young couple exchanging numbers, smashing into their high-top table and bouncing off it like a ball. She didn't bother to stop or apologize. Instead, she stole another glance behind her and darted toward the Foyer without hesitation.

That wasn't like Gertrude.

She was clearly in a hurry to leave, but why?

What had spooked her?

# FOUR

I didn't have time to dwell on my exchange with Gertrude because the line for drinks grew as more eager participants funneled in. I filled wine glasses and watched guests become more animated and at ease as they sipped wine and mingled. The room grew thick with the scent of perfumes and cologne mixed with the earthy aroma of the hors d'oeuvres.

Light melodies floated from the speakers, blending with laughter and clinking glasses. The velvet green curtains that framed the large arched windows provided a glimpse of the darkness settling in outside. But the ballroom was charged with energy and anticipation and warmth.

It helped me take my mind off Scarlet and the mysterious note from Natalie, at least momentarily.

When the line finally died down, I took a few pictures we could use on social media and in the store newsletter, and then I texted Liam.

Liam was working at the Stag Head tonight, but I promised to keep him updated on the event and whether anyone found a love match.

> The dating games have begun!

> Packed house. Well done, Murray. Any bets on who's going to pair up first?

I scanned the ballroom. It was too early to tell, but clearly, even without Aaliyah's help, a handful of couples had already splintered off to private corners, cozying up between the rows of bookshelves in the back and at the two-person high-top tables scattered throughout the room. Others lingered over their surveys, considering each question with the utmost seriousness as if it were an AP exam.

> Not yet.

> As long as you don't get any ideas about joining in on the matchmaking.

> Me? Never.

> Good. Because I'm kind of into you, Annie Murray.

> Kind of?

I sent him the shocked face emoji.

> You can do better than that, Donovan.

> We're still on for dinner, right? I'll dazzle you with my delectable cuisine and superb conversation. You won't be able to resist my natural charms.

I chuckled.

Our banter was one of the things I enjoyed most about our ever-deepening connection.

> I'll be counting down the minutes.

He responded with a clock emoji.

I put my phone away and returned to serving drinks.

A middle-aged woman swept up to the table like a dancer or actress taking the stage. She swirled her skirt and picked up one of the questionnaires. I had to blink twice because she looked like the spitting image of Professor Trelawney from Harry Potter with her long silk scarves and a flowing shawl that stretched to the floor and surrounded her like a cloud of mystery. Heavy, ornate jewelry adorned her wrists and every finger—rings with large glimmering stones and bracelets that clinked as she moved. Her neck was draped in layers of beads, charms, and pendants.

"Are we supposed to fill these out?" She squinted at the form like it was difficult to see.

"If you're participating in the matchmaking events, yes." I motioned to the food and drink. "Please help yourself to appetizers and cocktails."

"Do you work here or for the matchmaker?" She folded the paper in half and creased the edge meticulously before securing it between the pages of the leather-bound journal tucked under her arm.

"I work here. I'm Annie Murray." I extended my hand in a greeting.

She rested the journal on the edge of the table. Instead of shaking my hand, she clasped it tight and turned my palm face up. "Annie, I'm Elspeth Prachett. Let me take a closer look at your heart, head, and life lines."

"What?"

"Don't worry. I'm a professional palm reader and psychic." She pulled my hand inches away from her face. "Oh, interesting. Interesting. I see a divergence of paths here on your life line. A significant event occurred. Something tragic. See how your lifeline is fractured here?"

I watched in stunned silence as she traced the lines on my hand with the tip of her finger.

"This was in the past. The lines split, but you're on your new path now. I see good things for your future and what a strong, solid heart line. You have deep emotion and a sensitive soul. It's a strong combination with your head line—analytical thinking, creative problem-solving, and high intelligence. A tendency to take too much on. Is this resonating?" Her jewelry, along with the scarves and shawl, gave her an almost other-worldly presence.

Was she in my head?

She had pretty much captured my personality.

How?

By tracing the lines in my hand?

"Uh, I guess. I've never had my palm read." I tried to pull my hand back, but she kept a tight clasp.

"It's very revealing. Interpreting lines comes from years of palmistry practices. While individual readings may vary, the palm can tell us so much about our soul's purpose and emotional center." She followed a curved line that arched around the base of my fingers. "You have the Girdle of Venus. It's quite rare."

"What does it mean?" I asked, wary of her intensity. She could use some work on her personal space boundaries.

"It's a sign of heightened emotional sensitivity and intense passion. You have a deep appreciation for the arts, don't you?"

Well, I worked at a bookstore, so that wasn't exactly a stretch.

She released her grip and waited for my response.

"I do enjoy the arts," I acquiesced.

"You have a talent for them, too. I'm an artist like you. I'm working on a novel as we speak." She reached for her journal and massaged the leather, petting it as if it were a soft kitten.

I needed a minute to get centered. Her spontaneous palm reading had thrown me for a loop. She had nailed my personality, but how much of that was the lines etched in my hand versus her initial impression of me?

George joined us, clearing his throat and giving Elspeth a nod of acknowledgment. "Might I trouble you for a drink, Annie?"

"Sure, what can I get you?"

"I wouldn't turn down a glass of bubbly." His eyes drifted to the bottles of champagne chilling on ice.

Elspeth stared at him like his hair was on fire. I could only imagine the stories she was weaving in her head in preparation for "reading" him. I wished there was a way I could subtly warn him.

"One glass of bubbly for the mastermind behind tonight," I said, handing him his drink.

Elspeth looked at me with wild eyes and then back to him again. Then she gripped his arm, nearly spilling his champagne. She stared at him in horror, throwing her other hand against her chest. "Oh, dear. This is bad. I sense dark, dark energy around you. Your aura is black. As black as a starless sky."

George cleared his throat. "Excuse me?"

She pulled her hand away and looked at it like it was contaminated. She brushed her hands together and blew on them like she was attempting to rid herself of the energy. "You're in danger. Deep, deep danger."

# FIVE

Elspeth's coppery eyes were wild with fear. She waved her hands in tiny, rapid circles. Her scarves, baubles, and charms jangled as she spoke in a panicked rush. "Do you see it? Do you sense it, too? This is dark energy. The energy of death."

George chuckled and rolled his eyes. He raised his glass in a toast. "That's because I'm an old man."

"No. No." Her voice rose. "This is different. This is toxic. You're under a dark spiritual attack, sir."

George caught my eye and shrugged. He tipped the glass to his lips and chugged the champagne. Had she gotten under his skin, too?

I was speechless, which was rare for me. Elspeth appeared genuinely concerned for George, but was it an act? I half expected her to ask him for money next, suggesting she could rid him of the dark energy with a simple spell for the low, low cost of a thousand dollars.

"We need to cleanse your aura immediately." She closed her eyes and swept her arm from his toes to the top of his head.

"I'm fine." George stopped her, physically blocking her by

turning his torso toward me. "Annie, could I trouble you to top me off?"

"Of course." I caught his drift and refilled his drink.

"Wait, you can't just walk away." Elspeth sounded frantic. She tried to grab him, but he ducked out of her grasp. "You need an aura cleanse. A protection charm. Maybe more."

I was starting to wonder if there was more going on with her. Could she be emotionally unstable?

"I can and I will. My aura is fine and dandy." He lifted his fluted glass and tipped his head in a half bow before strolling away with a pronounced casual ease.

Elspeth wrung her hands together like she was trying to wash off the energy. "This is terrible. He's in danger. I've only seen a black aura twice in my career, and each time, they ended in death."

I wasn't sure how to respond.

She studied me with a new intensity. "Your aura, on the other hand, is a soft glowing blue. That represents calmness and tranquility. Blue auras are associated with clear and concise communication and signify truthfulness and honesty."

"Maybe it's the lighting in here," I suggested, gesturing to the dimly lit chandeliers. Fletcher intentionally turned the overhead lights on low to create a romantic atmosphere.

"No. That's not how auras work. His is black. Jet black. I see a midnight sky. He's in grave, grave danger." She swiped at one of the pendants around her neck and swung it from side to side.

"It's good you warned him, then." However, I had no clue what George was supposed to do with that information.

She squinted and leaned over the table, once again invading my personal space as she tried to peer into my soul. "You have bird energy around you. Yes, yes, I sense the birds are drawn to you."

I pulled away from her.

Out of everything she could have suggested—what were the odds it would be birds? My mind immediately flashed to the crows. I didn't want to give her any indication that she had hit on something that resonated. "We have large communities of crows and other birds that live in the gardens."

"No. It's not that. You carry the energy of the crow—intelligent, observant, and deeply intuitive. Crows are the guardians of hidden knowledge. You have the ability to see beyond the surface, just like the crows, uncovering truths others might miss. You should listen to what they have to tell you. If you open yourself up and pay attention, they'll share their secrets."

It was clear that there was no rationalizing with her. I decided the best approach was to try and refocus her attention. "Can I get you something to drink before you fill out the questionnaire? We're expecting a large turnout, so this might be a good time for you to chat with Aaliyah before things get busy."

"I'll take a glass of Cupid's Punch. I need to stay clear-headed." Her gaze followed George as he drifted toward the Foyer. The punch was a non-alcoholic mixture of cranberry juice, pomegranate juice, and ginger ale. Each drink was topped with a maraschino cherry, pink sprinkles, and a red-and-white-striped paper straw.

"And good idea. Maybe she'll be able to help me convince George that he's in peril. Please keep an eye on him. I can't begin to explain how terrifying it is to see a black aura."

"I will," I assured her.

I took a deep breath and turned to see a new line had started to grow as everyone was ready for a second round. I poured drinks and encouraged everyone to fill their plates and fill out their dating match surveys. Pri snuck behind the table and jumped in to help me.

"Hey, bestie, you look like you could use a professional barista." She pressed her hand to her chin and posed for me. Pri was tall with long, smooth dark hair, a heart-shaped face, and eyes that lit up any room. She was dressed in a pair of flowing khaki pants and a burnt-pumpkin V-neck sweater that brought out the warm tones in her skin.

I was always jealous. My fair skin burned at the mere sight of the sun. No matter how much sunscreen I applied after a few minutes outside, my freckles emerged like a dusting of cinnamon.

"I can always use a professional barista," I teased.

"Put me to work. How can I help?" She rolled up her sleeves and cracked her knuckles.

"Could you open a couple more bottles of champagne? It's the drink of the night." I poured the last of the bottle into a glass.

"Yeah, because champagne." Pri's mouth twisted into a goofy smile as she effortlessly uncorked the bottle. "One for the guests and two for me, right?"

"As long as you pour one for me, too." I winked.

We spent the next thirty minutes making sure everyone had a fresh drink in hand and understood they needed to complete their questionnaires and return them to Aaliyah.

When the line finally died down, Pri poured us glasses of champagne. "Here's to love."

"To love." I clinked my glass to hers. "Speaking of love, where's Penny?"

Penny, Pri's girlfriend, had become a dear friend of mine. Penny had moved to Redwood Grove last year and purchased the old Wentworth farmhouse on the outskirts of town. Her passion project had turned into a massive renovation. She'd spent months and depleted her bank account getting the house up to code and livable. Someone without her resolve and tenacity may have given up, but she was steady and solid. The payoff had been worth it. She had transformed the farmhouse into an elegant and comfortable home with gleaming original hardwood floors and new paint and light fixtures. Her aesthetic was a balance of modern and vintage. She had added rich wallpaper accents to the living room and bedrooms, restored the fireplaces, and pulled in touches of warmth and color with handwoven rugs, Northern California coastal artwork, and a statement piece in the form of stained-glass entry windows.

Her latest endeavor involved a major overhaul of the orchard, vineyards, and barn. Renovations were currently in progress. I had no doubt that Penny's vision of a family-friendly event space would come to fruition. Her plans involved summer concerts, wine tasting, apple picking, cider pressing, and so much more.

Her measured and introspective lens was a lovely match for Pri's big, bold energy. They balanced each other beautifully.

"She's got a big pitch for work, but she's going to join us for dinner tomorrow."

"Great."

"What about your vampire?" Pri stabbed her fingers into her neck like fangs.

She had nicknamed Liam "the vampire" after he'd dressed up like Dracula for Halloween.

"He's working at the bar tonight, but I'm going to stop by after we're done here if you want to join me."

"And third wheel your date? No way." She scowled as she took a sip of her champagne. "Have you seen Fletcher, though? Talk about smitten. He's fawning over a woman I didn't recognize."

"What?" I glanced toward the Foyer. Fletcher was still at the front counter, but he wasn't alone. He was leaning against the edge of the long wooden counter and chatting quite comfortably with a woman I didn't recognize. "Who's that? And is Fletcher Hughes actually flirting?" I clasped my hand over my mouth.

*Fletcher flirting.*

I never thought I'd see the day.

"Uh, I'd say that's a yes, but what do I know about flirting?" Pri lifted her arms up as if she was stumped. "I tried to get his attention when I came in just to say hi, but he was completely captivated, like literally hanging on her every word and they've been like that this whole time."

"I can't believe it. The irony is that he begged me not to set him up or involve him in any part of the matchmaking."

"Looks like love found him organically." Pri raised her glass in a toast.

I couldn't wait to find out who the mystery woman was and how they had hit it off so quickly, and was setting down my glass to scoot over, but just then a commotion broke out near the stage. I looked over to see that Aaliyah was on her feet, holding a young woman away from George.

"Hey, that's Linx," Pri said, frowning and putting her glass down like she was preparing to help break up the fight.

"Who's Linx?"

"She's training as a barista at Cryptic. We're doing a trial run to see if she's a good fit. She's been shadowing me for the last week. I told her to stop by tonight at the end of her shift because I've put her on coffee and pastry duty here tomorrow morning. I figured she should get a look at the setup. But why in the world is she yelling at George Richards?"

"Good question." I turned in that direction as the chatter and conversations in the crowded ballroom stopped.

Linx was as short as me, with neon red hair streaked with chunky sections of black. She was covered in piercings, and her fiery body language matched her vibe. George held her off with a book wrapped in brown paper. She lunged at him.

Aaliyah stepped between them.

"I just want to talk to him," she yelled, trying to get past Aaliyah.

Aaliyah stood firm like his personal bodyguard. "This isn't the time or place."

Had Elspeth warned her about George's black aura?

Why else would she feel the need to protect him?

George whispered something to Aaliyah. Whatever he said did the trick because she stepped to the side. He nodded to Linx, tucked the book under his arm, and motioned to the Foyer. They left together.

"That's weird." Pri watched them go.

"Do they know each other?" I asked.

"I don't think so. Linx just moved to Redwood Grove. She has previous barista experience and dropped off a resume at the shop. When I looked it over, I figured it was worth giving her a chance. She's skilled. She knows her stuff. The customer service side of things could use some massaging, but she's got a natural palate for coffee."

"Maybe they had an altercation at the shop," I suggested. "Could George have been rude to her, and she recognized him now?"

"I guess it's possible, but I never heard about it if it happened." Her brow creased as she concentrated like she was reviewing past interactions. "Plus, George is a teddy bear. He always gives generous tips and remembers little details about my personal life. I can't imagine him being rude, but I suppose he could have had a bad day."

That was my impression of George, too.

Something stirred internally. A gut feeling.

It was a feeling I was all too familiar with.

Something was off with George.

First, Elspeth's warning. Now Linx.

Like Pri, I'd found George to be nothing but kind. He didn't strike me as the type of person to inflame situations or instigate conflict, but I couldn't shake the ominous feeling settling over me that there was something going on.

# SIX

Aaliyah called everyone to attention. "Greetings, my love seekers, and welcome to a weekend that could forever alter the course of your future. Tonight, we're here to turn the page on your love story. No cliff-hangers. Only happy endings. Take a look around this room. The love of your life very well could be standing inches away from you."

Soft murmurs broke out as people glanced around the ballroom with hopeful anticipation.

"I've gathered your surveys and will begin making matches shortly. With the help of the staff at the Secret Bookcase, I've carefully curated a book for each of you. They'll play into tomorrow's events, so if you haven't picked up your book match, be sure to do so before you leave." She motioned to the dwindling stack on the table. "Feel free to stay and mingle for a while. Our next event kicks off at ten a.m. tomorrow morning. We'll gather here again for coffee and pastries. Then you'll be sent throughout the bookstore on a scavenger hunt to find your first match. We have a full day of activities, from a botanical garden tour to lunch on the terrace, followed by dinner, trivia, and karaoke at State of Mind Public House tomorrow night.

Rest up because you're in for a weekend of romance." She blew the crowd a kiss.

Everyone applauded.

"She's confident," Pri whispered. "What if no one makes a match?"

"I was wondering the same thing." I grimaced at the thought. I didn't want ours to be the first event that failed to couple people up. "In our planning conversations, she told me she has a one hundred percent success rate. She's never failed to match at least one couple."

"Yeah, but for how long? Like one date?" Pri focused her walnut-colored eyes on Aaliyah. "That's a bold claim. It could mean that she paired up two people who went on one date and then split. I'd like to see her long-term statistics. Like how many marriages have come from her matchmaking? I want to see hard numbers."

"Look at you, Ms. Skeptical."

Pri was typically on board for pretty much anything, from a spontaneous trip to the beach to watch the annual dog-surfing competition to a girls' night where we binge-watched *Gilmore Girls* and ate as much takeout food as we could possibly consume. She was also Redwood Grove's unofficial match-maker. She'd been instrumental in nudging me toward Liam and highlighting his best qualities and the fact that he had a crush on me.

"Show me the facts." She tapped her hand onto her palm like she wanted immediate proof. "That's all I'm saying. It feels a lot like a scam if you ask me. How much money is Aaliyah making this weekend?"

"A decent amount. She's taking forty percent of the cost of the tickets. The rest covers her expenses—our fee for renting the bookstore, food, etc. I'm actually curious to learn more about her business relationship with George. It seems like an odd thing for him to invest in, and when she started to tell me about how they met and how he got involved in the business, he cut her off like he didn't want her to go into detail."

"Probably because he's having second thoughts. He's a good guy, after all. I bet he took a closer look at her financials and realized how unethical it is—profiting from someone's desperation to find love. Who wants to back a company that preys on emotions and plays with people's hearts?" She made a face. "I don't like it."

"But it's also a fun weekend. I don't think the ticket price is outrageous and she does have some great events planned. If I were single, I would enjoy it even if I didn't find a match." I found myself defending Aaliyah, but it was true.

She blew a long breath through her lips like a motorboat. "Yeah, you're right. I know you've put a ton of work into this. I'm not trying to yuck your yum. It's a touchy subject for me."

"Matchmaking?" I was surprised. Pri had never mentioned anything about having bad experience with getting set up. She'd pined for Penny before working up the courage to speak to her, but otherwise, she always struck me as so self-assured.

"I never told you this, but my mom tried to get me to use an Indian matchmaker. It's still customary in Jaipur, her hometown. Matchmakers there are like dating apps here. She likes to remind me that she and my dad had an arranged marriage and that ninety percent of marriages in India are arranged."

"Really? I didn't know that. Did she put a lot of pressure on you?"

"You have no idea." Pri rolled her eyes. "This was before I came out to them. She would call at least once a week and say, 'Priya, I've found a good Indian man for you. You can meet him tonight for dinner at our house.'"

"Did you go?" This was a side of my friend I'd never known about. I was glad she was opening up about her family and past. "Was this before we met?"

"Yeah." She nodded. "This was during college and shortly

after. I couldn't take it anymore. Annie, the dinners were so awkward. The guys didn't want to be there either. When I finally worked up the courage to tell them the truth, I was so nervous. I thought they might disown me. But thankfully, they were much more supportive than I thought they might be, but then she started to try to set me up with other Indian women."

I chuckled. "I think it's sweet."

Pri furrowed her brow and groaned. "You try being set up by your *mom*, and then we'll talk."

"Yeah, you win." I threw my hands up. "I would never let my mom set me up. Never."

"Exactly." She nodded her head enthusiastically. "Now that Penny and I are dating, she's shifted her focus to wedding plans. She called this morning to ask me when we're getting married. I reminded her that we've been dating for less than a year. That didn't stop her."

I wrapped my arm around her shoulder. "Your mom sounds very similar to someone I know and love."

Pri gasped. "Annie, how could you? I'm nothing like my mom, and just for that, I'm going to sic her on you and Liam. Get ready for the full Indian matchmaking mom experience."

I laughed.

Her response to Aaliyah made much more sense. I wasn't going to argue with her about the potential for readers to find love. I was still holding out hope that guests would end the weekend with a new stack of reads and someone to snuggle up with.

Aaliyah finished her closing remarks and reminded everyone to be at the bookstore in the morning, ready to take on their first challenge. Pri got swept into a conversation with someone she knew from Cryptic. I snuck to the Foyer to get a better look at the woman Fletcher had been flirting with.

They were still deep in conversation when I approached the

front counter, clearing my throat loudly to make my presence known. "How are things going?"

Fletcher startled and grabbed his chest. "Annie, you scared the living daylights out of me."

The woman tilted her head back and laughed hysterically. "'Scared the living daylights,' who says that anymore?"

Fletcher puffed out his chest, standing taller. "It comes with the territory when you work here."

She batted her long lashes at him. "Don't I know it. It's refreshing to speak with someone in the industry."

I would guess she was in her mid-thirties. She was as tall as Fletcher, dressed in a red mini dress and high heels. She wore her hair in a tight, modern bun that gave off a no-nonsense, all-business vibe, like someone who made meticulous plans and always stuck to them. It was a strange contrast with her outfit, which was better suited for clubbing.

"Are you in the book business?" I asked with genuine interest.

Fletcher fumbled with a stack of books waiting to be wrapped and added to our blind date with a book display. "Oh, right. Annie, meet Victoria Carlton-Ivers. She works for Book Emporium."

*Book Emporium?*

Book Emporium was a big-box chain store with locations throughout California. It was notorious for undercutting pricing and offering aggressive discounts that stores like ours couldn't afford to match. Recently, it secured several exclusive deals with major publishing houses to get special releases from bestselling authors. Its massive advertising and marketing budget paled in comparison to ours. Two longstanding independent bookstores in Southern California had to close after a Book Emporium moved into the area.

I wouldn't go so far as to say that Book Emporium was our nemesis, but enemy, maybe.

"Nice to meet you," I said, extending my hand and glancing at Fletcher, trying to catch his eye. He wouldn't look at me. He kept his eyes on Victoria. "What brings you to our indie bookshop?"

"This event. I couldn't resist. I've been following Storybook Romances for a while, and when I saw they were partnering with you all, I absolutely had to come join in the fun." She tipped her head to the side and gazed at Fletcher with dewy eyes.

Was he falling for this?

I didn't trust Victoria for even the slightest second. It was highly unlikely she had ventured to Redwood Grove in search of romance—more like in search of trade secrets. She was probably planning on taking copious notes in order to copy our event.

Fletcher was oblivious.

She must have sensed that she could butter him up and glean information from him.

There was no chance I was going to let her use my friend.

"You should probably fill out the questionnaire. Aaliyah is starting to match people now." I pointed behind us.

Victoria hesitated. "Sure. I wouldn't want to miss out on a match."

Fletcher shook his head, looking briefly crestfallen but trying to sound upbeat. "No, don't let me hold you up."

"It's been a pleasure, Fletcher. I do hope we'll have a chance to continue our conversation as the weekend goes on." Victoria held her hand out like a character from a Jane Austen novel.

Was she expecting him to kiss it?

He froze like he wasn't sure what to do.

Victoria held her hand higher and wiggled her blood-red nails.

He clasped her fingers and shook them gently.

I wanted to jump in and save him, but Victoria pulled away.

"I'm looking forward to seeing more of you." She swept toward the ballroom, giving him a final glance that made it seem like a struggle to part from him.

"Well, well, well, Fletcher Hughes, what am I going to do with you?" I rested my elbows on the counter and narrowed my eyes at him.

He scowled as his eyes followed her into the Conservatory. "What do you mean?"

"Hanging out and sweet-talking the *enemy*."

"Victoria isn't the enemy." He threw his hands over his chest in a protective stance as his pale cheeks blotched with color.

"She works for Book Emporium, Fletcher. How many conversations have we had about your disdain for their business practices?"

"That's different. That's corporate." He picked up a ball-point pen and clicked it on and off nervously.

"Is she a bookseller?" It wasn't fair of me to assume her status in the company based on how she was dressed, but Victoria didn't strike me as the personality type to hand-sell books.

"Uh, I don't know. It didn't come up. She mentioned working for Book Emporium, but then our conversation drifted, and I never asked her what she does."

"I would bet money she works for corporate."

Fletcher sighed and doodled on a sticky note.

I hated bursting his bubble. I needed to dial it back. I didn't want to crush his hopes, but I also didn't want him to get caught up in something that could end badly for him. Then again, it probably wasn't fair of me to immediately assume the worst about Victoria.

"She seems nice," he said after a minute.

"I'm sorry for coming on so strong," I said, softening my tone. "When I heard Book Emporium, I guess I freaked out."

"Me too." He nodded. "But we were talking for almost an hour, and she's down-to-earth. We have a lot in common. I think you should give her a chance."

"I will," I promised. What I didn't say out loud was that I was also going to keep an eye on Victoria Carlton-Ivers. This weekend was about love, and I wasn't going to risk my friend getting his heart broken by a potential corporate mole.

# SEVEN

The rest of the evening was relatively uneventful. People lingered for a while. I took over the register for Fletcher. Sales were steady as readers left with new romances, candles, and bundles of blind dates with a book. As I'd hoped, they were a hit.

Hal wandered into the Foyer as the last of the guests trickled out. "Another smashing success, Annie."

"Thanks. I think it went well. Tomorrow is when the real fun begins."

He smiled, but it didn't reach his eyes.

"Is something wrong?" I asked, tucking cash into the register.

"I'm concerned about George." He rubbed the base of his neck. "He asked about coming up for a cup of tea or nightcap later. He said he had something he needed to get off his chest. Then he left with the barista, so I'm unsure if he's still planning to stop by. I tried to make light of things and mentioned that I'd be willing to take him on for a not-so-friendly late-night round of chess with a drink, but he didn't so much as crack a smile. It's not like him. He seizes any opportunity to rib me about our ongoing competition. He was distracted and out of sorts. Not at all like himself."

The Foyer was empty. Aaliyah was still in the Conservatory with Fletcher and Victoria, but otherwise, the bookstore was quiet. I hadn't seen George either since he left with Linx.

"Did you hear Elspeth's warning to him?" I wondered if that could be the cause of George's shift in behavior.

"No. Who's Elspeth?" Hal unbuttoned the top button on his cardigan and poured himself a mug of chamomile tea. "Would you like a cup?"

"I'm meeting Liam for a late bite soon." I shook my head. "I'm sure you saw Elspeth. She's hard to miss. She's the one wearing like a thousand scarves, necklaces, and gaudy jewelry. She's a writer and psychic. She told George his aura was black, which is apparently a bad omen."

"When was this?" Hal plunged the tea packet into the steaming water.

I tidied the counter and made sure everything was back in its original place. End-of-day store cleanup was the bane of every bookseller. We spent a good thirty minutes every night and sometimes longer reshelving items misplaced by customers. "Not long after we opened the doors."

"Hmm." Hal blew on his tea. "That's odd. I believe I saw them in the Parlor shortly before he left if she's who I'm thinking of. You said she's wearing a lot of scarves?"

"Yep. That's her. I wonder if she followed him. She was intent on cleansing his aura and doing some kind of protection spell on him. I think it's her thing. The minute she met me, she grabbed my hand and read my palm without asking if I was interested in her insight—if we can call it that. She was even more forceful with George. I have to admit, even though I'm sure her abilities are a practiced skill, she rattled me."

"I'm not sure I buy into palm reading and psychic predictions either, but I will say George was terribly upset when we spoke." Hal took a timid sip of his tea. Once he realized it had cooled off enough, he took a longer drink.

"Was this when you saw them in the Parlor?" I asked.

"No. It was later. I found him alone in the Mary Westmacott Nook. He was in tears, Annie." Hal's forehead creased into a frown. "He was quite distraught, shaking, inconsolable. That's when I suggested he come up for a drink later or a game of chess."

"Really." I thought back to the conversation between him and Elspeth. He appeared to blow her off in the moment. He didn't seem concerned about her warning or being in imminent danger, but perhaps he had masked his fears.

"I stayed with him. He was fairly incoherent, talking about his past and mistakes. I listened, but I'm not sure I was much help." Hal crossed his arms over his chest, not out of defensiveness, but like he was holding himself together while he thought.

"Don't sell yourself short. I'm sure having a listening ear and a friend nearby made a difference. He didn't say why he was upset?"

Could Elspeth's warning have hit him harder than he initially let on? I picked up on the tension between him and Aaliyah, and Linx had instigated an argument. Maybe George put on a brave face in front of me and everyone else and then slipped into the Mary Westmacott Nook to break down privately. A swell of sadness washed over me. George had always been incredibly kind and gone out of his way to make my day brighter whenever he came into the store.

What could have happened to cause him to break down?

"He wasn't making sense," Hal replied. "He was muttering about broken promises and big mistakes."

"Broken promises and big mistakes," I repeated.

Could he be referring to business partnerships gone bad?

Pri's perspective on George's involvement with Aaliyah might be correct. Perhaps he believed her efforts and vision were more altruistic than the reality. That could have led to conflict between them and explained why she was coddling him.

"Yes." Hal took a long sip of the tea, considering the words. "It's odd, isn't it?"

"Do you think it's related to his investment in Storybook Romances? Or other business ventures?" I remembered how he'd seemed to hover over Aaliyah despite her competence.

"Perhaps." He sighed quietly. "Although, it seemed personal, as if he had opened an old emotional wound."

"Is he still here? I could try to talk to him," I offered.

"No. He left out the back. He said he had things to fix."

"Things to fix. Did he say anything else?"

"Not a word. He clapped me on the shoulder and thanked me for being a good friend. That's why I'm upset. There was an odd finality to his tone." A quiver entered his voice, a telltale indication of the depth of his concern.

I didn't like the sound of that.

"Are you worried he might do something drastic?"

"I'm worried he's not himself." Hal cradled the mug. "As I mentioned, I offered to have him come upstairs for a cup of tea or nightcap, but his demeanor shifted. He left in a rush, claiming he alone had to fix this."

"Fix what?"

"That is the question, my dear."

"It must be related to something that happened tonight. Elspeth's warning, his fight with Linx, or maybe he's upset with how Aaliyah is managing the business."

"I suppose it could be any of those," Hal agreed with a slight nod. "I only hope he won't do something he'll regret."

"Are you worried he might harm someone? Or harm himself?"

"I'm simply worried." Hal released a long breath, letting his shoulders sag. "I've never seen George like that."

"Should we go look for him? I can cancel my plans with Liam."

"No, no." Hal refused my offer with a firm shake of his head. "Don't cancel any plans. I think that would only make things worse. I got the sense he wanted to speak in private. I'm sorry to burden you with this. I suppose I needed a listening ear myself. I'm likely blowing things out of proportion. If I don't see him tonight, I'll follow up with him in the morning."

"Are you sure?" Hal didn't like seeing his friend distressed, and I felt the same way about him.

"Positive." Hal rested his teacup on the counter. "Go have a nice dinner with Liam. I'm sure everything will look different come tomorrow."

Part of me wanted to go out in search of George anyway. Elspeth's warning already had me feeling uneasy. Whether or not there was any merit to her visions of dark auras remained to be seen, but it was clear she fully believed in whatever she'd seen. Now hearing that Hal was worried felt like too much of a coincidence.

"If something changes, you know where to find me," I said to Hal.

"Enjoy your night," he said, cracking a smile. "We'll regroup in the morning, and I'll lock up."

"Thanks." I left with a parting glance to the Conservatory. Aaliyah was gathering her things. Fletcher and Victoria were huddled together on a loveseat near the large arched windows. They looked content. I doubted they were leaving anytime soon.

"You should be more open-minded about her, Annie," I told myself as I grabbed my coat and bag from the rack by the door.

Maybe I had read her wrong. Maybe she was really interested in Fletcher. If that were the case, I wasn't about to put a stop to his chance at finding love.

# EIGHT

The air held a tiny hint of spring as I walked along the gravel drive from the bookstore that spilled out onto Cedar Avenue. February in Northern California tended to be cool and crisp, with sunny afternoons and the first blooms starting to break through. I was glad for my sweater as I drank in the refreshing smell of sea salt and took in the swath of stars overhead. Our proximity to the Pacific Ocean meant that Redwood Grove benefited from the salty sea breezes that wafted over the town square and the marine layer that would linger in the morning like a soft blanket.

The crows were roosted in the trees for the night, so the solar lights lining the drive were my only guide. I almost wanted to wake them. I would have felt slightly safer with them circling overhead. I tried not to think about the possibility that Scarlet's killer could be lurking in the shadows as I hurried along the pressed gravel drive.

A touch of relief came over me when I arrived at the village square and was suddenly engulfed by the cozy charm of downtown. One of the things that made our town unique was its varied architecture—mid-century modern, Spanish-style, and

Victorian-era buildings lined the quaint streets, each style reflecting the eclectic shops and restaurants within. I loved everything about our little village, especially the way each of the storefronts faced the square and was always decorated elaborately for the holidays. It was like the square had been painted pink for Valentine's Day. The large terra-cotta pots flanking the sidewalk overflowed with fuchsias, geraniums, and cosmos. Hanging baskets dripped with more color and greenery. Front windows sparkled with glossy heart cutouts and pastel candy displays.

The Stag Head was on the edge of the square. The pub was housed in a rustic building that matched its vibe. I went inside and was immediately greeted by the sound of music and the aroma of rosemary fries. The décor was intentionally distressed with original hardwoods, a long wooden bar, and booths and high-top tables situated throughout the open space. Dozens of cardboard stag heads were mounted to the walls, along with vintage black-and-white photographs of Redwood Grove in its early days. There were bookshelves filled with board games and cards and a small stage in the back where Liam hosted live music and trivia nights.

I fell into line at the bar and studied the chalkboard menu. With the frenzy of activity, I hadn't eaten much and was suddenly famished. Liam rotated family favorites and pub fare. Tonight's specials included a hearty chicken corn chowder and vodka penne.

Liam wasn't behind the bar, so I placed an order for a bowl of chowder and a glass of chardonnay and found an empty table near the band. It was a local college band that always drew a large following.

"Hey, Murray, when did you sneak in?" A familiar voice made me turn around. Liam was coming toward me, balancing a tray with a steaming bowl of chowder and a hunk of warm sourdough bread.

My breath caught.

Liam was devastatingly handsome with his rugged features, wavy hair that constantly fell over one eye, and sultry lips. He wore well-fitting jeans and a Stag Head fleece.

I would have thought that after dating for over four months, the butterflies in my stomach might settle, but so far they hadn't. The mere sight of him sent my heartbeat racing.

He kissed the top of my head, making my cheeks flame, and set the bowl in front of me. "I believe this is for you."

"How did you know?" I tried to regain my composure by drinking in a long, slow breath and sitting up taller.

"Everyone else is either wrapped up in an intense game of Settlers of Catan or here for the band." He motioned to a group of long tables that had been pushed together for gaming and then to the stage. "No one's ordering soup at this hour, and I promised to dazzle you with a delicious meal. Consider this your starter."

"Lucky me." I licked my lips. "Can you sit for a minute, or are you busy with drink orders?" A steady line remained at the bar where Liam's bartender poured frothy beers and fancy cocktails.

"They're good." Liam pulled out a barstool and sat across from me. "Fill me in. How was the matchmaking?"

"Not bad." I stirred the chowder, which was loaded with veggies, and finished with a sprinkling of bacon and white cheddar cheese. My stomach growled in anticipation.

"That sounds mild." He stared at me with his dark eyes, flecked with gold. "You were much more enthusiastic in your texts."

I dipped my spoon into the bowl and lifted it to my lips. "It got a little weird." I savored a bite and told him about Elspeth and George.

"A black aura?" Liam sounded skeptical. "I don't buy it."

"I know, it's unsettling, especially because Hal's worried

about him, too." I was about to tell him the whole story when Linx stumbled into the pub. She'd changed into black ripped jeans, combat boots, and an oversized hoodie that fit her more like a dress. She tripped over her own feet as she pushed her way to the front of the crowd gathered to listen to the band and then began dancing out of rhythm, bumping into people.

"Well, she's not getting served anything more tonight unless it's a cold glass of water or a hot cup of strong coffee," Liam said, raising his eyes.

I punched him softly. "That's Linx. She and George got into an argument shortly after Elspeth's dire warning."

"You're worried about her?" Liam rested his elbows on the table and looked from me to Linx. "Why would she have a reason to clash with George?"

"Excellent question. I have no idea. I asked Pri if they had potentially had a bad interaction at Cryptic, but Pri didn't think so. George is a teddy bear. I can't imagine him instigating an argument." I glanced at the dancefloor.

Linx jumped up and down, pumping her arms and singing along completely off-key at the top of her voice to the lyrics. How did she know the band? Pri said she moved here days ago. Maybe she was a superfan or a groupie.

"She seems harmless to me, Annie. Your classic drunk college kid. Unless you're one of the band members, I guess. Then, watch out. She's going to accost you for signed autographs and selfies." When he smiled, his chiseled jawline became even more pronounced.

I ignored the fluttery feeling in my stomach, which pulled me toward him like we were in our own magnetic forcefield. I scrunched my nose and made a face before taking another bite of the chowder. "It's silly, I know. I'm probably blowing things out of proportion. I just have a bad feeling about it."

"No. Don't mistake me. I'm not second-guessing your instincts. I didn't mean to blow you off." Liam lifted his hand to stop me as if wanting to make sure he clarified his meaning. "Your intuition is spot-on. I would never bet against you, Murray. Never. Okay?"

His gaze felt like it was boring straight into me.

I swallowed and let out a small sigh. "I guess it's one of those situations where something feels off. It feels wrong, but I can't put a finger on it. Linx does seem harmless. But if she's only been in town a couple days, why would she go after George in such a public way? George, of all people. He's beloved. I can't imagine what he could have done to set her off."

"Good question." Liam studied her with new interest. "Maybe George told her to tone down the energy? Or confronted her about drinking?"

"Could be. He pulled a grumpy old man move, and she shot back?" I chuckled as I ripped off a hunk of the sourdough and dunked it into the chowder. "This is amazing, by the way."

"Told you. My food lives up to the hype." He tilted his head to the side and gave me a sly, knowing glance.

"You're incredibly humble, too."

He turned serious, looking toward Linx again. "Is there anything I can do?"

"No. I'm sure it will be fine. I'll check in with George during coffee and pastry hour tomorrow morning." I pushed thoughts of George aside for the moment. I was eager to tell him about the documents and Natalie. "However, I do have two huge pieces of news to share."

"I'm listening." Liam raised one eyebrow and waited for me to say more.

I told him about Fletcher and Victoria and the letter I'd received from Natalie Thompson.

"I didn't see that coming." Liam shook his head in disbelief. "You haven't reviewed the documents yet?"

"There wasn't time. Plus, I want to be fresh. I don't want to miss anything. I'm going in early tomorrow so I can review everything while the store is quiet."

"Do you want company?" he asked hopefully.

"Thanks, but not yet. I will, for sure. First, I need to know what's in the documents, and then I'll likely need all the help I can get. I feel like I'm finally close, Liam. Really close."

"You are." He reached out and gently massaged my hand.

Liam never failed to surprise me. He'd listened to hours and hours of me relaying stories about Scarlet before her death and had spent a weekend combing through the police files with me after my meeting with Mark.

Having a partner as invested in the case as me was unexpected, and it was a healing gift I didn't even realize I needed. I just hoped I could do the same for him. Liam had trauma in his past, too, but he'd yet to open up to me about it. It was like a wedge or barricade between us. Until he was ready and trusted me enough to share, we were at a crossroads. I loved spending time with him, but if we were going to take our relationship to a deeper level, I wanted to know all of him.

"We're on for dinner tomorrow at Public House?" Liam asked. "Because I might have a surprise or two up my sleeve."

"You? Surprises? That doesn't sound like the Liam Donovan I know."

"Love is in the air. Anything can happen." He wiggled his brows.

"I definitely didn't take you for the Valentine's type."

"Ouch." He scoffed. "Don't let the stags hear you."

I glanced at the paper heart crowns adorning the stag heads. "You did that? I assumed it was one of your staff."

He pretended to be injured. "I'll have you know I was up until long past two in the morning gluing those hearts."

"Okay, I stand corrected. And yes, dinner tomorrow unless Aaliyah matches us with strangers."

He scowled. "You wouldn't."

"Never." I reached for his hand and squeezed it tight. "I'm quite content with my love life at the moment."

"Good," he practically growled, his voice filling with longing. "Because I'm a one-woman kind of guy."

I finished my chowder, and Liam walked me out. He leaned in for a long kiss before finally breaking away.

"Let me know what you find in the documents," he said as he left me at the door.

"I will." I made an X over my heart and left him with another kiss on the cheek.

Professor Plum was waiting for me at the front door of my cozy cottage at home.

"You shouldn't have stayed up," I said to the tabby, bending to pet his soft head. "It's late. Should we make a cup of tea and head to bed?"

Professor Plum rubbed my leg and mewed in response. He had been my faithful companion since Scarlet died, staying by my side in the days after her death, curling up next to me as I sobbed endlessly. I don't know how I would have healed without him.

He followed behind me like a dog while I heated water in the kettle and poured a cup of lavender tea with a touch of honey. Then he trotted upstairs to the bedroom and proceeded to tuck himself under my fluffy layers of soft blankets.

I leafed through my current read while sipping the tea, but my heart wasn't in it. I couldn't stop thinking about George. After I reviewed Natalie's documents, the first thing I was going to do was check in with him and see how I might be of service. He'd done so much for the community. I wanted to return the favor.

# NINE

I woke with the rising sun the next morning. Professor Plum hadn't moved an inch.

"Good morning, sir. Are you ready for breakfast?"

He stretched his paws like he was preparing for a yoga session.

"I feel you." I kissed the top of his head and scooped him up. I took a minute to snuggle him. "Today is a big day for us. I have new information about Scarlet to dig through."

I swear he nodded in response and nudged me out of bed.

It was a good thing Liam was a cat lover. That would have been a deal-breaker. Some people might think it odd to have full conversations with their four-legged friends, but not me. Professor Plum had been a perfect sounding board, or as Pri would say, "a purrfect sounding board." There was nothing I wouldn't do for him.

After pulling on jeans, a T-shirt, and fleece, tying my hair into a ponytail, and picking my favorite pair of tortoiseshell glasses, I headed to the kitchen to feed him and make myself a strong cup of coffee. I scarfed down a bowl of cereal and a banana while I waited for my coffee to brew. Once it was ready,

I put it in my favorite Nancy Drew reusable mug, added a splash of cream, and left for the bookstore.

The February air greeted me with a refreshing coolness. A sparkling layer of dew clung to the grass, glistening under the early morning filtered sunlight.

I cut through Oceanside Park. The park was my happy place. There was something magical and rejuvenating about starting my day amongst the redwoods and pathways that wrapped through the different sections of Redwood Grove's natural preserve. The children's play area was filled with climbing structures, swings, and a splash pad for those warm summer afternoons. Trails connected in every direction, leading to sweet nooks with picnic tables and benches. There were open grassy areas for morning tai chi classes and an amphitheater covered in ancient wisteria.

This morning was no exception. I allowed my thoughts to wander as I navigated the bark trail and breathed in the smell of the dewy grass and early blooming lilacs. A light breeze rustled the leaves still clinging to the ground, bringing a touch of the briny scent of the Pacific Ocean with it.

A hum spread through my limbs as I approached the turnoff to the Secret Bookcase. When Hal renovated the estate, he ensured the grounds remained open to the public. Our gardens are connected to Oceanside Park and farther out into a network of hiking trails surrounding the village, allowing guests to meander between both.

Peachy sunlight spilled onto the dewy grass and illuminated the orange and lemon trees, which were intermixed with eucalyptus and bay laurel trees. The redwoods and oaks stood tall, branches bare but hinting at new buds.

The landscaping shifted from the park's natural style to the manicured gardens that enshrined the bookstore. Trimmed hedges and topiaries, water features, marble statues, and ornate birdbaths made me feel like I was in the English countryside rather than a small, remote town in Northern California.

I breathed in the cool air, which held the last traces of winter. It was almost like I could feel nature stirring and waking up to spring.

Two crows circled overhead.

I froze and gazed at them, Elspeth's reading replaying in my head.

Did they have a message for me?

"Good morning," I said, feeling slightly silly that I was talking to the birds, but then again, I constantly had conversations with Professor Plum. What was the difference?

The crows soared so close I could almost reach out and touch their velvet black feathers.

I recognized the pair that hung out in the gardens like permanent guardians from the swatch of white iridescence on one of their wings.

Fletcher had adopted them and named them Jekyll and Hyde. He kept a five-pound bag of unsalted peanuts in their shells on hand, which he used to feed them. His ultimate goal was to train them to bring him gifts. He would leave small rocks, gemstones, and even Lego flowers next to the peanuts in hopes that the crows would reward him for his kindness with a gift in return.

Thus far, they hadn't reciprocated, but that had yet to deter him from his mission.

"We're going to have a murder of crows, Annie. Trust me. They're the most brilliant creatures. They're loyal and smart. Once they learn I'm a friend, not a foe, they'll be our protectors and watch over us. The Novel Detectives mascot will be our murder of crows."

I encouraged him. I enjoyed the wildlife that made their home in the garden—the gangly teenage geese, cottontail bunnies, hummingbirds, monarch butterflies, and redtail hawks that greeted me whenever I took my lunch break on the Terrace. It was wonderful to be surrounded by so much nature, but until last night, I'd never paid special attention to the crows.

Jekyll and Hyde squawked at me as I rounded the bend through an archway of roses.

"I'll send Fletcher out with your peanuts as soon as he arrives," I said to them, and continued along the pathway that led to the Terrace.

The Terrace was a large terra-cotta stone deck with built-in benches lining the perimeter and plenty of bistro tables and chairs for customers to enjoy a sun-drenched afternoon of reading. It felt like stepping into the pages of an Agatha Christie novel, which was always Hal's goal with any project related to the Secret Bookcase. Large potted palms and smaller planters with perennials and succulents gave the Terrace a pop of color.

As I got closer, I noticed someone sitting on one of the benches.

Odd.

It seemed early.

I checked my watch. It *was* early.

We didn't open for another two hours.

Was it an eager match seeker?

Or could it be an unhoused resident who needed a safe spot to spend the night?

Out of nowhere, the crows dive-bombed me.

I jumped and covered my head.

*What the hell?*

The crows had never attacked me before.

I scanned the skies, waiting to get swooped upon again.

They circled overhead, piercing the quiet morning with their screeching.

What had I done to make them angry?

I kept a lookout over my shoulder as I continued on.

They came at me again.

I ducked and shielded my body.

Geez. Why had the crows suddenly turned on me? Had I done something to upset them? Maybe they were being territorial—was it mating season?

Had Fletcher given them bad peanuts?

Or had I willed them to me by simply thinking about them?

They cried again, flying straight up and then swooping down so close to my head I could feel their wake on my face.

I froze.

This wasn't good.

I didn't want to start my day with a crow attack.

"What?" I called to them, changing my tactic. If Elspeth was right that I had a connection with the birds, maybe I was misinterpreting their message. "What's wrong?"

My palms got sweaty as I considered my options. I was only a few feet away from the Terrace, but it was like they were blocking me from getting any closer.

I could bail and take the gravel drive to the front of the store.

But would they follow me that way, too?

It was farther, which would give them more opportunities to strike.

I'd never been afraid of crows or any birds, but their cawing was almost painful. I stuffed a finger into my ear to block out the piercing sound.

Fletcher and I were going to have to have a chat about feeding them. Maybe it had been a bad idea. Instead of training them to bring him gifts, he'd trained them to attack. That was bad for me in the moment and would be bad for business. We couldn't have crows dive-bombing customers.

"I'm taking a few steps forward, okay?" I said as calmly as I could, holding my arms out in surrender.

This was ridiculous.

I was being held hostage by crows.

I took a timid step forward.

They continue to dart and dive above me.

I took another step.

I was surprised whoever was asleep on the bench hadn't stirred with all the commotion.

The crows yelped.

"Hey, it's Annie Murray with the Secret Bookcase," I announced myself as I stepped up onto the Terrace. I didn't want to spook the person.

The crows flew precariously close to the bench and then jetted straight up toward the wispy clouds like a rocket.

"Hello, good morning."

The person must be out cold.

I moved closer and threw my hand over my mouth, nearly spilling my coffee.

I recognized them.

It was George Richards.

He was slumped against the bench with his head hanging to one side like it was barely attached to his body. Huge, bright red welts erupted on his skin. His lips were puffed out like a botched plastic surgery job gone terribly wrong. A copy of *The Big Sleep* by Raymond Chandler rested at his feet with the discarded craft wrapping paper we'd used for the book matches. The cover was unique and one I didn't recognize from our collection.

I covered my mouth, gulped back the last sip I had taken, and set my coffee cup on the tile.

"George, George, are you okay?" I shook him slightly with urgency.

The crows landed on a nearby bay laurel tree and stared down at me as if to say, "This is what we were trying to tell you."

I shook George's shoulder harder, even though I had a sinking feeling he was long past saving.

"George?" My vision tunneled, darkening at the edges like the world was closing in on me.

His head flopped down farther.

I reached for his wrist. More angry splotches the size of golf balls spread up his arm.

I checked for a pulse.

There wasn't one.

I pressed my hand over my stomach to keep my coffee down. I wasn't sure what happened, but there was no question George Richards was dead.

# TEN

I reached for my phone and called 911. "This is Annie Murray at the Secret Bookcase; I found a body." My skin felt clammy and damp.

The dispatcher walked me through protocol while I waited for the emergency responders to arrive. I was trained in CPR and First Aid, but nothing was going to save George. I couldn't tell how long he'd been on the bench. Minutes? Hours? Longer?

What could have happened?

The angry red welts and patches on his skin made me think he'd had a fatal allergic reaction. But to what?

Bee stings?

Bug bites?

The skin around his puffy eyes and lips was tight and stretched like a rubbery mask. His face looked molted and uneven.

A crushing sensation gripped my chest as I studied his lifeless body.

Jekyll and Hyde remained in the tree, watching over me like guardians. I felt grateful for their presence and made a mental note to make sure they got extra peanuts later.

Sirens sounded nearby.

The good news was that the authorities would arrive quickly. The police and fire stations were only a few blocks away.

I thought I caught a flash of movement behind me.

I turned around but didn't see anything.

*Keep breathing.*

I sucked air in through my nose and closed my eyes.

Of course, I was skittish about finding George like this.

Who wouldn't be?

I opened my eyes and stole another glance at his lifeless body.

It certainly looked like he'd had some sort of allergic reaction, but could it also be poison? A drug?

What were the odds he would drop dead the morning after Elspeth's warning?

A crash sounded behind me.

I jumped, causing the crows to swoop from the tree toward me, cawing loudly.

"Yikes. Help."

I turned to see Victoria huddled behind a potted lemon tree, protecting her face with one hand and trying to shoo the birds off with the other.

"They're attacking me." She ducked down, holding her short skirt with one hand to keep it from flying up.

Questions swirled in my head, like, what was she doing here? Had she been here the whole time?

"They're harmless," I said, again feeling fortunate to have nature on my side.

Jekyll and Hyde must have sensed I wasn't in danger because they flew back into the tree.

Was Elspeth right? Did I have crow energy?

I shook off the thought and studied Victoria. "What are you doing here?" I asked, unable to mask my accusatory tone.

She brushed dirt from her white miniskirt. "Uh, I'm supposed to be meeting Fletcher. The front door was locked, so I came around the side to see if I could get in this way."

"You're meeting Fletcher now?" I glanced at my watch. A cold chill spread down my arms.

Sirens wailed as the emergency vehicles crunched over the gravel.

Help was close.

Thank goodness.

"What's going on?" Victoria arched her neck to try and see around me. Then she let out a little scream and stumbled backward. "Is that George? Is he dead?"

My internal radar spiked.

How could she have missed George?

If she was telling the truth about the front being locked, there was only one path to the Terrace, and it led straight past George.

That also meant she'd been hiding the entire time I'd been on the phone with 911.

I didn't trust her.

Not one bit.

Unfortunately, the flashing lights from the fire truck and ambulance brought our conversation to a temporary halt.

"Hang on," I said to her, rubbing my arms to stay warm. "Stick around. The police will want to speak with you."

"Me?" Her jaw dropped. She hoisted her sweater with its plunging neckline and rubbed her shoulders. She had to be freezing in the skimpy outfit. I would never judge another woman's fashion choices, but it was strange she didn't even have a coat with her.

"Stay here." I didn't have time to argue with her.

Two EMS workers immediately began assessing George. A police officer took my statement.

I couldn't stop wondering what he was doing here this early. Reading?

Waiting for someone?

"Dr. Caldwell is on her way," the officer said after I explained how I found the body and the approximate time. "She'll want to take an official statement."

"You should speak with Victoria," I said, pointing behind me. Then I gave them a brief rundown of my interaction with her.

As expected, the paramedics couldn't do anything for George either. Dr. Caldwell arrived shortly.

She easily and instantly took command of the situation, marching over to the scene in jeans and a puffy coat. Her short, white hair was cropped in a bob, and oversized black glasses framed her face. Her presence was naturally grounding. Being around her always made me feel like everything would be okay.

"Annie, good morning." She greeted me with a half nod. "I heard you found the deceased."

"George Richards," I said, motioning to the bench.

She opened her leather satchel and took out a notepad. "George Richards. What a shame. Our paths have crossed on a few occasions." She made a note and then moved closer to the body.

I hung back, but she encouraged me to join her.

Dr. Caldwell had offered me a position on her team, but ultimately, I decided to stay at the Secret Bookcase and strike out on my own with Novel Detectives. She had kindly mentioned she would consult with us on high-profile cases, but I didn't want to overstep.

"What do we know?" she asked the paramedics.

They gave her their report. She assessed the body.

"When exactly did you find him, Annie?"

"Ten minutes ago, at most." I peered at the crows and told her about how they tried to warn me.

"I would always put my faith in the birds." Dr. Caldwell adjusted her glasses and looked up to give them a nod of approval.

"Do you think he died of natural causes?" I asked.

"It's too soon to say. My first guess would parallel the paramedics'—an allergic reaction. I don't see any evidence of food or drink nearby. Did you see anything?"

"No, nothing, just the crows. And it's weird he'd be here this early. We don't open for a couple of hours." I shook my head. "I need to tell you about what happened last night, though, because it could be connected."

"I'm all ears." She directed the police officer to take crime scene photos, too.

We moved out of the way, and I told her about Elspeth's warning as well as George's argument with Linx.

"Hmm." She scowled and knelt to get a better angle. Then she pulled on a pair of disposable gloves and picked up the book, considering it with new interest. "As you know, I'm not a fan of coincidences. What are the odds George just happened upon the bookstore and experienced a medical emergency while reading?"

"Right?" I bobbed my head in agreement, feeling relieved she was picking up unusual clues as well. "That particular book is odd. Fletcher and I wrapped all the books for the event. The thing is, I don't remember that title being part of our list. It's a popular classic, but I don't recognize this edition. It looks old, like maybe a special edition."

"Hold that thought." She waved an officer over and handed them the book. "Bag this and the wrapping."

"Please continue," Dr. Caldwell encouraged. Her receptive style was one of the reasons she'd been my favorite professor in college. She never stood behind a podium and lectured for hours. Our classes were always conversations. She would push us to defend our theories and abandon our personal biases.

"I've been wondering if Elspeth could be involved. Her warning seemed staged. She made a big scene. George blew her off, but now I'm questioning whether it could have been intentional. Maybe she wanted to draw attention to him and away from herself."

Dr. Caldwell made a note.

I leaned closer and lowered my voice. "You should also speak with Victoria. She was here and pretended like she wasn't. She must have seen me find him. She was hiding behind a lemon tree and tried to give me a story about meeting Fletcher. I don't buy it."

"Who is she?" Dr. Caldwell asked.

"You're going to think I'm biased, and it's probably true." I shrugged. "Her name is Victoria Carlton-Ivers. She works for Book Emporium and claims to be in town for the matchmaking weekend, but I think she's using Fletcher, pretending she's interested in him to get insider secrets."

"Duly noted." Dr. Caldwell closed her notebook. "I'll speak with her now, but I'm inclined to agree with you. This doesn't feel right. We'll have to wait for more information from the coroner and the toxicology reports, which could take a while. In the meantime, stay vigilant. I don't have evidence to back anything up yet, but there are too many coincidences. Until we find proof otherwise, I'm treating this as a homicide."

# ELEVEN

I watched as Dr. Caldwell went to speak with Victoria. The Terrace, normally bathed in the tangerine California sun, was now covered in a tense stillness. Officers moved methodically, stepping carefully on the terra-cotta tiles while marking potential areas with evidence tags and stringing bright yellow caution tape around the perimeter. The scene was solemn and grim.

The police activity must have attracted attention from the village square because a small crowd had gathered near the ambulance and fire truck on the driveway below. Familiar faces, drawn in with curiosity and concern, stood in small clusters, trying to catch a glimpse of the unfolding investigation.

The scent of eucalyptus hung in the air, mixed with something new—something acrid, dusty, maybe metallic, but definitely ominous.

I waited until they removed George's body, and Dr. Caldwell gave me the all clear.

"I'll be in touch later this afternoon, but, as I mentioned, please do keep your eyes and ears open. I believe we're dealing with foul play. It's not clear how the killer initiated a fatal allergic reaction, but I'm certain that's what they did. I'll ask the coroner to look for a puncture wound and have my team review Richards' medical records to see if he had an allergy to bee venom or tree nuts."

"You think the killer injected him with an allergen?" If that were the case, whoever had killed him had put some serious thought into his murder.

"That's my gut feeling at the moment, yes." She pressed her lips together and nodded like she was trying to work out how.

Unlike some of my other criminology professors who solely taught based on procedures and the content of our textbooks, Dr. Caldwell encouraged us to tap into our intuition. She used to say that her gut feeling rarely led her astray. Which isn't to say that she wasn't meticulous when it came to documenting a crime scene and following protocol step by step.

"I'll be on high alert. Should we continue with the scavenger hunt or postpone events?" I glanced at the bookstore and then at my watch again. I couldn't believe over an hour had passed. It felt like five minutes. There was still plenty of time to prepare, but I understood if Dr. Caldwell wanted us to call it off.

"No, you can proceed as normal. It will be an opportunity to observe anyone George interacted with last night. Do keep me abreast of what you uncover, and I'll be in touch soon." She patted my arm. "I'm sorry you found him, but I'm glad you'll be assisting in the case."

"Technically, I don't have my PI license yet. My test is scheduled for next month."

"When have we ever let a little technicality stop us?" She gave me a conspiratorial smile.

"Good point." I shot her a thumbs-up.

"Annie, it's Annie, right?" Victoria asked, joining us.

"Yeah. It's Annie." I didn't bother to try to mask my irritation.

Dr. Caldwell gave me a knowing look and excused herself.

"I'm shocked. Floored. I can't believe George is dead." She fluttered her eyelids and reached into her purse. She took out a deep red lipstick and ran it over her lips like an artist carefully applying the first layer of paint to a canvas. "It's heartbreaking."

"It is," I agreed. In the flurry of finding George and everything after, I'd barely had a chance to process the loss. Tears threatened as I thought about the many tender and sweet gestures George had done for the community over the years. "I didn't realize you knew him."

"Me?" She pointed to her chest with a manicured nail. "Oh, well, George and I have been acquainted for a while through mutual business contacts."

"At Book Emporium?" This news surprised me because George had been such a staunch champion of locally owned, small businesses.

She struggled to put the cap on her lipstick. "I can't say much more about it at the moment, contractually speaking, if you know what I mean."

It didn't take a detective to read between the lines, but that wasn't going to stop me from pressing her for more information. If she and George were financially linked, that could give her a motive for murder.

"Are you hinting that you and George were in business together?"

"Like I said, legally, I'm not allowed to divulge more." Her speech was slow and deliberate, as if she was testing the waters.

"I thought George tended to finance small businesses." I had dozens of other questions for Victoria, but I didn't want to lose this thread yet. I also couldn't believe she wasn't a popsicle. A chill lingered in the air, making me long for the comfort of the toasty warm fireplace in the Sitting Room and a hot cup of cinnamon tea with honey.

"That's true. I wish I could say more. I'm not trying to play coy. Honestly." She shifted her weight from one foot to the other, swaying subtly and appearing uncertain. "I can tell by your face you don't trust me. I understand. This is a small town. Everyone is protective of the community. I get it."

"I'm not sure how that relates to George investing in Book Emporium."

"He wasn't investing in Book Emporium." She stuffed the lipstick tube into her cleavage. "That much I can tell you. I'm afraid I can't divulge more details. The one thing about George was that he knew a solid business opportunity when he saw it, and when I presented him with my plan and vision, he didn't need any convincing."

"Why the secrecy, then?" I noticed Jekyll and Hyde fly to a nearer tree and balance on a narrow branch as if they were keeping a close eye on us. Did they have similar feelings of distrust for Victoria?

"Contracts, negotiations. You never want to share the details until the ink is dry. Surely, you must understand that. You're in a similar process with the bookstore."

How did she know that?

*Fletcher.*

*Ah, Fletcher.*

I would have to remind him to play his cards closer to his chest.

"What were you doing here this morning?" I asked, ignoring her mention of the Secret Bookcase.

"I told you I'm meeting Fletcher. In fact, I wonder where he is?" She scanned the small crowd. "He offered to give me a full tour of the bookstore before things get too busy."

Why wasn't Fletcher here if they were meeting? And why was Victoria dressed scantily? Her miniskirt, tight, revealing sweater, and high heels weren't exactly hanging out at a bookstore attire.

"You must have seen me. You must have heard me on the

phone with 911. Why didn't you say anything?" I wasn't letting her off the hook.

"No. I didn't see a thing." She fiddled with the zipper on her purse.

I recognized the nervous habit.

"How did you get on the Terrace?"

"I came around the long way." She pointed to the back of the estate and drew a circle in the air. "I wanted to see all of it. Fletcher mentioned potentially expanding the grounds, so I figured I would take a look while I was waiting for him and give him my professional opinion. I've headed several store redesigns for Book Emporium. It's my area of expertise."

There was no pathway on that side of the building. She would have had to snake along the side of the estate, which was entangled in ivy and wild blackberry bushes. I inspected her outfit. It would have been a challenge to navigate the narrow, overgrown space in her high heels and tiny skirt.

"You went around that side?" I could hear how incredulous I sounded, but I didn't care. George was dead, and I intended to do everything in my power to bring his killer to justice.

"Yes, I came that way." She motioned to her left again. Then she lifted her foot. "I ruined a brand-new pair of heels, sinking into the wet grass, and got a tiny tear in the hem of my skirt, but it was worth it. The view from the back really gives you perspective in terms of how large the estate is."

The pointy tip of her black heel was muddy, but that could have been from walking up the gravel drive or the grassy path.

"Look, it's clear we got off on the wrong foot. I apologize if I made a bad first impression or came on too strong to your friend. I admit I have a crush. He's unlike anyone I've met, and his Sherlock knowledge had me up all night reading online articles about Sir Arthur Conan Doyle's serial work. We brainstormed a few ideas I think you might be interested in for the store. But my intentions with Fletcher are strictly romantic," she continued, running her teeth over her bottom lip. She left a streak in her lipstick. Normally, I'd alert a friend or even a stranger if they had lipstick on their teeth, but I wasn't about to afford Victoria that courtesy until I knew what she was really up to. "I plan to tell Aaliyah to take my name out of the matchmaking. I never imagined I'd stumble upon love. I figured I'd leave that to the professionals. The minute I met Fletcher, the chemistry was palpable. I don't know where it will take us, but I'm excited to see."

I desperately wanted to believe her, for Fletcher's sake.

"I hope you'll give me another chance. I'm sure my story sounds unbelievable." She exaggerated with her hands as she tried to plead her case. "The detective was as skeptical as you. I told her to check the cameras. Do you have cameras?"

Was she asking because she was trying to gauge whether she'd show up on the footage?

"We do," I said. "We installed them after an incident last year." I didn't expand on the fact that the "incident" had been another murder.

"Good. They'll have proof. Please share it with them." She leaned to one side to get a better look at Dr. Caldwell, who was directing her team on next steps. "You're close with the detective, aren't you?"

"We're friends," I said, keeping my tone neutral. Victoria and I were not friends. I rarely found myself this cold, but I was convinced she was lying. I just couldn't figure out about what.

"I got the impression she thinks someone may have killed George, and I don't think she's wrong." She raised her perfectly arched brows and watched my expression.

"You think George was killed?"

"I do." She glanced around us, worried someone might be eavesdropping. The only people nearby were the police. "You should talk to Linx."

"The barista?" How did she know Linx?

"Yes. I saw them together last night. They were arguing. Actually, let me amend that. Linx was arguing. George was simply standing there, taking her wrath. I can't say for sure, but I got the impression she was drunk."

"I saw them, too," I said. "He left the ballroom with her. I wouldn't describe it as wrath, but she did seem upset."

"No. This was later. This was after I left the bookstore." She shook her head and shot her finger toward the gravel drive. "Fletcher and I didn't stay long. Hal was leaving, so we didn't want to keep him. That's another reason we agreed to meet early. Fletcher stayed to lock up, and I headed for my hotel. I'm staying at the Grand Hotel. Fletcher told me I could cut through the garden and Oceanside Park. It was a nice night. I thought that was a great suggestion, so I walked along the driveway." She nodded to the gravel pathway with its strings of Edison-style lights and pink and red bunting we'd hung for the occasion. "It's wonderful to be in a place that's so safe. I didn't have a care in the world walking to my hotel in the dark, but I had a scare when I came upon them in the garden, right over there." She made a little circle with her finger and pointed to one of the fountains. "Linx was screaming bloody murder at him, and George was crying."

"He was crying?" I tried to piece together the timeline. I'd seen the two of them leave the ballroom. Could they have come out to the gardens then? Or had Linx confronted him a second time?

"He looked despondent. I couldn't make out what she was saying. She was hysterical, waving her arms in his face, spouting insults, and he stood there and took it without saying a word."

"What did they do when they saw you?" I was interested in exploring this new thread, but not ready to rule Victoria out as a suspect yet. She could be intentionally trying to shift suspicion away from herself and throw Linx under the bus.

"I made sure they didn't see me. I turned around and went

in the opposite direction. I didn't want any part of their drama. I was still floating on cloud nine from meeting Fletcher. Maybe I should have broken it up, though. I told the detective she should speak with Linx immediately. If anyone killed George, it must be her."

# TWELVE

I took a minute to process Victoria's accusation. "What makes you think Linx murdered George?" I asked, and quickly followed up my question with another. "Did you tell Dr. Caldwell all of this?"

She brushed her fingernail with her thumb like she was trying to buff her glossy red polish. "Yes. Obviously. I'm a professional. I'm an upstanding member of the community."

I wanted to interject, "Not this community," but I let her finish.

"I gave the detective every detail and then some. I'm confident she'll bring Linx in for questioning shortly. It's not an exaggeration to say I was rattled by the way she was berating the poor old man. If he was killed, she did it," Victoria asserted again.

She was nothing if not convinced about her theory.

"Oh, there's Fletcher now." She wiggled her fingers to get his attention. "Fletcher, over here!"

He and Hal were part of the small crowd the police had contained to the drive. People mingled, speaking in hushed murmurs with the occasional gasp of suspicion.

"Would you mind if I go say hello?" Victoria asked as if I were in charge.

"Not at all." I watched her practically dance over to Fletcher and greet him with a kiss on each cheek like we were in Paris.

Why was I feeling so protective of him?

Fletcher was a grown man and could make his own mistakes, but after what he'd told me about his dating woes, it was hard not to want to guard against him getting his heart broken. The problem was that Victoria was lying. There wasn't a shred of doubt in my body about that. From the outside, it looked like she was using him, but maybe she was lying about something else, like her future endeavors with George.

I sighed and left the Terrace, passing an officer bent over a spot near the bench.

Another uniformed officer kept onlookers at bay. He lifted the yellow tape for me to duck under. My feet crunched on the walkway. Clouds framed the village in the distance with a soft orange blush.

Hal hurried up to me, his brow crinkled in concern. He was wearing pajama bottoms, slippers, and a thick sweater. The commotion must have roused him from bed. "Annie, is it true? Is it George?"

I nodded. "He's dead." I stepped forward and put my arms around him.

Hal rubbed my shoulder and firmed his grip. I let myself lean into him and my sadness. We stood there in silence for a few minutes, maybe longer. Time seemed to slow. I was grateful to have Hal next to me and equally worried about him. He and George had been close, and last night, he'd been so worried. The news had to be a shock.

I brushed a tear from my eye and pulled away. "How are you holding up? I'm sorry about George."

"As am I, my dear. As am I." His eyes turned to the entrance gates at the end of the drive, where two police cars and a firetruck waited. "I heard sirens. They woke me, and I kept thinking they were passing by until the flashing lights lit up my bedroom like a 1970s disco. My heart dropped. I thought something could be wrong with you or Fletcher. Then, once I came down, rumors were already circulating that it was George. What in the world was he doing on the Terrace at this hour?"

"That was my first question, too." I filled him in on what I knew.

"I can't help but blame myself." Hal made a small circle with his slipper in the pea gravel. "I should have done something. He never stopped by for a drink or that game of chess I promised him. I should have forced the issue. I knew he was upset about something."

"This is not your fault." I hated seeing him broken up. "We couldn't have known this would happen. I understand. Trust me, I keep replaying Elspeth's warning, but let me repeat again, this isn't your fault. Whoever killed him is responsible, and I'm going to do everything I can to help Dr. Caldwell track them down."

He patted my shoulder and gave me a sad smile. "That's our girl."

"Did you hear anything last night?" I scanned the long drive. The gardens to our left were bursting with succulents, citrus trees, and manicured lawns. The creamy exterior of the estate on our right was draped with ivy snaking toward the pitched roofline. Strings of pink and red bunting flapped in the slight breeze. If it weren't for the flashing police lights and officers in blue scouring the grounds for evidence, it would have been like an ordinary day at the Secret Bookcase.

"Like what?" Hal pulled his sweater tighter around him as if shielding from the chill.

"Screaming? An argument?"

Hal wiggled his earlobe. "Afraid not. These old ears don't

work like they used to. I made myself a cup of tea, read two chapters of my latest book, and dozed off. I didn't hear a peep until the sirens this morning. Why?"

"Victoria claims she saw Linx yelling at George in the garden when she left."

"Hmm." Hal's lips narrowed as he thought about it. "I haven't made my mind up about her yet. She latched on to Fletcher quickly, didn't she?"

"Yes! Right?" I noticed a couple of heads turn in our direction. I didn't mean for that to come out quite so loudly. "Sorry, yes. I'm glad you feel like that, too. I don't trust her motives. I'm worried she's using him to get information about the bookstore."

"Were you aware she and George met yesterday?" Hal's bushy white eyebrows shot up as he glanced in their direction.

Victoria was draped over Fletcher, cooing in his ear. It was either love at first sight with the two of them, or she was up to no good.

"No, when did she meet with George?" I found it interesting Victoria had failed to mention that during our conversation.

"He said something in passing." Hal kept his gaze focused on Fletcher and Victoria. "He didn't go into detail, but he did ask me if he could buy me a drink later this weekend and pick my brain about the book business because he was considering some sponsorship with her. He was light on details. I wish I had asked more at the time. I never considered he wouldn't—" Hal didn't finish his thought.

I squeezed his arm. "I know."

A police officer interrupted us to take Hal's statement.

I left him and headed for the front.

If George wanted Hal's input on the book business, that supported what Victoria had told me. What were they partnering on? Why was she so mysterious and tight-lipped about it?

Another thought took hold.

What if things had taken a bad turn in their negotiations?

Could George have decided to back out?

That would give Victoria a solid motive for murder. Maybe the paperwork was already signed, and he had second thoughts. She could have killed him before he had a chance to make any changes.

I sighed as I reached the entrance. The store was a sight for sore eyes. I took a second to let the crisp air, tinged with a hint of the sea, fill my lungs, holding it in and then slowly releasing the breath. I repeated the centering breathing technique twice.

My body still felt shaky, but I was in control of my emotions.

That was an improvement.

The estate was washed in brilliant sunlight, casting a sepia-tone glow over the shingled roof and chimney stacks. Decades-old ivy clung to the siding like well-loved stories woven into our beloved library. Planters with pink, red, and white tulips flanked the front door, and paper hearts peeked out of the windows.

The Secret Bookcase was the perfect retreat from the chaos on the Terrace. I was glad to have a moment alone. I unlocked the front door and locked it behind me again. We weren't ready to open yet despite the small gathering outside.

I went through the motions of brewing coffee and heating water for tea. Gone were my plans for the day. I had hoped to steal some time to analyze Natalie's letter and consider its implications for Scarlet's murder, but George's sudden death—and apparent homicide—changed everything. It had to take precedence, which felt like the story of my life when it came to Scarlet. Just when I was on the verge of having a major breakthrough in her cold case, another crisis swept in, pushing the mystery of her death to the backburner again. This new drama would once more crowd out my focus when I was so close to uncovering the truth.

I sighed and poured myself a cup of tea.

*It's okay, Annie. One thing at a time.*

I started the computer to check on any online orders that may have come in overnight. Once everything was set up in the Foyer, I moved into the Conservatory to assess what needed to be moved for brunch.

Fletcher had done the bulk of the work last night.

I'd have to thank him later.

The long tables where we'd served drinks and appetizers needed fresh tablecloths, and the flower vases needed fresh water. Otherwise, the ballroom was in good shape.

I checked the time. Guests would be arriving within the hour.

I still needed to get plates, napkins, and cups, walk through the rest of the store, set up each room for the day, and package the online orders.

*Damn.*

There wouldn't be enough time for me to look through the paperwork Natalie had sent. It felt like the universe was conspiring against me.

*Prioritize, Annie.*

This is where I shined.

My organizational skills were my superpower.

If I could devote the next half hour to checking off everything on my to-do list, I just might be able to carve out enough time to at least give the documents a cursory glance.

I hurried to the basement for breakfast supplies. Then I went room by room, turning on lights, the electric fireplaces, and flameless candles. I made sure the Sitting Room had tea ready to serve and set out special chocolates and bowls filled with candy sweethearts in the Mary Westmacott Nook.

Our children's story hour would take place in the Dig Room

instead of the Conservatory because Aaliyah had opted not to use that as part of the scavenger hunt.

I was packing a box of cozy mysteries when someone pounded on the front door.

I looked up to see Elspeth waving wildly. She was dressed similarly to last night in a new gauzy robe with three scarves tied loosely around her neck and dozens of jangly necklaces weighing her down.

Why was she here already?

I was so close to being done.

The documents were right above my head, waiting in my office, and yet here I was, deterred again.

I sealed the package with tape and went to unlock the door.

"You've heard the news?" She was breathless and sweaty. A dew like the one that formed in the garden on cool mornings misted her face. "He's dead. George Richards is dead. I predicted this very outcome. Like I said last night, a black aura is inescapable—it signals imminent death and danger."

"Do you want to come in?" I asked, instantly regretting my decision. I had a feeling that if Elspeth came in, she wouldn't be leaving anytime soon, so Natalie's files would have to wait a while longer.

She didn't bother to answer but rather pushed past me and scanned the Foyer like she expected to see his killer hiding nearby. "I feel a dark presence now. A heaviness."

I wanted to say I felt the same. I didn't think it had anything to do with auras but everything to do with the fact that George had been killed on the Terrace.

She waved her hand in wide patterns, like a conductor guiding their orchestra. "Do you feel it? We need to cleanse the bookstore. You can't have anyone come inside until we do. It's not safe. Where's your incense?"

"Incense?"

"Yes. I need incense, a sage wand, candles, and preferably

some crystals." She rummaged through the canvas bag looped over her shoulder and through the display of candles next to the stack of blind dates with a book. She picked up a tin candle, removed the lid, and inhaled deeply. "This will work. I'd prefer sage, but peppermint will do in a pinch."

I could barely keep up with her zigzagging thought process and movements.

"What about the incense? Do you have any?"

"Yes, we have some incense packages in the Sitting Room."

"Go get them. There's no time to delay." She flicked her wrists to encourage me to move. "You can put it on my tab. Go. Go. I'll start here. Where are the matches?"

Her level of urgency made my heart rate spike.

I wasn't worried I was in danger from any dark auras, but I was starting to wonder if I could be in danger with her.

# THIRTEEN

"Please, hurry," Elspeth pleaded. "I can't be responsible for another death."

I froze.

*Responsible?*

*Did she slip up?*

*Was that an admission she killed George?*

"Why are you standing there?" She tapped her fingers rapidly on the countertop. Her rings and gemstones clicked sharply with each tap, echoing her impatience. "We must cleanse this energy. No one will be making a love match with this dark density. I fear someone else could meet an untimely fate if we don't cleanse this space."

Her erratic behavior put me on edge. In a situation like this, I usually follow up with a round of questions, but something told me not to.

"I'll be right back," I said, keeping one eye on her as I left the Foyer.

Elspeth lit the candle and began waving it around the room, making sweeping circles from the floor to the ceiling and chanting.

As I walked to the Sitting Room, I wondered if there was another reason she wanted to cleanse the space. Could she have left evidence behind, and this was her excuse to retrieve it or find it?

I grabbed a package of incense and hightailed it back to the Foyer. I didn't want to give Elspeth any leeway to venture off into the store alone.

Questions brimmed to the surface as I hurried down the long hallway.

What was the real nature of her relationship with George?

He had been instantly dismissive of her warnings.

Was that simply because he didn't believe in her abilities, or could there be another explanation? What if they were already acquainted? Maybe he'd been short with her because he recognized her and wanted to get away.

But if that were the case, what was their connection?

And how could I find out?

Elspeth was unstable, or at least pretending to be. Questioning her like a normal suspect would be like trying to herd cats, so I was going to have to devise a different tactic to get anything out of her.

Only there was a huge problem.

She was gone.

I froze.

The Foyer was empty.

Where could she have gone?

It had taken me less than two minutes to grab the incense.

"Elspeth," I called, peering into the Conservatory.

The aroma of the peppermint candle permeated both rooms, but there was no sign of Elspeth.

I never should have left her alone.

She couldn't have gone far.

Was she hiding behind the bookshelves or on the stage?

I did a quick search, but there was no sign of her.

"Elspeth," I called louder. "Where are you?"

No response.

Were those footsteps upstairs?

She wouldn't have gone into our private space, would she?

There was clear signage posted on the door to the former servant's stairwell, alerting customers that the area was off-limits.

I couldn't imagine what would possibly make her think it was okay to go upstairs. Not only were our offices on the second floor but so were Hal's private living quarters.

A strong waft of peppermint assaulted me as I opened the door to the stairwell.

Yep, she had come this way.

*What the hell?*

*Talk about a violation of our personal space.*

"Elspeth, are you up here?" I yelled, not bothering to hide my annoyance. I was angry. Furious actually. Blood rushed to my head as I took the stairs two at a time, passing by framed original covers of Agatha Christie's novels and photos of her house, Winterbrook. Hal had lined the hallways and stairwells with an assortment of photos of the prolific mystery writer, along with playbills, book covers, and old magazine clippings. They were all part of his personal collection, not intended for public consumption, just his own enjoyment. If I had to wager a guess, I would bet Hal's Agatha Christie collection was one of the biggest in the world. He had framed, signed original plot sketches and first edition copies in his room, which he kept behind lock and key.

When I made it to the second floor, I scanned the hallway. Elspeth could only have gone in the direction of our shared office and the storage room. The other side of the second floor where Hal resided was locked. Unless she'd managed to steal a key, she couldn't get in.

"Elspeth, where are you?" I repeated, my voice cracking with anger.

The smell of peppermint continued in the hallway.

She was in my office.

*Unbelievable.*

I'm not typically prone to outbursts, but this was unacceptable. Elspeth had crossed a line.

I threw the door open.

She was huddled over my desk.

"Elspeth, what are you doing?"

She whipped around and held the candle in front of her like a protective barrier. "Cleansing."

"You're not allowed up here." I stood in the doorframe and motioned for her to get out. "This area is off-limits."

"Not for dark auras, dear. Negative energy knows no bounds. It has no walls. I have to start on the upper floor and work my way down to clear it." She twisted the candle in concentric circles like a tornado swirling into formation.

I glared at her. "No. You need to get out of my office."

"There's no need to be testy. I'm simply trying to help. Without clearing the energy, your event will be a disaster, and I can't guarantee everyone's safety." She held the candle in her left hand and squeezed her right arm toward her body like she had something tucked under it.

"It's not your job to guarantee anyone's safety." I squinted to try and see if she did have something under her arm. I couldn't tell, and I didn't want to stand around and debate. "Let's go."

She ran the candle over the top of the desk in large sweeping motions like a ballet dancer stretching before a performance. "Okay, that's better. All clear," she said in a singsong voice, finally coming toward the door.

"After you." I waited for her to go first. I didn't trust she wouldn't bolt.

"You found the incense. Excellent." She stopped and thrust

the candle at me. "Use this to light it. Then, follow my lead. You want to create a vortex with the smoke, working low and then going higher." She demonstrated her technique for whatever it was worth.

"I don't have time for this," I said, pointing to the stairwell with the package of incense. "I need to finish opening procedures."

"But we haven't finished the cleanse." Her pupils grew wide like saucers, making her eyes appear almost black. She ran her hand over the door leading to Hal's quarters. "I sense the area behind the locked door needs my attention."

"We'll have to risk it." My voice dripped with sarcasm that was lost on her.

"Dearest, it's not worth the risk." She jiggled the door handle. "I sense dark, dark energy here."

"Nope." I pointed to the stairwell, firming my feet in a stance that gave no room for discussion, and waited for her to move.

She muttered something under her breath but went downstairs without a further argument.

"I should at least do the ballroom," she said, angling the candle in that direction. "Can I have the incense? It's more potent than a candle."

I handed it to her. "Go ahead, but do *not* go anywhere else, understood?"

"I'm sensing you're upset. There's no need to hold on to anger. We're a team in creating a safe space for your readers." She plastered on the most serene smile I'd ever seen.

"I don't have time for this. Like I said, don't go anywhere else."

That put an end to our conversation.

I watched her carefully. The only reason I agreed to let her "cleanse" the Conservatory was to get another look at her from behind. Her right arm remained plastered to her body like superglue. She was definitely hiding something under her flowy scarves and clothes.

Was it evidence linking her to George's murder?

She must have found it while we were separated.

What could it be?

The needle used to inject him?

Something else?

I intended to watch her like a hawk while I figured out a way to see what she was hiding. I ran through possible scenarios —I could accidentally bump into her or toss something at her, like a throw pillow. I had to get a look at what she had under her sleeve. I was more convinced than ever that her ESP was a cover for what she was really up to.

# FOURTEEN

Fletcher and Hal came inside, followed by a team of police officers.

"What is that?" Fletcher waved his hand in front of his face and stuck out his tongue. "It smells like a candy cane coated in patchouli."

"Pretty close," I replied, tipping my head toward the Conservatory. "Elspeth is cleansing the bookstore's aura."

"Now, that's a new one." Hal scrunched his forehead. "How did she get inside?"

"She knocked." I shrugged and shook my head. "I shouldn't have let her in. She's insistent that the bookstore is heavy with dark energy, but I left her alone for two minutes, and she snuck upstairs."

One of the police officers stepped forward. "We'll need to speak with her about her whereabouts."

"Feel free." I swept my arm out like an invitation. "She's all yours. You might check to see if she's hiding anything under her arm."

The officer went to speak with Elspeth. The others pointed to the hallway. "Dr. Caldwell wants us to do a quick walkthrough before you open to the public. Make sure there are no signs of forced entry, broken windows, that sort of thing."

"Yes, by all means." Hal pressed his hands together in gratitude. "I, for one, will feel much better if you have a look."

"I turned on lights throughout the store and set up coffee and tea here and in the Sitting Room," I said, nodding to the drink station. "I hope that's okay."

The officer saluted me with two fingers. "It's not a problem. Since the victim was found outside, we won't be sweeping for prints or anything like that. Dr. Caldwell asked we do a once-over as a precaution."

They left to complete their task.

"If you two will excuse me momentarily, I'll pop upstairs and put on something more practical." Hal tugged at his pajama pants.

"Of course. Go ahead," I encouraged.

"Annie, Hal said you found him?" Fletcher asked, unwinding his houndstooth scarf and hanging it on the coat rack near the front door. He wore khakis and a black button-up shirt with a pink carnation pinned to the breast pocket.

"Yeah." I shuddered remembering George's puffy, swollen face. "He was outside on the Terrace."

"We heard." Fletcher made a tsking sound. "How awful. And George Richards, of all people. If it was murder, who would want to kill George?"

"My thoughts exactly." I shook my head. "I know this is going to sound odd, but I think your crows tried to warn me— Jekyll and Hyde were going bonkers before I found him. At first, I thought they were attacking me."

"They would never attack you," he interrupted, shaking his head vehemently.

"I realized that once I got closer and saw George's body. I told them we owed them extra peanuts."

"Consider it done." He gave me a sharp salute to reinforce

his complete agreement. "We must reward the behavior we want to see in them. It's an essential part of their training."

My gaze flickered toward the window, wondering where they were now. "I've started a suspect list in my head, and Dr. Caldwell asked for our support with the investigation."

Fletcher perked up. "She did? As in a real case for the Novel Detectives?"

"Potentially, although she can't pay us a consulting fee until the business is legal, but yes, she explicitly requested our input. Speaking of that, do you remember wrapping a Raymond Chandler title for the book matches? George had a copy of *The Big Sleep*."

"Um, maybe." He tapped his chin as he thought. "We have quite a few titles in stock, but to tell you the truth I've wrapped so many books between the event and the blind date display, I can't remember. Is it important?"

"I'm not sure yet. Maybe." I paused for a second to think about how to phrase what I wanted—needed—to say. After a moment of consideration, I decided that being direct was the best route. "Fletcher, you might need to take a step back from the investigation, though."

"Why?" He pulled his neck toward his body.

"Because Victoria is one of the top suspects." I met his gaze.

He blinked rapidly and gulped. "Victoria? What? She would never. She couldn't."

"She was at the crime scene this morning. I caught her hiding behind one of the potted lemons. She claims she was meeting you and didn't see you at the front, so she decided she'd wander around the back of the store and then somehow wound up on the Terrace."

"Is that her story?" Hal appeared dressed and ready for the day in a plain cardigan and slacks. He looked at me and grimaced.

"Yep, and it's filled with holes—gaping holes," I replied.

Fletcher sputtered, stumbling over his words. "No, well, that's not right. We were supposed to meet, but I was running a bit late, so I texted her to let her know. She's not lying about that."

"Okay, fine. Why did she opt to traipse through the overgrown underbrush on the back side of the estate versus walk down the nicely pressed gravel path?" I countered.

"She has a penchant for English architecture." A touch of worry crept into Fletcher's voice, making it sound sharp and pitchy.

"And why did she hide? She had to hear me when I found his body. Jekyll and Hyde were squawking and swooping down over me. I called 911 and was on the phone for at least three or four minutes. She never budged. She never announced her presence. That's weird."

"Maybe she was scared," Fletcher suggested. He picked up a teacup and held it to the light to inspect it. Then he cleaned it with his sleeve and returned it to the coffee and tea cart.

"Possibly," I agreed. "Can either of you imagine standing by and doing nothing?"

Hal shook his head, raising his hand ever so slightly to encourage me to tread lightly. He wasn't wrong. I didn't want to ruin Fletcher's chance at love, but I did want him to proceed with his eyes wide open.

"There must be an explanation." He twisted his carnation so that the flower was upright. "She was upset when I spoke with her outside. I'll talk to her again."

"Good. See if she'll give you any details about what she and George were working on. She mentioned contract negotiations."

"With Book Emporium?" Hal sounded incensed. "George wouldn't invest in a corporate bookstore."

"I said the same thing. She claims they were working on something new together but couldn't go into further details for legal reasons."

Fletcher stared at the floor.

Did he know more about the deal Victoria was trying to ink out with George?

I dropped it for now. I trusted Fletcher with every bone in my body. He would eventually see through Victoria's façade if she was lying. I'd made my case. Now I needed to give him space to figure out if Victoria was worth pursuing.

Aaliyah appeared at the door, balancing a heavy box. Her outfit was as striking as last night's yellow dress. She wore a silk teal dress that almost looked metallic. Its ombre layers caught the light, creating a mesmerizing glitter between the opaque and translucent hues.

Hal let her in and helped her with the box.

"What an utter disaster." She thanked Hal for his assistance as she set the box on the counter. "George is dead. There goes my business."

I was taken aback by her lack of grief. Was she really more concerned with how it impacted her and the future of Storybook Romances at a time like this?

"We're all in shock," Hal said gently.

Aaliyah seemed to realize her sentiment might not have come across the way she intended. "Yes, yes, yes. Me too. It's a tragedy. A real tragedy. A life ended way too soon." She closed her eyes and massaged her neck as if trying to soothe herself.

"Will his death impact Storybook Romances?" I asked.

"Do you mind if I help myself?" She picked up a mug and reached for the coffee pot. "I need some serious caffeine to get through this day."

"Please, that's what it's there for," I encouraged.

"To answer your question, I don't know." Aaliyah poured coffee to the brim and pressed her lips to the mug with reverence. Her hair tumbled in loose, soft waves that shone like the shimmering material on her dress. She reminded me of a mermaid. "The specifics of his estate are unclear to me. I need to dig out our contract and read the fine print. I'm not sure whether funding will continue now that he's deceased."

If that were true, it would potentially drop her lower on my suspect list. Losing George's generous financial backing would make it more likely she would want him alive unless she had a different motive for murder.

"What do we do about the day?" Aaliyah clutched the mug with one hand and pulled a packet from the box. "I was up all night matching readers. I've succeeded in matching everyone, which is a feat. There were a few questionable profiles, but I pushed through and found someone for every participant. George was thrilled with my success rate. He didn't think it was possible until I showed him the spreadsheet."

"When did you show him the matches? Last night?" Aaliyah might very well be the last person to see George alive. This was a critical clue in terms of the window in which he had been killed.

"No. I didn't finish until close to three. I texted him this morning, and we met for a coffee. He wanted to review the matches with me."

"Is that normal? Did he typically get involved in that piece of the business?" George had come across as a hands-off partner. I got the impression he vetted companies and small business owners and then let them do what they did best—run their businesses with an influx of his cash.

"No. Never." She savored the coffee, staring into the mug as if it had the answers she was seeking. "I know he's a morning person, so I expected he would text me back, but I never anticipated he would want to meet. I was going on three hours of sleep at that point. Hence why I'll be drinking gallons of this all day." She raised the mug.

"When did you meet?" I asked, wanting to firm up the timeline.

"Six thirty." She fluttered her eyelids. "Early. At Cryptic

Coffee. It was fairly empty, just the usual caffeine obsessed, getting their fix on their way to work. We had a drink. He asked me to print everything out. He was old-school that way. He looked over the paperwork, and then he said he had a minor change he wanted to make, which was also out of character. George isn't a matchmaker. That's my domain, but I couldn't argue with him. I told him to let me know what he wanted changed, and then I headed back to the hotel to shower and get ready. I figured he'd be here when I came in, but I never imagined he'd be dead." Her shoulders heaved as she sighed.

"When did you leave George, and did you see where he went?" I could feel my body begin to hum. This was a big break. George had been alive at six thirty, and I found him less than an hour later, which meant there was a narrow window when he was killed.

"I didn't even have time to finish my latte. He was in a hurry. He scanned the document, took a few sips of his coffee, and then took off. It was before seven, I think." She glanced at the ceiling while trying to remember. "Yeah, it must have been because when I got back to the hotel, there was a young couple wrangling two toddlers at the breakfast buffet, and I overheard the mom complaining that seven was too early for vacation breakfast."

"And you met at Cryptic?" I clarified. I could check with Pri to see if she saw George leave.

"Yes. The cute, restored garage right downtown. Good coffee, too. Although I'm still going to need about five hundred more cups of this to get me through the day." She took a long drink to prove her point. "What about the schedule of events? Are we good to go?"

I forgot I hadn't answered her first question. "Yes, the police gave us the green light to proceed with the scavenger hunt and dinner. We may need to re-work the garden tour, depending on how long they'll have the Terrace cordoned off."

"I need to set up, then." Aaliyah chugged the rest of her coffee and reached for the box.

"Let me finish this last order, and I'll come help," I said.

The truth was I needed to text Dr. Caldwell and Pri immediately. George had been killed sometime between seven and seven thirty. That much I knew for sure. More questions lingered, though, like why George had suddenly become so interested in Aaliyah's matches. And if she was the last person to see him alive, could she have slipped something fatal into his coffee at Cryptic?

# FIFTEEN

After Aaliyah left to begin setting up the matches in the Conservatory, I texted Dr. Caldwell and Pri.

Dr. Caldwell replied instantly to let me know she would drop by the bookstore soon to take Aaliyah's statement personally and review the surveillance footage.

> Nice work, Annie.

She responded with a thumbs-up emoji.

Pri wasn't quite as responsive, likely because she was pulling strong espresso shots for customers. Her text came through a few minutes later when I went to the basement to grab extra supplies.

> They were here. He ordered an Americano no cream. No sugar. Old school. Classic. Although Linx managed to mess it up and had to remake it for him. Aaliyah had a skinny vanilla latte. They didn't stay long. Maybe twenty minutes. He left first. Seemed rushed. Can't believe he's dead. 😭😶

I'll be there soon with coffee, pastries, and Linx. Btw, she's wrecked from last night. More importantly—how are you?!? What can I bring you? A double chocolate muffin? A raspberry latte?

I smiled at my screen and let her know I was fine and didn't need anything extra. Pri was such a good friend. I wished I could sneak off to Cryptic and grab a coffee with her. I loved our chats. We carved out time every week to meet either at the coffee shop or the bookstore. She would always make me a special drink and use me as her test guinea pig. It was a rough job, but someone had to give her feedback on her layered Neapolitan coffee or vanilla tea latte. We always got lost in our conversations, covering every topic, from our love lives to the potential existence of UFOs. Pri was a solid yes on that topic. She was an avid sci-fi fan and like to dabble in conspiracy theories.

It was such a whirlwind with George's death and the event that time with Pri would have to wait for the moment.

I felt satisfied that I'd at least helped point Dr. Caldwell in a new direction. My mind latched on to Aaliyah as a possible suspect. From a financial perspective, it didn't make sense. There could be another explanation. What if George threatened to pull his backing? Could she have killed him to ensure her funding continued?

Pri's perspective on matchmaking lingered in my mind. What if Aaliyah learned George no longer intended to support her endeavors to grow the business? That was certainly a motive. If he was planning to draw up a new contract that put an end to his investment, perhaps she murdered him before he had a chance.

Or was it personal? He had hovered last night, watching over her like a hawk. Maybe she was upset about him micro-managing and interfering with her matchmaking. Yet, she had also babied and spoken to him like he was hapless. Something didn't add up.

And murder seemed like a big leap.

I was struck by the fact he wanted to see the matches. There had to be a reason. But I hadn't seen any paperwork near his body. Only the book. Unless he'd tucked it inside the pages. That was another point to make sure I mentioned to Dr. Caldwell.

If he was concerned about how she was running the business and using his money, that felt like a critical detail, but I couldn't land on what yet.

*Give it time, Annie.*

*Let it simmer.*

Learning to trust the investigative process had been a hard lesson for me. My brain wanted to pick away at the puzzle until I came up with a solution. That rarely worked. Instead, the better option was to give it a little space and continue working through various scenarios.

I found Aaliyah unpacking papers into stacks in the Conservatory.

"How can I help?" I asked. I felt distinctly underdressed compared to her.

She held up a color-coded spreadsheet. "This is the master list of matches. Each of the packets in this stack contain the first clue."

I picked up the top packet, which was labeled with the participant's name.

She tapped the next stack. "These are numbered. They'll need to be hidden throughout the store. I've made notes on the corresponding rooms for every clue."

"Does it matter where we hide them in the room or just the room?"

"Just the room."

There were six stacks of clues, including the initial puzzle that would send couples on their quest. "Let me recruit Hal and Fletcher to help, and we'll take care of the hiding. Pri and Linx from Cryptic should be here any minute to set up coffee and pastries. Is there anything else you need?"

Aaliyah shook her head. "Uh, yeah, an IV of coffee wouldn't be so bad."

I chuckled. It felt good to laugh, even for a second. This was supposed to be a weekend about love and connection. I didn't want to lose sight of that. Yes, it was terrible George was dead, and there was no escaping the heavy energy of that, despite Elspeth's cleanse. Yet, this was Redwood Grove, a place where we cared deeply for one another. I looked around; the bookstore glowed with radiant light. The dainty pink and red hearts strung from the chandeliers and the bouquets of flowers served as a reminder of my purpose—we were here to create love matches. Book love matches, which, in my humble opinion, were the best kind of matches.

"I'll keep a fresh pot brewing," I said with a smile, feeling a bit lighter and resolved to ensure everyone had a good experience today. Seeing couples pair up and set off on a book hunt through the store might just be the antidote we needed.

I checked the time. Guests would be arriving in a half hour, so I grabbed the first stack, which was labeled SITTING ROOM, and went to find Fletcher and Hal. They eagerly agreed to hide the other clues in the Parlor, Mary Westmacott Nook, Library, and Study. I suspected that, like me, having a positive task to focus on was a happy distraction.

The police had finished their sweep of the bookstore, so I went to work tucking clues in between the pages of Mary Higgins Clark and P.D. James novels. I tried to get tricky with my hiding spots, stashing some under the soft pink heart pillows on the wingback chairs and the cushions as well as behind the curtains and among the candle and tea display.

When I was done, I returned to the front to find Gertrude pacing from the door to the counter.

"Annie, I've been looking all over for you." Her eyes were puffy and bloodshot like she'd been crying. The wadded tissue balled up in her hand confirmed my suspicion.

"What can I do for you?" I asked, observing her with new interest. She looked distraught and shaken.

"Is it true?" Her bottom lip quivered. "Did a man die here this morning?"

"I'm afraid so." I nodded.

She sucked in a breath through her nose, her shoulders quaking as she tried to take in the air. "Was it the man who was here last night? The older gentleman about my age?"

"Yes, George Richards. Did you know him?" I leaned closer. It was clear Gertrude was distraught.

"No." She dabbed her eyes with the tissue. "That's what's so unusual and disturbing about hearing he died. He reminded me so much of my Walter. He could have been his brother. I wish you could have met Walter. He was so handsome. My girlfriends called him a 'dreamboat,' and he was. His eyes had a mischievous twinkle, like he was always up to something. That's what made him so handsome to me—his impish personality. He kept me on my toes and laughing."

"He sounds wonderful," I said.

"Oh, you would have loved him. Everyone did." Gertrude batted tears back, her eyes turning glossy.

I thought back to last night when Gertrude had looked like she'd seen a ghost. That was why—George reminded her of her long-lost love.

"I couldn't bring myself to talk to him last night. I was so rattled thinking that Walter was still alive after all of these years. It shook me to my core and threw me back into that grief and sadness like it was just yesterday that he died. I went home and cried for hours, looking through old photo albums. It's hard to think that an entire lifetime passed Walter by. He missed so much. Everything in fact." She squeezed her lips together and shook her head like she couldn't believe it was true. "I finally worked up the courage this morning. I was going to ask if he wanted to partner with me. Is that odd? Saying it now makes me feel silly." She wiped a tear from her cheek with the back of her hand and scrunched the tissue in her palm repeatedly like it was a fidget spinner.

"I don't think it's silly. I think it's sweet."

"I was so overcome when I saw him. Looking through the photos of Walter and me when we were young was quite cathartic. I had boxed them away because it was too painful. I know it wouldn't bring him back, but I thought maybe I could have some closure if I spoke with George. It was almost like pretending he was Walter, and fate had a different plan for us. We had grown old together instead of him dying so young."

I recognized the long-term grief etched in the lines around her eyes. I felt the same about Scarlet. Every once in a while, I'd see a stranger from behind at the grocery store and think it was her and then have to remind myself she was dead all over again.

"How young was Walter?"

"Twenty-five." She clutched the tissue tighter and placed her other hand over the ring dangling from her necklace as if to steady herself. "We were engaged. The week before the wedding, he was on his way home from his stag party—that's what we called them in those days—and he was killed by a drunk driver."

"Oh, I'm so sorry, Gertrude. That must have been awful."

"It was." Her voice broke as tears welled in her glossy eyes.

One thing people who hadn't experienced loss didn't realize was the platitudes they shared were lies. Things like, "Time heals everything." Not true. Not for me. Not for Gertrude.

Time changed my grief, but it didn't take it away.

It shifted like it was now part of me. A piece of Scarlet lived on everything I touched. I could sense the same was true for Gertrude even after all these years.

"I'm sorry, dear. I'm a bit of a mess, aren't I?" She patted her eyes with the tissue and forced a smile.

"You don't need to apologize." I reached for her arm. "I lost my best friend ten years ago, and it's still raw. I'll be fine, and then a memory surfaces, or I hear a laugh that sounds like her, and the emotions come rushing to the surface."

"Yes." Gertrude nodded, her eyes wide, recognizing a kindred spirit in grief.

"Would you like a cup of tea?" I motioned to the cart.

"That would be lovely, thank you." She pinched her cheeks and fluffed her white curls. "I will pull myself together. Am I early, by the way? I'd be happy to help if you need assistance with anything."

I glanced at the clock. The doors would be opening in twenty minutes. Everything was ready to go minus the coffee and pastries, but Pri and Linx would bring those right before the event started so they were fresh and hot.

Gertrude sounded hopeful. Maybe she needed a distraction. I could relate to that, too.

"Actually, I could use some help getting the Dig Room ready for our children's story hour. They're making paper valentines and having special snacks. The supplies are already in there. It just needs to be set up."

"Count on me." Gertrude patted my shoulder and tossed the tissue in the garbage. "It will feel good to do something."

"Yes, I know the feeling. I'm assisting Dr. Caldwell with the investigation. The distraction of having to focus on that and today's events is quite welcome." I handed her a cup of tea. "Let me walk with you and show you where to put everything."

"You're assisting the police? I didn't realize you were an official member of the team. I've heard some talk around town about a private detective agency coming to the bookstore, so those rumors must be true." Gertrude carefully balanced her tea as we walked to the back of the store. She appeared slightly wobbly, almost struggling to steady the mug as she weaved to the left.

"Can I take that for you?"

"Oh no. I'm fine." She shook her head, which made her nearly trip.

She didn't look fine to me.

"Dizzy spells." She flicked her wrist dismissively. "Another joy of aging. Here's my advice: stay young."

"I'll try." I smiled and slowed my pace, hoping that might help her retain her balance. "In terms of your question about the detective agency, yes, that is in the works. Those rumors are true, but we haven't officially opened yet."

"You mentioned helping with the inquiry into George's death. What do the police think? I assumed he must have had a heart attack." She stopped as if processing her thoughts and walking were too many tasks to handle at once. "They don't believe someone killed him. Certainly, that couldn't be true. Not in Redwood Grove. Things like that don't happen around here."

I wanted to correct her and explain that nowhere (Redwood Grove included) was completely immune to crime.

"Unfortunately, it appears that way," I answered truthfully.

"Oh, dear. That's terrible." She didn't move. "We aren't in any danger, are we?"

I shook my head. "The police believe this was an isolated event. George was targeted. They wouldn't allow us to proceed if they were concerned anyone else was in danger."

Gertrude took a tentative step forward. It was more of a shuffle. She moved slowly with intention, keeping her eyes on her footing. "Who would have ever thought such a thing could happen? I'm sure you're correct. I have faith in our police. I'll try not to fret too much, but rest assured, I will keep my eyes open and let you know if I see or hear anything out of the ordinary. One pro of aging is no one pays attention to you. You wouldn't believe how many conversations I've overheard and witnessed while going about completely unnoticed. I'll use that to my advantage."

I appreciated her wanting to do her part to find George's killer. Gertrude exemplified our connected community here in Redwood Grove, but I didn't want her to put herself in harm's way, especially when she seemed so rattled and unsteady.

After I dropped her off in the Dig Room with instructions on setting up for story hour, I returned to the front.

Could Gertrude be rattled for another reason? Could she have been involved somehow?

If George strongly resembled Walter, could she have had a dissociative event? Maybe the overwhelming flood of grief caused her to snap.

I sighed, not satisfied that theory had strong legs.

Why would she harm him?

If she had thought it was her long-lost love, she would have been overjoyed.

I felt even more resolved to piece together whodunit. Gertrude was right about one thing—things like this *shouldn't* happen in Redwood Grove, and the sooner we could find George's killer, the sooner we could sink back into normalcy, embracing our village for the sweet, safe place it was and always would be.

# SIXTEEN

Linx and Pri were setting up the coffee and pastries in the Conservatory.

"Morning," I said, taking in the intoxicating aromas of buttery raspberry-filled croissants and the nutty roast. "I followed the magical scents of Cryptic, and I am not disappointed with my nose."

Pri handed me a spiced vanilla latte and opened a box of strawberry tarts. "I know you said you didn't need anything, but, trust me, coffee will help and you should probably taste test to make sure your nose is up to the task."

"If you insist." I breathed in the sweet, spicy aromas of the coffee and swiped a bite-sized tart from the box and popped it in my mouth. The flakey crust paired beautifully with the homemade strawberry preserves. "I could eat the entire box."

"Good thing we brought extras." Pri winked and nudged Linx. "Can you make sure the carafes are filled with milk and cream?"

Linx moved at a snail's pace, as if every muscle in her body had been weighed down by a rough night. I wondered how long she'd stayed at the pub. Dark mascara and eyeshadow smudges lined her bloodshot eyes. She was wearing the same outfit I'd seen in her at the Stag Head last night—ripped jeans and the oversized sweatshirt that hit her at the knees.

Pri rolled her eyes as Linx dragged her body to the other end of the table and twisted off the cap of an oat milk container like she was attempting to break into a vault. "Can you say *hangover?*"

I winced and sipped the creamy and comforting drink. "She looks like she's hurting, for sure."

Linx squinted while filling the pitcher like she was blinded by the soft lighting in the ballroom.

"I'm sort of convinced she's still drunk. You should have seen her trying to make George's order. It was almost comical. How do you mess up an Americano?" Pri whispered, arranging the tarts on a ceramic cake stand. "I'm worried about leaving her, but we don't have extra coverage at the shop, and there's no chance I'm letting her near a steaming wand."

"That's okay. She'll be fine. All she needs to do is stand behind the table and restock pastries. Everything is self-serve." I helped myself to a second tart to prove my point. "See, look at me. I'm so self-sufficient."

"I just hope she doesn't snap at anyone." Pri brushed crumbs from her hands. She wore linen pants and a tangerine sweater that accented her dark features.

"She doesn't seem like the snapping type." I cradled the coffee in my hands, grateful for the drink and Pri's thoughtfulness. "That's why I found it strange she and George got into it. I heard they fought again last night. Do you have any idea what it could be about?"

Pri shook her head. "No. I wish. I don't get it. Like I mentioned, George was nothing but jovial and upbeat with everyone at Cryptic. I've been wracking my brain to try and remember any instance of the two of them even interacting, and I've got nothing. Zip. Zilch." She made an O with her hands.

"He seemed fine this morning. Rushed. Distracted. But they were both fine with each other. Of course, I have no idea if Linx even registered it was him. She was struggling to keep her eyes open."

"Having her here will be good. Once the scavenger hunt kicks off, I'll see if I can get anything out of her." I stole a glance at Linx. Her spiky, streaked hair was messy like she'd rolled out of bed, and her makeup was smudged. Had she slept last night? Pulled an all-nighter?

I knew that George was alive as of seven this morning, so she couldn't have killed him last night, but could she have slipped something in his drink? She'd made his Americano. That certainly gave her an opportunity.

I couldn't silence the litany of possibilities.

Aaliyah tested the microphone, yanking me out of my head, at least temporarily. "Test, test? Are we ready to make some love matches? It's two minutes until ten—time to open the doors and let love in."

She was unusually upbeat, given the circumstances.

I looked at Pri for confirmation. She swept her hand over the mouthwatering spread and nodded. "I think we're good," I said to Aaliyah, finishing my latte. Then I went to the Foyer where Fletcher, Hal, and Gertrude were waiting.

"Hal suggested I help usher children to story time so there's no confusion," Gertrude said with a touch of pride. She kept one hand on her ring like it was a talisman. "It's a delight to see young readers. I never had children of my own. Walter and I wanted a large family, but fate had other plans..." She trailed off.

I caught Hal's eye. He gave me a slight nod to let me know we were on the same page. I was glad he found another task for Gertrude.

"Excellent. That will be a big help," I said to Gertrude.

Then I checked with Fletcher. "All of the clues are hidden, right?"

Fletcher picked up a clipboard with Aaliyah's spreadsheet. "I've marked everything off. Now it's up to the participants to find their matches. There are a couple of names that have been withdrawn, so use this as the master list."

"People got cold feet, huh?" Hal asked.

A blush crept up Fletcher's long neck. "Well, yeah, uh, some of them were technically not intending to be involved to begin with. Like Victoria. She's more interested in watching the event rather than participating in it."

*I bet she is,* I thought to myself.

Fletcher busied himself with making another mark on the spreadsheet. "Anyway, I'm a yes for opening the doors."

I dropped it. I intended to keep Victoria within my sights today, but I didn't need to crush his dreams in the process. At least not until I had a better sense of her motives. I opened the door to an eager line of customers.

Gertrude led a little parade of tiny readers to the Dig Room. It never got old watching our youngest patrons trot in, their tiny eyes wide with excitement, and then leave later with their tiny hands clutching the hems of their parents' coats and colorful picture books. The room buzzed with the happy chatter of the next generation of readers, full of anticipation for our special Valentine's story time.

Fletcher and I directed hopeful matches to the ballroom. Hal offered opening remarks, including a moment of silence to honor George. Once she took over, Aaliyah was all business. I was glad Hal had at least acknowledged the tragedy. Aaliyah seemed to want to gloss over the fact that her business investor was dead.

I understood that she was responsible for ensuring the event went smoothly, yet to show absolutely no remorse for George was a glaring red flag.

Pri snuck past me as the last of the participants trickled in. "Keep an eye on my trainee and text me if I need to come intervene. I told her to guzzle coffee and put on a fake smile. We'll see. She's barely upright. Also, we need a full debrief about everything; once you're done, come by the shop, okay?"

"Yes, on all counts." I held the door for her and watched as she headed down the driveway. Sunlight spilled on the pathway and drenched the grounds with brilliant light. There was nothing that compared with a blue California sky. February in other parts of the country might be dreary and cold, but here it almost felt like spring.

Tender green shoots pushed up along the driveway. A few patches of wildflowers, eager to greet the season, dotted the lane with soft purple and yellow hues.

I was about to close the door when I noticed Dr. Caldwell approaching.

"Good, Annie. I was hoping to speak with you." She quickened her pace. "Is this a good time to review the surveillance footage?"

"Of course. Aaliyah is giving everyone instructions, and Gertrude jumped in to help corral our youngest readers during story time." I waited for her to come inside. The ballroom was buzzing with energy as people gathered with drinks and treats and waited for their next steps.

The desk was empty. Fletcher must have left momentarily to track down a book or direct a customer to a specific section.

"You can come behind the counter," I told Dr. Caldwell, clicking into the security files. "Where do you want me to start?"

"We'll need to recover everything the camera recorded for the last few days, but I would like to take a quick look at the footage from, let's say, six forty-five until you arrive on the scene."

I opened the file and waited for the video to load.

"You can speed it up until we see any movement." She leaned over my shoulder as I dragged the cursor so the video ran in double time.

The Terrace sat empty except for Jekyll and Hyde, who flew in and out of the frame a few times.

"There. Pause." Dr. Caldwell tapped on the screen.

George stumbled up the steps and collapsed on the bench, clutching his throat and gasping for air. The book in his hands dropped to the ground.

I didn't want to watch him take his last breath. It had been hard enough finding him dead, but this was part of the job. I sucked in a long drink of air through my nose and placed my hand on my heart.

Dr. Caldwell gently placed her hand on my shoulder in a rare show of affection. It wasn't that she didn't care deeply for me and our community. Her personality just wasn't effusive, which was likely due to the nature of her work. "I can take it from here."

"No, it's okay. I can handle it." I swallowed hard and concentrated on the details. "George was already in trouble when he showed up here."

"Exactly." Dr. Caldwell reached for her notebook. "Hit pause."

She made a note.

"So he had already been exposed to whatever killed him," I pondered out loud as Aaliyah ran through the scavenger hunt rules. I studied her for a second. The evidence that she was the last person to see him alive continued to point to her. I lowered my voice. Not that anyone could hear us over the noise from the microphone. "Unless George bumped into someone on his walk from Cryptic to the bookstore, Aaliyah was definitely the last person to see him alive. What if she put something in his coffee? It might have taken a minute for him to feel the effects."

"That could be what we're seeing on the screen," Dr. Caldwell agreed. "Can you hit play?"

I clicked the video. We watched in silence as George struggled for air, eventually losing the battle.

She inhaled slightly and bowed her head. "We have the official time of death."

"It's a tight window," I said. "Both Pri and Aaliyah report seeing him leave the coffee shop shortly before seven."

"And he was dead fifteen minutes later." Dr. Caldwell made another note. "Whatever killed him interacted with his system quickly."

"Poison?"

She made a circle at the top of her notebook. "Possibly. I'm still leaning toward an allergic reaction. The paramedics agree the swelling, the welts, and the condition of his airway align with anaphylactic shock."

"So the question is how? Or could we have it wrong? Maybe he was stung by a bee, and no one killed him."

"Except for the bee." Dr. Caldwell twisted her lips together and readjusted her glasses. "Arresting a bee might prove challenging."

"You think he was murdered for sure, don't you?" I studied her face.

She pressed her lips tighter. "I do. Certainly, we can't rule out the possibility of other factors—a food allergy or a bee sting. His medical records will give us clarification, as will the autopsy, but to answer your question, yes, my instinct is that he was killed."

"Mine, too." She'd given me another possible thread to follow—a food allergy. Could the killer have known about a nut allergy? What if they'd intentionally given George a slice of cake or a latte laced with the allergen?

That gave me two possible suspects: Aaliyah and Linx. I

told Dr. Caldwell about Linx and how she had made and served George his last drink.

"Let's rewind and take another look for any signs of Victoria," Dr. Caldwell suggested.

I went back to before George came wobbling up the steps.

"Can you zoom in?"

"Not in the app." I inched closer to the screen to see if I could spot anything out of the ordinary.

"That's fine. My team will be able to do that once we receive the digital files."

We both paid close attention to the top of the frame.

My stomach fluttered in anticipation. What would it mean if Victoria showed up? Could she have slipped George something at the front of the drive and then snuck around the side of the estate to watch him die?

I shuddered at the thought.

"Right there." Dr. Caldwell sounded pleased with our sleuthing abilities.

"What? I don't see her." I squinted.

"Slow it down." She placed her finger on the bottom section of the screen. "Pay attention right here. It's fast, but she shows up and must duck behind the tree because she disappears again."

I watched. Sure enough, Victoria's face briefly flashed on the screen and vanished.

"Check out the time stamp. She got there almost immediately after you." Dr. Caldwell scribbled the time on her notebook and circled it three times.

# SEVENTEEN

Dr. Caldwell and I scanned the video footage for another few minutes. Victoria hadn't lied about sneaking around the back of the estate, but why had she gone out of her way not to be seen? And what was she doing at the bookstore at the crack of dawn when most people were enjoying a leisurely cup of coffee or reading the morning news? Was she really meeting Fletcher or was that her cover?

"It feels like she was intentionally trying to avoid being seen by the cameras," I said to Dr. Caldwell.

"Yes." Her face was severe as she took another look at the footage. "Agreed. And yet, while I took her statement, she insisted I check the video, claiming it would prove her whereabouts."

"Maybe she realized there are cameras on the Terrace and decided to change her story on the spot."

"It's possible." Dr. Caldwell closed her notebook. "Can you send the digital files to my team? We'll need the last three days."

"No problem." I emailed the files while I still had the screen open. "They're headed to you."

"Excellent. I'll keep you in the loop." She nodded to the

hallway. "I'm going to do another walkthrough before I leave as long as that's all right with you."

"By all means."

I wondered if she was onto a new theory after seeing Victoria lurking on the Terrace. I was perplexed. Victoria's movements didn't add up. Could there be another reason she was sneaking around the property unrelated to George's murder? Was she scoping out the bookstore for whatever future project she had lined up with George? Could she have been working with an accomplice?

I rubbed my temples and wrinkled my nose. Something was missing. Forcing it wasn't going to help.

I took a minute to check in with Liam. Hearing Gertrude speak about her lost love, Walter, made me more grateful for my connection with Liam and the many ways he showed how much he cared about me, from our long Sunday morning hikes in the redwoods to homemade dinners at his house, him taking the time to read my favorite novel and show up on my porch with a bunch of wildflowers and hot-from-the-oven chocolate chip cookies.

> Just wanted to say I'm thinking about you this morning. I'm sure you'll hear the news about George soon so I wanted to tell you first.

I gave him a brief recap of my morning.
He texted right away.

> I'm so sorry. What can I do? I can be there momentarily.

I explained the store was busy and promised I'd check in later. It felt good just knowing that Liam was in the loop and thinking about me, too.

"Are you okay, Annie?" Fletcher asked, joining me at the counter and pulling me away from my phone screen. "Sorry, I slipped away for a minute to help a customer. I didn't miss a sale, did I?"

"No. You're fine. I've been helping Dr. Caldwell review the surveillance footage." I tucked my phone in my pocket.

"Is Victoria on it?" His voice was barely audible as he stared at the floor like he already knew the answer but couldn't face it.

"Yes." I watched him trace a pattern on the hardwoods with his shoe.

He looked up at me with a glimmer of hope. "That's good, right?"

"I'm not sure," I said gently. "Dr. Caldwell's team will review the videos from the last few days and take a closer look. Are you sure about Victoria?"

"Annie, I'm sure." He cleared his throat and ran his index finger along his jawline. "You trust me."

"I do."

"Then, trust me on this. I know I'm not the best when it comes to small talk or flirting or really anything dealing with the opposite sex unless the topic of Sherlock Holmes comes up." He picked up a letter opener and flipped it in his hand. The blotchy blush that seemed to appear whenever he talked about Victoria crept up his neck. "I believe Victoria, and if you give me a little time, I think she'll tell me the truth about what she and George were partnering on. She was close to telling me last night. I don't think she's trying to be secretive. I think she's worried that if she says anything, she's in breach of her contract and will ruin the deal. Will you at least give me the rest of the day to see what I can find out?"

"Yeah, I will." I felt bad that he needed to defend himself. That wasn't my intention. "You're right. If we're going to be partners, then I need to trust you completely, and I do, Fletcher. I just feel protective of you, in a little sister sort of way."

He returned the letter opener to its spot on the counter. "You're like a sister to me, too. I've got this, though."

"Okay." I bobbed my head in agreement and dropped it.

"What's the plan for the rest of the morning?" He peered into the ballroom.

Aaliyah was doling out instructions and the first clues. As soon as she finished, readers would be set loose through the store to start the hunt.

"Should we tag team managing the front desk and floating through the store? I'm not anticipating many sales until story time wraps up."

"Sounds good. I can take the first shift here." He picked up one of the schedules. "Hal's in the Dig Room. Do you want to check in in an hour? I wouldn't mind taking a look at the surveillance footage while it's slow up here."

"Perfect. That will give me a chance to speak with Linx." I told him Linx and Aaliyah were likely the last two people who interacted with George before he died.

"Good." He perked up at other names being floated as potential suspects.

"Hey, before I go, did you give Jekyll and Hyde extra peanuts yet?"

"Of course." He beamed with pride. "I praised them profusely and commended them on their advanced cognitive abilities. Did you know they can use tools to solve problems and recognize human faces? Studies have shown that they hold grudges against people who behave poorly, and they can pass that knowledge on to other crows, teaching them to be wary of certain individuals. They're bonded to you now, Annie. You're going to see a lot more of them. They're probably not going to leave your side. You have two new friends for life—watchful friends."

"That's amazing." I was glad they befriended me. "I'll take any extra protection I can get. I'm feeling slightly on edge after getting the note from Natalie last night. I'm sure it's in my head, but I keep feeling like I'm being watched."

"It's probably the crows. They're definitely watching you." Fletcher's tone was matter-of-fact. "Have I shown you what they've left me lately?"

"No." I shook my head. "I knew you'd been training them, but I didn't realize they'd actually left you anything."

He scooted me to the side so he could open the top drawer on the checkout counter. "Look at this. These are trinkets they've left."

I glanced in the drawer as he pulled out a set of keys, earrings, and a handful of coins. There were also glossy rocks, pebbles, and paperclips.

"I'm forming my own murder, Annie. My personal murder of crows. Well, now *our* murder."

"I'd noticed the junk in the drawer but assumed it was items kids had left around the store. These are all from the crows?"

"Every single thing." He raised a silver dime to the light. "I leave them peanuts. They pay me in shiny objects."

"Well, I'm glad they received extra peanuts today. They deserve it." I wasn't surprised the crows had left him trinkets and treasures. Given my experience with them this morning, there was no doubt they were astute observers and much smarter than we gave them credit for.

He tossed the money back into the drawer. They landed next to the keys. "Consider it done."

"Whose keys are those?" A vision of crows storming the village square and swiping objects from unsuspecting tourists flashed in my head. I could imagine the headlines now: "Local Murder of Crows Responsible for String of Robberies." Fletcher and I might inadvertently send the crows out to steal from strangers to pay us for extra peanuts.

"No idea, but according to Jekyll and Hyde, they belong to us now." He gave me an evil smile. "Holmes himself would appreciate the intellect and cunning nature of our murder."

"So what you're saying is I need to keep a tight grasp on my bag when I'm walking through Oceanside Park because our crows are flying around town seeking shiny objects to pay the piper?"

"If you put it that way, you make me sound like a mob boss. However, my goal is to get them to bring us cash. We're working our way up from nickels and dimes. Think about it. It's another revenue stream for the bookstore."

I rolled my eyes.

"You laugh now. Just wait until they're depositing hundred-dollar bills on the Terrace."

"That they've stolen from an innocent bystander," I retorted, raising one eyebrow.

"Stolen?" He ran a bony finger along his jawline. "That's a bit harsh. Borrowed feels like a better description."

I chuckled as I left him and moved into the ballroom to have a chat with Linx.

Fletcher's personal murder of crows was fitting. Now, if he could only train them to show us who had killed George.

# EIGHTEEN

The ballroom cleared out as readers clutched their first clue and scattered to every room in the bookstore in search of their love matches. Laughter and banter echoed off the high, ornate ceiling, blending with the big band mix we had selected for the weekend. A few couples held hands, their fingers intertwined as they headed out on their quest, while others stood close, their bodies angled at each other as if waiting to see who would make the first move.

I found Linx alone at the coffee and pastry table, which looked like locusts had swarmed it. Pri wouldn't be pleased that Linx hadn't restocked any of the cake stands or muffin baskets or that she was propped against the wall scrolling through her phone.

"It looks like people enjoyed the breakfast treats," I said, keeping my tone upbeat.

She rubbed her jaw and peered at me through tiny slits in her eyelids like they were too heavy to open. "Huh?"

"The pastries. Coffee." I motioned to the table. "People went through everything."

"Oh yeah." She sounded disinterested but turned off her phone and shoved it in her pocket.

"Are you completely out, or are there additional items to restock?" I'd seen Pri show her the extra boxes filled with scones and jelly donuts. As much as I wanted to speak with her about her relationship with George, I was in charge of the event and wanted to make sure everyone was well-fed.

"Um, yeah, I think there's more." She didn't move.

"Would you like a hand?" I didn't bother to wait for her reply. I walked around the long tables and reached under for the tubs.

Linx took the hint and pulled on a pair of plastic gloves. "Okay. Yeah. Thanks."

Pri's assessment might be right. She was acting and moving like she was still under the influence.

I put on a pair of gloves, too, and began arranging double chocolate, cinnamon chip, and blueberry lemon muffins in a basket.

By the time I finished filling the baskets, Linx had managed to open one box of assorted cookies and place a single chocolate-dipped shortbread on a tray.

"Did you have a late night?"

"Huh?" She squinted as she set a second cookie on the tray and stared at it like she wasn't sure how it had gotten there.

"I saw you in the mosh pit at the Stag Head. I heard the band played until closing."

Linx brushed a strand of hair from her eyes. "They went hard. We closed the place down. They had to kick us out. This town isn't exactly a hot spot for nightlife."

I made a mental note to ask Liam about kicking people out. Had he and his staff had to remove Linx and her friends physi-cally? Had things gotten out of control? I wasn't sure how that potentially related to George's murder, but if she was drunk and angry about being forced out of the bar, maybe that prompted her to seek revenge on George and plot his murder.

*While drunk, Annie?*

My mind ping-ponged on ideas.

"Is anywhere else open late?" I already knew the answer, but I wanted to hear what she'd done next.

"No. This town is kind of lame but also chill, you know?" She plopped another cookie on the tray. Watching her move like sludge made me want to jump in and take over. "We tried to go to Public House, but they close at midnight. One of my friends offered up his place, so we hung there."

"And then you had to get up bright and early for work."

"Don't remind me." She rubbed her forehead. "I maybe got an hour of sleep on the floor before my alarm started blaring. I would have called in sick, but I need this job."

"You're a student, right? I remember the days of scraping by when I was in college."

She closed her eyes and pressed her fingers into her temples like she was trying to block everything out. "I *was* a student. I'm not anymore. I'm done with that scene. It's not for me."

This was new information. Maybe the hangover was making her more willing to open up. "I thought you mentioned you were a college student."

"Yeah, I was. I dropped out." She ran her hands through her spiky, streaked hair.

"Was this recently?"

She nodded, twisting one of the piercings in her ear counterclockwise. "Like yesterday."

"Can I ask what made you decide to drop out?"

"I don't like it. The books. The studying. Cramming for tests. Regurgitating a bunch of facts and useless information I'm never going to use again, let alone remember." She deposited a final cookie on the tray and stuffed the empty box under the table. "Coffee is my thing. Getting the job at Cryptic is a big win. I worked at another corporate chain last semester, and I hated it. The coffee was so bad. This is the real thing. Small batch roasting. Hand-pulled shots. It's an art form. I don't need a college degree when I'm doing what I love."

I couldn't argue with her about that.

"It sounds like you know what you're passionate about and what you want."

"Yeah." She fiddled with her studded earring. "Try telling that to old people around me who want to dictate what I do with my life."

It was impossible not to pick up on her hint. "Do you mean George?"

Why would his opinion matter?

"You heard, too? God, did he tell everyone? Geez, that guy couldn't shut up. Why does the whole town need to know our business?" She dragged her fingers under her eyes, smudging her black liner.

"I didn't hear anything. I didn't know you and George were connected."

She reached for one of the coffee carafes and poured a cup. "Want one?"

"No thanks." I shook my head, not wanting to get off topic. "Did George tell people you were dropping out of school?"

"I don't know what he said." She shrugged. "He liked being my savior and got pissed when I told him I was done."

"Being your savior?" I was confused. "How was he your savior?"

She gulped her coffee. "He was financing my school."

This was a huge breakthrough. I tried to keep my emotions in check and stay neutral. I wanted her to keep talking. "He was paying for school?"

"Yeah. I didn't know that until a couple of weeks ago. I got an anonymous full-ride scholarship. My high school counselor found it for me. She had me apply, and the money showed up."

That matched George's other philanthropy.

"How did you make the connection that he was your bene-factor?" I asked, trying to ignore the dozens of questions fighting for space in my head.

"We got to talking at the coffee shop one day. He was a nice enough guy. He was a good tipper. I told him where I was going to college, and he mentioned it was his alma mater. That's why he set up the scholarship."

That also made sense. George tended to fund projects that were near and dear to his heart.

"I mentioned I could never afford to attend without the scholarship, and that's when he must have realized that it was his money." She took another drink of the coffee and poured more.

"Is that when you told him you were dropping out?" Between her and Aaliyah, we were barreling through the coffee today.

She started to shake her head, but it must have hurt because she stopped and winced as she pressed one finger to her fore-head. "No. I told him two days ago. I wanted to be honest with him about my decision. I told him the truth: I was grateful for the experience, and I had learned a lot, but school wasn't for me. I want to work in the coffee industry. I want to own a shop one day, and the best way to do that is to work my way up the ranks."

"He was upset with this news?" I reached for a cookie.

"More than upset." She let her tongue hang out. I noticed she had another piercing on the side, which made me wince. Ouch. "He told me I was making the biggest mistake of my life, and then he wouldn't stop. He started harassing me. He left me notes at work and sent me dozens of emails with stats about college dropouts and how hard it is to go back and make any money as a small business. It was nuts. It's not his choice. I didn't owe him anything. Plus, the scholarship can go to someone else who wants to get a degree."

I understood her frustration, but I could also imagine that George had the gift of distance and was probably trying to advise her on some of the potential pitfalls of dropping out of college, especially if her degree was free.

"Is that why you were arguing with him last night?" It was hard to tell if her closed-off body language was due to the fact that she was hungover or holding back.

"Yeah. I told him to get off my back. He's not my dad. He's not my grandpa. He's a stranger. What I do with my life is my choice and my choice alone. I was done with the lectures. I told him to knock it off."

"What did he say?" I fixed a stack of pink cocktail napkins, fanning them to create a pretty pattern.

"Not much. He rambled on about mistakes he made when he was young and how he was only trying to protect me and prevent that from happening to me, too. I told him his argument didn't really add up. If he dropped out of college and made so many mistakes, he was doing just fine. He's like a millionaire."

She had a point.

"I told him to chill out, you know. Let it go."

"Did he?"

"No. When he saw me last night, he was at it again, going on and on about never being able to recover from mistakes. I was like, okay, man, I've had enough. I didn't have to listen. It's borderline abuse at that point."

"You served him this morning, right? Did he bring it up again?"

"What do you think?" She gave me a hard stare.

"Did you get into another fight at the coffee shop?"

"Kind of. I told him to leave me alone. It was my choice to make—not his."

"How did he react?"

"The same as always—insisting he was looking out for me."

"And that made you angry?" I wanted to push her a little, but I wasn't sure how far I could go.

"Yeah, it made me angry. Wouldn't it make you angry?"

"Probably. The issue is that George died shortly after he left you. You might be one of the last people he interacted with."

"Wait. Hold up." She thrust her free hand in my face. "What are you saying? You think I did something to him?"

"You were angry with him." I didn't specifically answer her question.

"Why would I kill him? Was he killed? I thought he died?" She shielded her eyes from the light.

"The police believe he ingested something that sent him into anaphylactic shock." My eyes landed on the coffee carafes.

"No way. What the hell? You think I put something in his drink? Why would I do that? How would I do that? I don't even know what causes anaphylactic shock. I'm a barista. No, I'm not even a barista. I'm a barista-in-training. I know how to make like five drinks. How would I know how to poison someone or whatever happened to him?"

She sounded genuinely shocked at my light implication. That didn't mean she wasn't lying. There could be another side of her story. What if George had tried harder tactics to keep her in school? What if he threatened something drastic, like forcing her to repay his financial contributions to her education?

Knowing that she was financially tethered to George changed everything. I wasn't sure whether it meant she was the killer, but she was suddenly a very viable suspect.

# NINETEEN

I asked Linx a few more specifics about what she'd served George, if she noticed anything unusual about his behavior, and whether or not she'd seen him with anyone besides Aaliyah. She answered my questions without any pushback.

I left her to finish restocking the pastry table, albeit slowly.

My initial impression was she was telling the truth, at least about her level of irritation with George meddling in her personal life.

Pri texted to check in on her barista-in-training.

> How's my caffeine cadet doing?

>> Funny you should ask. I was just grilling her about her relationship with George. Apparently, he was funding her education.

> What? How did I not know this?

I gave her a brief recap of my conversation.

> I wish I had time to swing by and chat over a chai.

Don't worry. I'll keep my little eye on her and see what else I can learn. See you tonight.

Pri was not only a good friend but also an invaluable sounding board. She had an uncanny knack for asking the right question when I felt stuck or found myself spiraling down a rabbit hole with no way out. I was glad she was in the loop and had zero doubts that she would keep a watchful eye on Linx.

I did a quick survey of the ballroom and Foyer. There was a sense of joyful suspense in the air. The store was alive with the promise of new connections and the flutter of the possibility of finding love.

By all appearances, the event was off to a great start.

My thoughts drifted to Liam again. This was becoming a habit. He occupied more of my headspace than I cared to admit. Maybe it was because he wasn't afraid to show me how much he cared. Given the contentious start to our relationship, I never would have imagined he had such a soft and tender side. It was a side I kept seeing more of the longer we were together, making me fall even harder for him.

It wasn't anything grandiose, but rather, his sweet gestures left a lasting impression and made my heart skip a beat whenever he was near or even just in my head. It was the simple things like fixing the loose knob on my kitchen cupboard that fell off any time I tried to open it, buying me a footstool so I could reach the upper shelves, and tucking a blanket around my feet when I fell asleep on the couch while watching reruns of *Murder, She Wrote*.

I smiled at the thought.

Hopefully, the couples dashing through the store searching for hidden clues would find a partner like Liam in each other. Everyone deserved the kind of happiness I was experiencing— even me. For so long, I had carried the guilt of Scarlet's death with me, believing that if I went on living after her life had been cut brutally short, it was some form of betrayal. That I was letting her down. I wrapped myself in that narrative, convincing myself that if I felt joy, I was abandoning her memory. Nothing could be further from the truth. I was finally starting to understand that the best way to honor her legacy was not by hiding away and making myself small but by embracing life fully—living with a passion and purpose that she never got to experience. In choosing happiness, I wasn't letting her down, I was keeping her spirit alive.

I pressed my hand to my chest and sighed, taking a minute to lean into that truth. Then I checked the antique typewriter clock. I had some time to spare—enough to pop upstairs to see if I could find more information about George's scholarship.

I appreciated the upbeat banter and palpable romantic tension in the air. The entire bookshop smelled of fresh-cut roses and jasmine, with a lingering hint of Elspeth's sage and peppermint.

When I opened the door to the staff stairwell, the scent was almost overpowering, as if it had been locked inside a box waiting to be unleashed.

The smell was equally strong in my office. I opened the window on the gardens to let fresh air in. Smoke curled from chimneys in the distance, and sunlight filtered through scattered clouds. It was shaping up to be a gorgeous afternoon.

I went to my desk and gasped. Natalie's file was sitting front and center.

What?

I clutched my throat and swallowed.

Was I remembering wrong?

I was sure I left it in my top drawer, but it was resting on my desk calendar.

Had Fletcher come up to take a look at it while I was busy with Dr. Caldwell?

He wouldn't do that, not without me.

I glanced around to see if anything else was out of place.

Maybe I was just imagining things. I'd been in a hurry. I guess I could have left it on my desk.

*No, you didn't, Annie.*

Beads of sweat formed on the back of my neck. My body went on high alert like prey being stalked by a wild animal.

Someone had been in our office and moved my file.

Who?

Elspeth?

I'd caught her "cleansing" the space.

Could that have been a ruse?

Had she dug through my desk to find Natalie's file?

Possibly.

But that didn't make any sense.

She had no connection to the case or Silicon Summit Partners.

I sat in my swivel yellow chair and propped a fringed pillow behind my back. Fletcher teased me for accessorizing my side of the office. That was fine. At least my half of our shared space was cute and organized.

I logged on to my computer and searched Elspeth's name. Numerous event postings appeared for past readings at county fairs and holiday bazaars. I scanned through dozens of hits, but no initial connection with Silicon Summit Partners showed up. I added her name to my spreadsheet and would be sure to tell Dr. Caldwell about my suspicion she moved the file.

The other possibility was that she was looking for something else—something tying her to George's murder. Maybe she moved Natalie's file while searching for evidence she left behind.

However, that didn't explain how said evidence would have ended up in our office.

I scowled and opened a new browser window to search for public records of George's collegiate scholarships.

I was much more successful with this line of inquiry. George's various philanthropic endeavors, including Linx's scholarship, were conveniently listed on his website. The scholarship, aptly named George Richards' Legacy, was awarded to five deserving Northern California students each year, representing unique areas of study, including fine art, sciences, math, political science, and humanities.

It was impressive that Linx had landed one of the prestigious full-ride scholarships. The website had a section tracking former recipients and what they had gone on to do. George's investment in education had paid off in the form of future doctors, city managers, museum curators, and professors.

Maybe he was worried that Linx dropping out of school would be a blemish on his pristine track record.

Again, I wondered if he could have threatened her with some kind of consequence she found untenable. Could that give her enough of a motive for murder?

I made some notes for Dr. Caldwell and checked the time. I still had ten minutes before I was due to relieve Fletcher from front desk duty. I seized the chance to skim Natalie's files.

My heart thudded against my chest as I opened the large envelope and pulled out the paperwork. She had taken grainy photos of photos and documents. The photos looked like they were taken in the early 2000s long before every cell phone had high-resolution cameras built in.

Natalie must have been concerned about leaving digital breadcrumbs. Given how tech-savvy Silicon Summit Partners was, it was likely a wise move.

I thumbed through blown-up black-and-white photos of people I recognized from my previous research, including the CEO of the company, Logan Ashford. I'd never met Logan in person, but I'd spent countless hours researching everything about his past and present. I felt like I knew him, and his highly styled headshot told me everything else I needed to know about him.

Yes, sure, Dr. Caldwell had warned me about making rash judgments based on appearances, but Logan oozed smarminess. His slicked dark hair looked like it had been dipped in a pool of expensive gel. I could tell from his disingenuous, smug smile that he was untrustworthy and a smooth talker.

Natalie had circled other faces in the photos where Logan was posing with people in expensive business suits in front of the courthouse and Silicon Summit Partners' headquarters. She'd listed names with arrows pointing to each person. A few of the names jumped out at me, like the mayors of Cupertino and Sunnyvale, as well as two congressional reps and a senator. It was no surprise Logan moved in circles with high-ranking government officials. Silicon Summit Partners poured millions into the local economy.

What was the significance of these players?

I turned to the next pages and immediately latched on to a very familiar face—Mark Vincent.

When I met with Mark in December, he insisted he wasn't involved in any sort of a cover-up. He claimed he was worried about his own personal safety, and that's why he left the company and moved to New York. During our dinner conversation, I believed him, but that changed instantly when I learned he had rented a Tesla for the weekend. Coincidently, shortly before our meeting, I had been run off the road by a Tesla.

I escaped fairly unscathed, short of some minor bumps and bruises, but ever since, I'd been leaning into the possibility that Mark could be the key to all of this. Natalie's photo of Mark with his arm wrapped around Logan's shoulder proved I had to be on the right track.

## TWENTY

Mark and Logan looked quite chummy in the photos. Natalie had marked dates below the picture. It was going to take time and concentration to check the names and dates against the database I'd created, so I flipped to the last pages.

These were photocopies of a contract.

My heart sunk as I read through the contract.

As Mark had shared, Scarlet penned a deal with Logan, agreeing to join the firm.

Why?

She must have had a reason.

I'd been wrestling with what the reason could be since Mark had revealed the news.

Was it her cover?

Her way in?

Or had Logan attempted to pay her off? Her silence in exchange for a large chunk of cash? I knew Scarlet had student loans she was worried about, but was she concerned enough about her collegiate debt to work for Silicon Summit Partners?

*No, Scarlet would never.*

I shook off the mere thought.

Maybe she hadn't realized at first that Logan was involved in the high-scale cover-up. Once she figured it out, it was too late. She confronted him, and he killed her. Or maybe had her killed. Something about his Machiavellian grin made me think he had "people" to do his dirty work.

An overhead announcement on the speakers brought me back into the present.

It was time for me to check in with Fletcher and time for the matchmaking participants to break for lunch.

I put the files away underneath a stack of vendor receipts and special orders in my desk drawer. If it was moved again, there was no question someone else had touched it. I wasn't taking any chances or second-guessing myself, so for extra protection, I locked the door behind me.

Fletcher and I never locked the office door, or the door leading upstairs, but there was a killer on the loose—George's or maybe even Scarlet's. Although the latter was a stretch. As much as I had been rattled by my run-in with the Tesla, the odds that Silicon Summit Partners had someone tailing me in Redwood Grove were slim at best. Either way, they weren't getting back inside.

There was a small line waiting to check out at the Foyer. Couples queued to purchase vanilla candles and collections of poetry.

I jumped in to help.

Ringing up orders and packaging books was my favorite part of the day. It never ceased to bring me joy to watch happy customers trot out of the store with an armful of new reads. However, I had a hard time concentrating. I couldn't stop thinking about Logan and Scarlet.

"Has it been busy for long?" I asked Fletcher once we'd gotten through the line. "You should have called me. I would have come right away."

"No. It's been dead." He stopped, scrunched his nose, and

chewed on his bottom lip. "Sorry, bad choice of words today. It's been slow until Aaliyah made the announcement for everyone to convene in the ballroom."

"You didn't happen to go upstairs by chance?"

He shook his head. "No, why?"

I told him about the file and what I read in the documents. "Something feels off about it. I would swear I had left them in my desk, but I admit I was in a rush."

"I'll be eager to look them over. It's my duty as your future partner in crime. Scarlet's murder is our top priority for Novel Detectives," Fletcher said. "Maybe you meant to put them in your desk but ended up placing them on top instead. We've had so much going on the last few days. I feel like my head isn't screwed on straight."

"Yeah, probably," I agreed, but I was sure I had left them in the drawer. "Any new developments?"

"Yes, as a matter of fact, I spoke with Victoria, and she's willing to talk to you. She's in the Sitting Room now, waiting for you." He stabbed his finger in that direction.

"Waiting for me?" I pointed to my chest.

*Why is she waiting for me?*

He nodded. "I told her it would be better if you heard everything straight from her. That way, it doesn't get lost in translation."

"The two of you already spoke?"

"We did. It was slow, so she hung around. I feel confident that once you hear her side of the story, you will believe her, too." His soft blue eyes were wide with hope, and his voice teetered on the edge of downright begging.

"Don't you want a break?" I shot a glance into the ballroom, where Aaliyah instructed everyone to return from lunch by two for the next activity.

"I'd rather have you speak with Victoria first." He pushed

me in that direction. "Hal said he'd be here in a minute anyway."

It wasn't worth arguing. Fletcher wasn't going to budge. I owed him at least having a conversation with her.

I headed for the Sitting Room, passing a couple who clearly had hit it off. They were wrapped in each other's arms, nuzzling necks, and completely oblivious to my passing by.

As expected, Victoria was waiting in one of the plush chairs in front of the faux fireplace in the Sitting Room. I felt like I was stepping back in time for a formal afternoon tea.

She raised her finger in a greeting. "Good. I'm glad you agreed to speak with me. It's important for me to clear things up, even if it jeopardizes my contract with George. I suppose now that he's dead, the contract is worthless anyway."

I sat next to her.

Her polished, perfect posture made me sit up taller. Although I had a feeling she was keeping her back erect so as not to spill out of her low-cut shirt.

"I can tell you don't like me." She crossed her legs and gave me a formidable stare. I couldn't decide if she was trying to figure out how to get through to me or whether she could control me.

"I never said that."

"You didn't have to." She moved her head from one side to the other, studying me like a therapist or doctor trying to assess a new client. "Listen, I like Fletcher. That's the only reason I agreed to talk to you."

"I'm not forcing you to speak with me."

She rolled her neck to the other side and made a small circle like she was warming up for yoga class. "I'll be straight with you and get to the point. I didn't come to Redwood Grove to find love."

Shocker.

I wanted to say, "Duh," but instead, I leaned back and waited for her to continue.

"I'm here for some competitive research."

"For Book Emporium," I offered.

"No. That much is true. What George and I were working on is entirely my own. I've been desperate to break away from them for years, but the reality is I make a decent living and have health care through the company. It's hard to give that up, especially in California where our cost of living is double anywhere else."

I couldn't argue with her on that point. There was nowhere I would rather live than California. In less than an hour, I could be strolling along the golden coastal beaches, hiking through redwood forests, or snowshoeing on a mountaintop. But our rich lifestyle did come with a price tag, especially regarding real estate. Housing costs had spiked in recent years with no signs of slowing down.

"I met George at a networking event in San Francisco for women-owned start-ups. It's kind of like the matchmaking you're doing here. There were a number of investors, and we went table by table, pitching our ideas. George and I hit it off immediately. He loved my concept and talked at length and with passion about the importance of funding small, community-based businesses."

That sounded like the George I knew.

"To tell you the truth, I never thought we'd go much further than that initial conversation. You know how it is with these things: you do the pitch, and people are excited, but when it comes to formalizing contracts and signing off on payments, well, that's another story." She stared at her nails with interest, as if she were remembering past failed experiences.

"George followed through, though?" I prompted, wanting to keep her on topic.

"Enthusiastically. He reached out to me. That never

happens. I couldn't believe it. It was like a gift from the heavens. He gave me a tight timeline, asking for a full business plan, marketing plan, and financials within a month. He didn't want to waste time. He wanted to move fast."

I wondered if there could be a reason George wanted to push their partnership forward quickly.

As if reading my mind, she answered my question.

"He would tease that he was in his elder teen years and had to get projects finished before someone took away his keys."

"Took away his keys?"

She pretended to dangle a set of keys with her fingers. "Revoke his driver's license."

"Ah, got it. That's kind of an odd statement."

"He was a kidder and an astute business adviser. I was worried about the timeline because I had to maintain my day job and work on the proposal for him at night, but it turned out it was better to have a tight deadline. It forced me to dive deep." She shifted in the chair, tugging at her skirt hem as she crossed her legs.

"Did you pitch him on the final proposal before he died?" I was very curious about where Victoria was going with this.

"I did. We met three weeks ago. He loved the pitch even more than my first attempt to secure venture capital. He said he'd have his lawyer review everything, and a contract would be drawn up for us to sign within the week. I couldn't believe it would move that fast, but he was a man of his word. The contract appeared in my inbox three days later."

"Is that why you're here? Were you and George meeting in person to finalize the contract?" I felt like I was missing something.

"No. I signed the contract already. I've been waiting for George to sign it. It's just a formality. The big issue is that I signed an NDA—a nondisclosure agreement."

I knew what an NDA was, but I didn't bother to interrupt her because it felt like we were getting close to the juicy part.

"That's why I've been on edge about saying anything. Since the contract is technically not complete, I don't want to jeopardize it, but now..." She trailed off.

"Did you follow George here hoping to get him to sign it?" I repeated the question because she hadn't answered it, not directly.

"Not at all. George suggested I visit the bookstore as part of my competitive research and for potential inspiration for our project." She gestured toward the bookshelves.

I tried to keep my expression neutral, but inside I was fuming. My initial take on her had been correct—she was trying to steal our ideas.

"I was already aware of the Secret Bookcase. You have quite the reputation. I read an article about a cute mystery bookshop housed in an English estate in the California Independent Bookseller's Association newsletter a while ago, but it didn't do justice to this." She paused and looked around the Sitting Room with awe. "It's a charmer. It gets under your skin, and I'm brimming with ideas for my project now."

She wasn't even subtle about her motives. How was Fletcher so dazzled by her that he was blinded to her intentions?

"George mentioned the Valentine's extravaganza, and I thought it was the perfect excuse to come take some copious notes and have face time with him."

"I have to be honest. I appreciate your openness, but it's hard for me to hear you being so blatant about ripping off our ideas for your new bookstore. Maybe things are different working for a big corporation, but in the indie bookselling world, we're always happy to share, brainstorm, and even cross-promote, but it's hard to want to do that knowing you've been sneaking around taking notes and plotting how to recreate our events."

Victoria gasped and patted her chest twice. She leaned forward like she wanted to reach for my arm but decided against it at the last minute. "Never. I would never. No wonder you don't trust me. I wouldn't trust me either. You have the wrong impression. I'm not opening a bookshop with George's investment."

"You're not?" I was genuinely confused.

"We're rolling out a modern version of the bookmobile. Our working name is the Book Bus, but I'm not tied to that. I want to bring books to underserved communities. There are dozens of small towns, mainly in rural areas, that don't have a bookstore within one hundred miles. My vision is to change that. Our bookmobile will sell books, offer free little library services to those who can't afford to shop, and do literacy outreach and events. That's why George was eager for me to see what you're doing here at the Secret Bookcase. I could never pull off anything on the same scale, but I want to create an event calendar and bonus activities to draw kids and families in. Books are a point of connection, and my vision—our vision—for the bookmobile was just that."

I wouldn't have predicted a rural bookmobile would be what George and Victoria were partnering on.

"Now that George is dead, I don't know what will happen. I'm hopeful his estate will honor projects like this that he was passionate about, but there's no way to tell."

I took a minute to process everything. No wonder Fletcher was crushing on Victoria. This was a completely different side of her. Her drive and dedication came through when she spoke about the bookmobile. Bringing books to bookless communities was a noble project in my mind, but there were still some major gaps in the timeline and some serious questions left to answer, like why was she sneaking around the side of the estate this morning and hiding behind the lemon tree with her future business partner dead on a bench nearby?

# TWENTY-ONE

Victoria stood and walked to the window, staring into the gardens with a wistful gaze. "I believed with George's guidance and financial backing, we'd be able to achieve great things. I was prepared to give Book Emporium my notice when I returned home. I suppose it's good I waited. It looks like I'll be stuck in corporate book hell indefinitely."

"Surely, your contract must have stipulations for this," I said, following her gaze. A couple was walking hand in hand through the rose bushes, neatly pruned in preparation for spring. I couldn't wait for rose season when the garden would be lush with peachy, pink, and brilliant red blooms.

"We'll see. The issue is I don't know whether or not George formally signed the contract. I could be floating in limbo for months if not years." She drew her eyes away from the window. "I hope this clears the air between us. I'm sorry if you misunderstood my intentions, and I am serious about Fletcher. He and I had an instant connection. I'm interested in seeing where it takes us."

"I appreciate your honesty." I stood up, too. Speaking of

Fletcher, I needed to check in with him. "You've reported what you've shared with me with the police, correct?"

She hesitated, her eyes flitting outside again. "Most of it."

"I would advise you fill Dr. Caldwell in on everything." I started to move toward the exit but stopped. "By the way, what were you really doing this morning? Why were you sneaking around the side of the building?"

Her body stiffened. She sucked in her cheeks like she was deciding whether or not to tell me the truth. "Listen, I didn't say this to Fletcher, and I haven't told the police yet either because I want them to review the footage first. Otherwise, I might be implicated."

"They've already reviewed the footage." I didn't think Dr. Caldwell would mind me sharing this piece of information, especially if it prompted Victoria to admit what she was doing.

"Really? Oh, excellent. Good. That's very good." She paced from the tea cart to the first row of books and back again. "As I mentioned, Fletcher and I were supposed to meet early. He was going to give me a tour of the bookstore, and I wanted to pick his brain about ideas for the bookmobile. I was waiting for him near the gate when he texted to let me know he was running late. I would have stayed there, but I saw George."

"You saw George?" I couldn't believe how many people had seen and interacted with George prior to his death. "Do you know what time this was?"

"I'm not sure. I wasn't really paying attention. I would guess shortly before seven. Fletcher and I were meeting at seven. I got here first."

Had everyone in town seen George right before he died?

"He had a book and some papers in his hands and coffee in the other. I thought he might be drunk or maybe having a stroke because he could barely stand upright."

"Where was this?" I interrupted.

"Right over there." She pointed to the rose garden.

"Someone was with him. I knew it was a woman because she had a long skirt and a flowy coat. They were arguing, but I was too far away to hear what they were saying."

"Did you see the woman?" A long, flowy coat certainly matched Elspeth's style.

Victoria shook her head. "Only from behind. Again, I was all the way at the far end of the drive." She motioned with her right hand. "I'm not proud of this, but I guess my curiosity got the best of me. I justified it by telling myself that I was doing my due diligence if George was going to be a business partner, but the truth is I was snooping."

I could hear the embarrassment in her voice. I wasn't going to judge. "That's understandable. I probably would have done the same thing."

Her eyes grew wide. "Would you? Doubtful. I'm a grown woman. I should have left it alone. George's personal life had no bearing on our business relationship."

"So you followed him?"

"I couldn't. It would be way too obvious. I eavesdropped for a few minutes, but I couldn't hear anything." She gazed out the window again as if replaying her movements. "Fletcher texted me to let me know he was running late, and I guess my curiosity got the best of me. That's why I went around the backside of the property. If I walked along the drive, they would have seen me for sure, but I figured I could sneak along the house and hide on the Terrace since they were right over there." She tapped the window to point out the spot.

I moved closer to see exactly where she was pointing. It was the same spot the crows had swarmed me. She likely could have overheard their conversation if she had hidden out on the Terrace.

Her story was adding up, at least so far.

If only Fletcher could train the crows to speak, we would know for sure.

She sighed. "I feel ridiculous, but it's the truth. I couldn't hear what the woman was saying, but George was pleading with her, begging her."

"Begging her for what?"

"I don't know." She shrugged. "That's why I snuck around the building. It wasn't my proudest moment and I'm surprised I'm not more scratched up or covered in spiderwebs. I didn't exactly dress for bushwhacking. I was trying to impress Fletcher with my outfit." She pressed up her cleavage and adjusted her bra straps.

"Yeah. We don't maintain that side of the property." I wanted to keep the conversation to the investigation and not how she was trying to entice Fletcher.

"Why would you? There's no reason except for snoopy booksellers like me." She frowned.

"Were you able to hear or see them?"

She shook her head. "No. George had already collapsed on the bench. I was going to see if I could help, but then you showed up, and the crows were going wild, and I got spooked. I figured you and the police would think I killed him."

"How long did it take you to get around the building?"

Her eyes raised toward the ceiling as she thought about it. "Longer than I'd like to admit. I had to pull away branches, and I kept getting caught in spiderwebs. These heels aren't exactly made for hiking." She lifted a black two-inch pump. "The woman must have taken off right away. I never saw her."

"Could you describe her?"

"I wish I could." She shook her head with regret. "I only caught a flash of her long white skirt and flowy black coat. I say flowy because it almost reminded me of a witch's cape."

"You're sure you didn't recognize her? How tall was she? Or did you see her hair color?" I needed specifics.

"I've got nothing. Nothing. That's another reason I didn't want to tell the police what I was doing because I can hear how flimsy my story sounds. Who's going to believe me? I wouldn't believe me. The only thing saving me is the security footage. George must have already been feeling the effects of whatever killed him. That would explain why he was stumbling and slurring his words. He must have died quickly."

I considered her story. Who was the mystery woman?

Her description pointed to Elspeth, but so far, I didn't have any solid evidence linking her to the crime scene.

The timeline surrounding George's death was shrinking by the minute. I must have found him right after he died. Victoria was there, too, and I knew Linx and Aaliyah had interacted with him at Cryptic. One of them might have followed him. Or Victoria could be spinning her own web of lies.

## TWENTY-TWO

"Isn't it a shame we were both so close and yet neither of us could save George?" Victoria scrunched her face like she was trying to force tears.

I chose not to comment on that but rather direct her to Dr. Caldwell, who needed to know this immediately. "I realize you're embarrassed, but this is critical information for the police. You probably saw George's killer."

A third possibility entered my mind in terms of how George had been killed. There was the coffee or his food at Cryptic. Dr. Caldwell's theory that he could have been stuck with something was also compelling. What if the mystery woman had coated the papers or the book with a substance? Was that a viable method for murder?

Something toxic to the touch—peanut residue perhaps? Assuming he had a deadly allergy.

The idea felt equally absurd and potentially plausible. If that were the case, the killer must have known George intimately in order to plot such a cunning method of murder. I'd have to sit with it and ask Dr. Caldwell if they'd recovered the papers or book.

"Yes, I know. You're right. Knowing the footage matches my statement should shut down their interest in me." Victoria picked her purse up from the floor and looped it over her wrist. "I'll speak with the detective now."

"Thank you." I walked to the hallway with her. "And thank you for telling me the truth about your relationship with George. I hope the bookmobile can proceed as planned, and I'll be happy to lend any insight I can about events and outreach."

"That would be wonderful." She crossed her fingers. "I'll be crossing my fingers and toes."

We went to the front together. Hal sat on the stool behind the desk, reviewing a spring catalog from one of our top vendors. It was hard to imagine that Redwood Grove would be in full bloom in a couple of months, with swaths of California poppies and golden sun-drenched afternoons stretching into the evening.

"Tell Fletcher I'll be back soon," Victoria said as she left.

"Detective Annie, what did you discover?" Hal asked once she was out the door and out of earshot.

"Am I that obvious?"

"Only to me because I love and adore you. And because a little birdie who just went to feed his birds told me." Hal winked and dog-eared a page in the catalog before setting it on the counter.

"I have a feeling that's because he's desperate for me to prove she wasn't involved. Jekyll and Hyde know the truth. Fletcher needs to up his training game and teach them to speak."

"I'd put my money on Fletcher in that bet." Hal stood and wandered over to the candle display. He twisted the label on a heart-shaped candle so the label faced out like the rest of the stack. "Was she involved?"

"It's too soon to say for sure, but I'm leaning toward no." I rearranged the rack of Valentine's stickers that had been picked over and told him about our conversation.

"I never would have imagined so many people harboring ill feelings for George. The George I knew was a dear friend, a kindhearted soul who spent his last days building a legacy of community for the next generation." Hal rubbed his shoulders as if there was a draft in the bookstore. "I suppose it goes to show that we only know the parts people allow us to see."

"Not you, Hal Christie. I doubt any skeletons are hiding in your closet."

The briefest flash of sadness crossed his face before he smiled. "Same for you."

"I keep wondering about George's past. How much do you know about what he did? Could he have come into his fortune in less than reputable ways?"

"I've been pondering that as well." Hal turned up the thermostat a notch. "George was tight-lipped about his past. He was vague in our chess games if the conversation drifted to our early days. It's hard to articulate why, but I got the sense he had regrets."

"Doesn't everyone?" I thought about how much time I'd wasted beating myself up for not being able to solve Scarlet's murder. If I could travel back and meet my younger self, I would encourage her to be much kinder to herself. But then again, I'd learned a lot through my mistakes and missteps.

"Certainly." Hal gave me a knowing nod. "George was different. When the subject came up, he would go quiet, painfully quiet. It was as if it was too heavy for him to face. He was quite distressed and kept mentioning broken promises and big mistakes. I believe he was depressed and somehow felt guilty and perhaps even responsible for whatever happened in his past."

My thoughts immediately returned to Scarlet.

For years, I'd been unable to speak about her death and,

subsequently, her life. The Secret Bookcase had changed that. Hal, Fletcher, Pri, Liam, Penny, and my entire crew had helped crack me open. As I'd said to Gertrude, the grief lingered, but it wasn't quite as raw.

"Maybe the killer was seeking revenge for something in George's past." I checked the coffee and tea station, which needed refreshing. The candy hearts had been a hit, as had the red velvet hot chocolate. I stole a quick glance into the ballroom. Linx was long gone, and the food tables were empty.

"It's strange to imagine anyone seeking revenge against my friend, but I suppose it could be true." Hal sighed and ran his hands along his beard pensively. "It is all women on your suspect list, isn't it?"

"Good point. I'm not sure that's ever happened." I hadn't made that connection; Aaliyah, Gertrude, Linx, Victoria, and Elspeth—they were all women.

"I hate to even bring it up, but is there a chance George could have been inappropriate with any of them? He wasn't inappropriate with you?" Hal stared at me in horror as if he'd just had the worst revelation.

"Not at all. The opposite. I found him to be thoughtful and respectful. He had good boundaries. I didn't witness that kind of behavior from him, and I haven't heard any other rumors like that. You would think if he had a history of issues with women, it would have come up."

Hal relaxed a bit. "Good. I would hate to hear that. Sadly, as you well know, some of my peers are, shall we say, less evolved when it comes to gender roles and stereotypes."

"Another reason you're a true Renaissance man and ahead of your time." I smiled.

He waved me off.

"I should reset the tables before everyone comes back from lunch. Are you still game to lead the garden tour?"

He gave me a salute. "My Wellies are waiting and ready."

Hal's Anglophile obsession stretched from his choice of garden boots to British tea. He was convinced the Great Dame of Mystery was his grandmother due to a long-unsolved mystery surrounding Ms. Christie. She went missing from her home in Berkshire for eleven days and was later found at a hotel in Harrogate with memory loss attributed to a car accident. A public search ensued before she was discovered safe and sound. Rumors ranged from her attempting to exact her revenge on her husband, who wanted a divorce, to the psychological effects of depression. According to Hal, she vanished to give birth to his mother, who was put up for adoption and raised with no knowledge she was the descendant of the world's most famous mystery writer.

"Let me clean up, and then we'll swap spots." I ducked into the Conservatory, which was empty. I gathered empty cups and plates and took off the tablecloths. Hal's observation sent my brain in new directions.

George didn't strike me as chauvinistic or predatory. He was intentionally investing in women-owned small businesses. Was there a reason for that?

The angle of a woman scorned didn't seem to fit in this case, with the exception of Gertrude. Everyone was twenty or thirty years younger than him, and I hadn't picked up on romantic gestures on George's or any of the suspects' part.

There had to be some other explanation.

I covered the tables with fresh tablecloths, rearranged the flower vases, and set out new bowls of candy and mints. We weren't serving any additional meals at the bookstore. Dinner tonight was at State of Mind Public House, and tomorrow, we would meet at Cryptic before the morning hike.

Hal would lead the newly matched couples on a garden tour, complete with a history lesson in native California plants and herbology. Then there would be a break until we reconvened and took over Public House for cocktails, dinner, dancing, and karaoke. The rest of the afternoon, as far as book sales went, should be manageable.

I was hoping for a chance to talk to Fletcher about Natalie's case files and George's murder. Having someone to bounce ideas off of and listen to my ever-changing theories was helpful. Fletcher was a worthy partner when it came to puzzling through clues and evidence. I wanted to hear his thoughts on George and see if he had learned anything new.

I had a chance after Hal and Aaliyah wrangled the new pairs outside for the garden tour.

Fletcher deposited a handful of shiny objects in the drawer under the cash register. "More crow money. They were very generous today. Check this out." He held up a gold band. "A ring. They brought me a ring."

"That looks like a wedding ring, Fletcher." I moved closer to get a better look.

"I know. They're heeding my cues to bring me better gifts." He tossed the ring into the drawer with the other objects.

"We're going to end up on a most-wanted list," I teased.

"No way. I'll claim it was you. They love you now." He made a heart with his hands. "But I will make an announcement in the next newsletter that we found a ring."

"Good idea. Some poor lonely soul is missing a ring because your crows have to pay up." I rolled my eyes and chuckled. "Before I forget, can I just ask again for my own sanity, you're sure you didn't move things around on my side of the office?"

"You're not turning into Mr. Monk on me, are you? Did I accidentally put one of your Sharpies in the wrong tin?"

"Mr. Monk is *the* OG detective. I'll take that as a compliment, but no, I'm still thinking about who moved Natalie's file, and I think there's only one person."

Fletcher's face went slack. "Who was upstairs?"

"Elspeth with her cleansing," I said with more inflection than intended. "I haven't seen anyone else, but we keep the door unlocked." I motioned to the door leading to the second floor. "Anyone could have snuck upstairs. When we officially open Novel Detectives, we need to install locks everywhere. We can't have sensitive material lying around." There had never been a need to lock doors short of those leading to Hal's private living space. Our customers were respectful. The PRIVATE signs had done the trick up until now. Running a detective agency upstairs required extra precautions. I didn't like the thought of a stranger rummaging through my things, but I was glad I caught Elspeth earlier because it highlighted the need to call a locksmith.

"Fair point." He checked to make sure no one was around. Everyone was outside admiring the topiaries and taking pictures with bunches of wild rosemary and lavender. "I just saw Elspeth when I was gathering the trinkets from the crows. She was on the Terrace staring at the roofline like she was going to scale the building."

"Odd. Was she looking at something?"

"The crows. They were perched on the peak. She launched into a new round of warnings about what a bad omen the crows were and how we needed to get rid of them. Her exact words were, 'Crows portend to murder.'"

"We had a murder this morning." I knew I was stating the obvious, but so was Elspeth.

"You took the words right out of my mouth. She insisted she 'sees' another murder." He ran his hands up and down in waves, mimicking her exaggerated gestures. "A murder connected to the bookstore."

"George's murder was connected to the bookstore."

"Agreed. And, again, my thoughts exactly. However, Elspeth wagged her long finger in my face and said that this time, the victim would be one of us." He tapped his chest and then pointed to me.

"Us—as in you and me?" I was quickly tiring of Elspeth's

antics. This was serious. A man was dead. We didn't have time for her party tricks.

"As in a bookstore employee." Fletcher rolled his eyes. "That woman is in another world, Annie. I don't take a word she says with seriousness."

"Right." I agreed, but there was one problem: regardless of Elspeth's alternative reality, she had accurately predicted George's death. If she was warning Fletcher, that could mean the killer was about to strike again, and one of us could be next.

# TWENTY-THREE

I didn't want to worry Fletcher, so I let it go and asked him what else he'd heard about George and the suspects. Elspeth was the most likely candidate to have moved things in my office. What could she really have been looking for? I felt like we were getting so close, but there were still a few key pieces I was missing. Victoria's description of the woman she'd seen arguing with George before he died certainly matched Elspeth's description. But what was her motive? Could she have a connection with him from the past? Neither of them had given me the impression that they were already acquainted when she'd warned him about his dark aura, but perhaps that was intentional.

At dinner tonight, I intended to have a one-on-one chat with the psychic. I didn't trust her, and I didn't like her warning Fletcher about another murder. Could it be because *she* was planning to take one of us out?

One of my first theories had been that she was responsible for his death, and her warning was a smoke screen. In criminology, we are trained to explore any and every possible theory. Perhaps the reason Elspeth had been at the top of my mind immediately following George's death was because she was the killer.

The rest of the afternoon proceeded without incident. Hal's garden tour was a hit, and more couples emerged as the day wore on. I had to credit Aaliyah. Her system appeared to be working. There was no denying the electricity in the air. It was thick and palpable, like if I were to strike a match, we'd set the entire building on fire.

Sales were steady as newly formed couples left with packages of books and dewy smiles. I couldn't help but get caught up in the spirit. We wrapped orders in pink paper, tied them with shiny red strings, and sent everyone off with parting chocolates.

Aaliyah waited until the last few stragglers were gone and then collapsed dramatically on the front counter. "What a day. I'm spent."

"Can I get you something? A drink? A snack? We keep a secret stash of protein bars upstairs in our office."

"Oh, I know. I took a couple earlier. Pastry and coffee can only sustain you for so long before you come crashing down from the sugar high. I was so busy, I never had a chance to step out for lunch."

I tried not to clench my jaw too tight. She had taken bars from our office? I would gladly share, that was a non-issue, but she was admitting she'd been upstairs. Could it have been her who moved Natalie's file?

And if that were the case, I had the same questions about what she was really looking for.

"I didn't know you went upstairs," I said as casually as possible.

She lifted her head. "Is there a problem with that? Hal mentioned you kept snacks up there. I'm happy to pay you."

"Keep your money. You don't need to pay me," I replied. Obviously, I needed to do a better job of playing my cards closer to my chest. "I would have offered to pick you up lunch, that's all."

"There was no time to eat." Aaliyah brushed off her silky dress and then stretched an arm over her head. "It's been match, match, and match."

"People seem happy," I agreed.

"Happy? That's an understatement. We're sitting at twelve successful matches, and the event is only halfway through. If the matching continues at this rate, everyone will be paired by the end of the weekend. I'm calling it now—a massive, massive win for me and for love." She placed both hands on her chest and closed her eyes, swaying to the overhead music like she was basking in the glory of her matchmaking talents.

The fact that she snuck "and for love" at the end of her declaration told me everything I needed to know. Aaliyah remained singularly focused on the success of Storybook Romances.

"It's too bad George isn't here to witness your success." I watched her reaction.

She smoothed her hair with her hand and inhaled, shaking her head in disbelief. "I refuse to believe he's gone. It doesn't feel real. I've been trying to throw myself into the event today as a distraction. I haven't been very successful. I keep expecting him to amble up with his sweet smile and ask me who's been lucky at love. That's what he wanted our new tagline to be, well, a version of that concept—Storybook Romances, where lucky meets love."

"That's good. Clever. Do you know where things stand with his investment now that he's dead?" I cut right to the point. It was late. I needed to get ready for dinner and knew I didn't have much time with her.

"I'm not sure I follow." One side of her lip tugged up as she looked at me like I was speaking a foreign language.

"His investment in Storybook Romances. Is that in jeopardy?" She couldn't be surprised by my question. George was her business partner.

"No. Why would it be?" She sounded irritated I would ask such a thing. "He's already invested. His trust will take over. It won't impact me or the business."

How was she so confident?

Her reaction was exactly the opposite of Victoria's. Both women had financial connections to the philanthropist.

Aaliyah might feel more confident since George had already invested in the business, but I couldn't imagine being nonchalant about the viability of continued financial support. Did she know more than she was letting on?

"Does he have a trust?" I asked. The financial aspect of their partnership was a critical piece of either removing her from my suspect list or catapulting her to the top. Was George as enthusiastic about Storybook Romances as Aaliyah wanted me to believe, or had he had a change of heart? If he intended to pull his investment in the business, it gave her a clear motive for killing him. And she seemed more knowledgeable than anyone else about George's emotional state. Why? Could he have confided something? His deep, dark secrets from the past that even Hal didn't know? I had to at least entertain the possibility that there was more to their story than just Storybook Romances.

"Why so many questions? Are you working with the police?" She wrapped her cashmere sweater tighter around her shoulders.

"Actually, I am. I'm assisting Dr. Caldwell in her investigation." There was no reason to lie to her. If anything, as Fletcher and I inched closer to launching Novel Detectives, I wanted to be intentional with my investigation methods and ensure people recognized our expertise.

She flinched but recovered her composure by stretching again. "Good for you. That makes sense. A mystery bookseller investigating a mystery. Next, you'll tell me you're writing a book about it."

She'd deliberately changed the direction of the conversation. Why didn't she want to discuss George's role in the business? Was she hiding something?

What if he had decided to pull his funding?

Maybe he wasn't pleased with her results or the sales trajectory and told her he wouldn't be renewing any financial contributions or intended to terminate their partnership. That could have prompted her to act swiftly and kill him before he could make any changes to their contract.

I wished I knew the exact nature of their partnership. There was one way to find out—ask her, although I had a feeling she was unlikely to divulge much.

"Was George a partner or owner in Storybook Romances?" I asked, quickly adding a personal element, hoping it might make her more willing to open up. "I'm wondering because Fletcher and I are currently negotiating plans to buy Hal out, and we're looking into different scenarios where he might stay on in some capacity—perhaps as a silent partner or consultant."

It worked because she gave her body a half shake, like shaking off her need to protect herself. "George was a silent partner, although he wasn't very silent. I don't recommend it. That generation of older men find it impossible to give up their power, especially to strong young women like us. George didn't have a say in how I run the company or go about making matches, but that didn't stop him from inserting his opinion."

*This is good, Annie. Keep her talking.*

I nodded sympathetically, even though the opposite was true with Hal. He had always sought my input and advice and given Fletcher and me complete autonomy in running events and managing the store.

"George had two personalities." Aaliyah spoke as if she were in a trance and I wasn't even in the room. "There was his public-facing personality. The sweet, old man who generously doles out his cash and champions women-owned small businesses. And then there's his other side."

I gulped in a breath as I waited for her to reveal what his other side was.

She didn't speak.

She hung her head and stared at the floor.

"What was his other side?" I finally nudged.

"Huh?" She looked up at me like she'd lost her train of thought.

"You said George had two sides. What was his other side?" I repeated.

"Right. Uh, it was a side not many people got to see. He did a good job of masking it, but the man had some nasty demons."

This was a first. No one had mentioned nasty demons or a different side of George's affable personality, except for Elspeth, of course.

Did the demons line up with Elspeth's visions of his dark aura?

"What kind of demons?" I asked Aaliyah.

"Things from his past. Dark things from his past. I don't know what they were, but I saw him snap every once in a while. It was like going from Dr. Jekyll to Mr. Hyde. It wasn't pretty, I can tell you that much."

My thoughts drifted to the crows.

Was it just a coincidence Aaliyah used the literary analogy?

"It scared me. I kept my guard up around him because when he slipped into that darkness, it was like he was wrestling with imaginary monsters. Whatever happened in his past, I think he was trying to make amends with his philanthropy, but I don't think he succeeded. Whoever killed him, they've been waiting, watching, ready to exact their bloody revenge."

# TWENTY-FOUR

Aaliyah's words sent a chill running down my spine.

"Listen, I need to go. I have a million notes to take on my new matches." She gathered her things, bringing an abrupt end to our conversation that left no room for me to ask her anything further.

"One more question before you go: do you remember if George took a book last night?"

"Book? You mean the wrapped books?"

I nodded.

"I couldn't say for sure. I never saw the titles. You wrapped them, but come to think of it, I did see him holding a book. I remember thinking it was odd at the time because he wasn't participating in the matching."

"Did you see where he got the book?"

"I can't say for sure; I wasn't tracking his movements. He could have taken a book from one of the other stacks." She looped her purse over her wrist. "You'll be at dinner, yes?"

"I'm looking forward to it." I nodded.

"See you soon." She lifted one hand in the form of goodbye and drifted out the door in a swirl of blues.

Our chat had been enlightening on two fronts. First, learning she had been upstairs. Whoever had gone through our office was looking for something. I was convinced of that much. Second, her revelation of George's dual personality struck a chord with me.

The façade he shared with me and the public was warm, open, generous, and kind, but what about his shadow side? Could he have had secrets from his past lurking in the shadows that finally caught up to him?

But what?

What were they?

Who was the real George Richards?

I massaged the base of my neck, wishing I could connect the dots.

Dinner tonight would be a good opportunity to watch the suspects. Maybe one of them would slip up, or better yet, come clean with me.

I checked in with Fletcher and Hal after finishing closing procedures.

"Go try and have some fun. It's been a day." Hal said, switching the sign on the door to CLOSED. "Caroline invited me to her place for her vegetarian lasagna. She won't tell me what the secret ingredient is, but my bet is tofu."

"Yum?" Fletcher sounded trepidatious as he pretended to gag. "Tofu, yeah. Good. Sure."

"Oh, no. It's wonderful. You'd never know it's tofu—that is, if I'm right."

"I'm sure you're right." I turned off the computer and handed Hal the end-of-day sales report. He still preferred a hard copy to review with a glass of brandy or malbec before dinner. "What about you, Fletcher? Are you joining in the festivities at Public House?"

He coughed. "Uh, me? Uh. Well." He cleared his throat

and became suddenly extremely interested in fixing a paper heart in the window. "I have plans."

"*P—lans.*" Hal stretched out the word as an impish smile tugged at the side of his lips. "Tell us more."

Fletcher removed the heart and secured it again with a new piece of tape. "I told Victoria I'd show her around town, and she suggested we get dinner afterward. She loves Italian, so I made reservations at the Pizzeria."

"Fletcher Hughes, you're going on a date," I announced, clapping softly and trying to catch his eye.

He tweaked a few of the other hearts. "It's casual."

"That's the best way," Hal said, looking at me.

"Agreed." I resisted the urge to warn Fletcher to be cautious. I'd warmed to Victoria, and her revelations about her partnership with George, as well as the video footage, made me tend to believe she was being truthful. All signs pointed to a love match.

I was happy for my friend.

"See you in the morning, then," I said as I left. I wanted stop by my cottage to change, feed Professor Plum, and take a minute to sit with everything I'd learned today.

Jekyll and Hyde flew above me as I retraced my steps from this morning, happy to see the police had removed the caution tape and not a single sign remained of George's death. Their inky silhouettes contrasted against the sky. They soared in a figure eight pattern, creating an infinity sign over my head.

"More peanuts for you tomorrow," I said to the crows as I reached the entrance to Oceanside Park.

The sun was already to sink on the horizon, bathing the wild, tame space in a demure, iridescent light. The short walk was a chance to clear my head. I took my time, pausing intentionally to admire the rough bark of a redwood tree and breathe in the fragrance of the dainty cherry blossoms.

I turned onto my cul-de-sac and could feel the weight of the day sloughing off at the sight of the yellow cottages decked out for Valentine's Day. I was years younger than most of the other residents in my neighborhood, who were predominately retired. They spent their days playing pickleball at the park and gathering for outdoor chess and bocce ball in the shared green space. Every holiday was an opportunity to showcase their creative aesthetic. Giant five-foot-tall foam hearts greeted me at the entrance. Plastic pink flamingos dotted lawns, and flower baskets overflowing with pink and white geraniums hung from porches.

As was typical, a silver platter filled with raspberry muffins and a note from my neighbor waited for me on the side table next to my rocking chair. The note read: Hand Baked With Love, Enjoy.

I picked up the tray and unlocked the front door. Professor Plum greeted me at the door as usual with a hungry meow.

I scooped him up and nuzzled his head. "You have no idea how happy I am to see you. It was a rough day."

While I fed him, I recapped everything that had happened, letting the emotion I'd been holding back rush to the surface. My cheeks warmed, and my heart rate picked up as the image of George's body played like a scene from a horror movie in my mind. "I'm going to solve this, Professor Plum. Mark my words. I'm close to figuring out who did this. Too many good things are happening at the Secret Bookcase and in Redwood Grove. I'm not letting the killer make us live in fear. Once I piece it all together, I can't wait to watch Dr. Caldwell make an arrest."

Professor Plum slipped between my legs to encourage me to feed him faster.

I set his kibble and wet food on the floor and poured myself a glass of water. "We've made progress on Scarlet's case, too."

Why was talking to a tabby cat so cathartic?

I could feel my blood pressure drop as I told him about Natalie's files and how Scarlet had inked a deal to work with

Silicon Summit Partners. "She must have had an angle, don't you think?" I sipped the water. "Maybe it was her way into the firm?"

Professor Plum ignored me as he devoured his dinner.

I didn't blame him. I was suddenly famished.

I headed upstairs to change. I tied my hair up and washed my face. Then I applied blush, lip gloss, and mascara. Dinner wasn't particularly fancy or formal. State of Mind Public House was a casual eatery serving craft beers and California-inspired fare—hearty salads with citrus and avocados, grass-fed, natural beef burgers, and Cali-style burritos loaded with beans, salsa, grilled chicken, and French fries.

My closet consisted of simple skirts, jeans, and leggings. I dug through the back until I found a dress I hadn't worn in ages. I'd bought it years ago for a dance we hosted at the bookstore. The dress was black with white trim. It hit me above the knee, and its scoop neck accentuated my pale skin and freckles.

I fluffed my natural curls and left my hair loose.

*Not bad, Annie.* I stood back to appraise myself in the mirror.

There was no need to dress up, but I was meeting Liam Donovan after all. Every time I was near him, my heart went into flutter mode, so I wouldn't mind if I returned the favor.

"Good night, Professor. Don't wait up for me." I bent over to pet his head and locked the door behind me on the way out.

The sky was full of stars as I retraced my steps to the village. State of Mind Public House was in a Spanish-style building in the center of the square. Its warm reddish stucco and terra-cotta roof always made me feel like I was in the Mediterranean. Outdoor tables with large umbrellas and heat lamps offered an inviting space to hang out with a cold beer. Inside, the space was cozy, with high ceilings and mood lighting. An impressive bar ran the length of the building with dozens and dozens of tap handles and a large chalkboard menu. Comfortable armchairs and low tables surrounded a rustic fireplace, shared communal tables, bar seating, and a gaming area in the back with retro video games and a karaoke machine.

They had strung red and white heart-shaped twinkle lights from the ceiling for the holiday.

Aaliyah had reserved the fireplace area. The tables were marked with signs reading RESERVED FOR STORYBOOK ROMANCES.

I spotted Pri, who had scored seats near the fireplace. I motioned that I was grabbing a drink, joined the line at the bar and studied the menu. After deliberating between a hoppy red ale and chocolate stout, I decided on the red and a California bowl—which featured quinoa, spicy garbanzo beans, artichokes, red peppers, grilled chicken, goat cheese, and finished with an avocado lime dressing. The basic rule was as long as there was an avocado in it, anything could be called a "California" bowl, burrito, burger... you name it.

Pri waved from one of the chairs in front of the fireplace once I had my beer in hand.

I made my way to her.

She jumped to her feet to hug me. "Love the dress. So chic. Liam's going to flip out when he sees you."

I did a half twirl. "I figured the occasion called for something slightly fancier than my usual leggings and oversized sweater."

"You look fantastic." She blew me a kiss. "And you look more like yourself than you did earlier. Are you feeling better?"

"Yeah, the shock has worn off, and I had the entire day to break down potential motives and speak with everyone on my suspect list." I motioned to her outfit, a slim cream pantsuit that she'd accessorized with chunky gold jewelry. Instead of wearing her hair down, she'd slicked it into a tight, high ponytail and added two-inch dangling gold earrings. "You look amazing! You belong on a red carpet, not in Redwood Grove."

"They're one and the same, aren't they?" She winked and patted my waist. "I got here early to score the best seats by the fire."

"Well done. Where's Penny?"

"Running slightly late. She should be here in fifteen or twenty. What about Mr. Donovan?"

"I haven't heard from him. I'm guessing he'll show up anytime." I took one of the chairs she had positioned strategically around the fireplace and set my beer on a side table. "I'm surprised Aaliyah's not here yet."

"She is. She just put out the name cards and set the tables. I think she went to check on the food." Pri pointed to the communal tables where place cards with match names were set out along with single-stemmed roses and boxes of Red Hots candy. "Fill me in. Tell me everything you've learned. The rumors were flowing faster than espresso shots at the shop this afternoon."

"I don't know where to start." I reached for my beer.

Pri took a sip of her wine. "Knowing you, I'm guessing you have a theory or a few theories."

"That's true." I was about to launch into my many theories of who killed George when Liam and Penny walked in as if they'd timed their entrance.

"Hey, speak of the devil. Hold that thought. Sip your beer. You've been through enough today. I'll be right back." Pri jumped up to greet them.

Liam caught my eye across the room, sending my head spinning. He looked deliciously handsome in his khakis and navy sweater. He was carrying a bundle of wildflowers and a package wrapped in red paper. "Gorgeous," he mouthed, making me bite my bottom lip.

I managed to wipe my sweaty palms on a napkin before they joined me.

"Hey, Murray, you look nice." Liam leaned down to kiss my cheek, letting his lips linger for a moment.

I closed my eyes and savored his soft touch and how he smelled like fresh-cut wood and cedar. He scooted his chair closer to mine. "These are for you." He set the flowers and gift in front of me and wrapped his sturdy arm around the back of my chair.

"Thanks." I picked up the bouquet and buried my nose in the aroma of lilies and lilacs. "They're beautiful."

"As are you." His voice was husky and thick with emotion. "How are you doing? I've been so worried about you."

"I'm good. Well, at least better. I was just saying to Pri that the shock has worn off a bit."

He cupped my face in his hands and kissed my cheek softly. "I'm glad you're here, and I'm sorry you had to go through that."

"Hey, I'm here. Hi, it's me, Pri. Your friend and current third wheel." Pri waved her arm between us. "Love the sentiment. I couldn't agree more, but how about we save the lovey-dovey stuff for later?"

Liam smiled and leaned back. "Sounds like it's been a harrowing day. Do you want to talk about it or drink a beer and forget about it?" He held his pint with his free hand in a toast.

I lifted my glass and clinked it to his. "Talk for sure."

We waited for Penny to return with her wine.

Penny greeted me by touching her chest and shaking her head. "I'm so sorry, Annie. Priya gave me the rundown. It sounds awful." She sat next to Pri. "Poor George. I didn't know him well, but whenever I bumped into him at Cryptic, he remembered me and would chat about work, the weather, and how things were going with renovations at the Wentworth estate."

"Everyone has said that about him." I leaned against Liam's arm, grateful to be surrounded by the people I loved.

"He was that way at the pub," Liam added, gently

massaging my shoulder. "Knew people by name, went out of his way to make conversation, bussed his own dishes. He was a very humble guy. I wouldn't have guessed he was rich if it weren't for his philanthropy. He gave us a generous donation to cover food or drink for anyone who happened into the pub and couldn't afford to pay."

"Really?" I felt more torn about George. Everything he did in his personal life spoke to his giving nature, but how did that align with Aaliyah's perception of his "dark" side?

"We've fed dozens of people off his donation." Liam raised his glass in George's memory. "He told us anytime we ran low to reach out, and he'd cut us another check."

"It's such a shame George had to die," Penny said, snuggling up next to Pri. "There are enough terrible people in the world. Why can't it be one of them?"

"But how well did we know him?" Pri interjected. "I mean, I agree. Don't get me wrong. I thought he was the sweetest. But short of some small talk, I couldn't tell you anything about him. In fact, I've been recalling our conversations, and the more I think about it, the more I realize he never talked about himself. He deflected and changed the topic back to me whenever I would ask him questions. I don't know a single detail about his personal life. Was he married? Did he have a family?"

"Those are all things Dr. Caldwell and her team are researching," I replied, filling them in on what I'd learned.

Our conversation was cut short when Aaliyah called everyone to attention. "Welcome to the dinner hour, my loves." She fanned her face. "The heat in this room is off the charts, and I don't think it's because our bartenders cranked up the thermostat."

People whooped and cheered.

"Let's go over the ground rules for dinner. If you're happily matched, please continue to enjoy an amorous evening together. If you're still seeking love, you'll have a notebook and pen waiting at your seat with your next task. Hint, hint: it involves some beer tasting, so get your palates ready. Here's to finding your perfect match." She motioned for everyone to find their place cards.

My attention was diverted to the bar where it looked like Elspeth was causing a scene. I couldn't help myself, I abandoned my drink and moved closer to listen in. "She's at it again," I said to Liam, resting my beer on the side table. "I'll be right back."

"Death! I see death and darkness in Redwood Grove. Despair is everywhere." She closed her eyes, swaying one hand out in front of her and tapping the other against her eye. Her jewelry and fluttery clothing flowed with her body movements as if swaying to imaginary music that no one else could hear. "There's danger in this very room tonight."

I approached the bar.

She continued her tirade. "Listen carefully. The spirits are awake. They don't come lightly. I see them here, surrounding us." She wafted both hands in the air, making concentric circles like tornados. "Danger, danger is within these very walls and closing in."

# TWENTY-FIVE

"You need to close the bar immediately." Elspeth waved her hands like two warning signs in the bartender's face. One of the many bracelets adorning her wrists slipped off and bounced along the bar like a spinning top. "There's dangerous energy tonight."

Justin, the bartender, caught my eye and shrugged as if to say he had no idea how to respond. He and I had connected during the first case I assisted Dr. Caldwell with and had remained friends ever since. I was glad Justin was behind the bar. It took a lot to rattle him. "You want a drink? We have a Shadow Stout on tap that's dark and delicious—maybe that's what you're picking up."

His attempt at humoring her failed.

"This is no time for jokes." Elspeth's eyes scrunched tight. She shot daggers at him with her look of fury. Her tone turned sharp and almost frantic. "This is no laughing matter. The spirits are angry. They're not to be toyed with. When they show me a message of death—death is imminent."

"Elspeth, let's step outside for a second." I jumped in, took her by the sleeve, and moved her away from the bar.

"Wait, wait." She scurried to retrieve her bracelet.

I stood near the door, not wanting a repeat of this morning.

The ferocity in her eyes made me recoil slightly as she shoved the bracelet on her wrist and stormed toward me with thundering footsteps. Light spilled from the streetlamps lining Cedar Avenue, giving her a villainous glow. I couldn't read auras, but I could read body language, and she was furious I removed her from the restaurant.

"What's going on?" I asked, trying to calm her rage by lifting my palms as I spoke softly and calmly. "I realize we're all on edge with George's death, but Aaliyah's goal tonight is to move past that and recenter on couples finding love."

Elspeth scanned the outdoor patio. "I wouldn't be dismissive if I were you."

"What does that mean?"

"I warned Fletcher earlier. I see more darkness. More death." Her eyes narrowed like two lasers. Her bracelets clinked together like cymbals as she wagged her finger at me. "George wasn't the last. You're in danger. You, Annie. You're in serious danger. Consider this your last warning."

I ignored the flip-flopping in my chest. Her scare tactics weren't going to work with me. "I can take care of myself."

"Can you?" She clasped her hands and pointed them at me with a single clap. "You have no idea what you're up against. You are in way over your head, honey."

My throat tightened. The wild look in her eyes rattled me. "I don't understand."

She rubbed her hands together like she was trying to create friction. "You are in deep trouble. I see it all around you. It's haunted you for years, hasn't it?"

I gulped, trying to force the growing lump away. She hit a nerve. I rubbed my shoulders, suddenly aware that the warmth of the afternoon had vanished.

"You've been carrying darkness like a shadow, but there's no escaping it now. You're surrounded by death, and unless you stop this tireless quest for the truth, you are next. Mark my words, Annie. You are next."

I shivered. I didn't like how her body swayed as she spoke, as if in a trance. Nor did I like her implication. What did she know? Could she actually know about Scarlet? Or was this part of her act? It wouldn't have taken much research. My name would appear in old articles about Scarlet's murder. Was she trying to scare me? Or was this why she'd snooped around my office—to find information to use against me? Was that her angle? She discovered people's pain points to use as a "revelation" in her premonitions?

Could she have done the same with George?

"I'm trained in criminology. I can take care of myself." I repeated the sentiment again, directly and with more force this time. It was true, but I had to admit her manic behavior sent shivers down my arms and into my fingertips. It was either that or my Raynaud's. I suffered from a condition that made me susceptible to the cold. I blew on my hands and rubbed them together to create friction.

She grabbed my arm. "You don't understand. This is so much bigger than you. They know. They're watching."

"Who?"

She dropped my arm and shook her head so hard it made mine hurt. "You're in danger. That's all I can say." Without another word, she took off down the sidewalk.

I stood stunned and confused.

Nothing she said made sense.

Was she a fraud?

Was her warning a distraction from George's murder? She knew I was helping Dr. Caldwell with the investigation. Maybe she was trying to scare me off.

But our interaction felt different.

It was like she was in my head.

Could her warning be linked to Scarlet?

But how?

I chewed the inside of my cheek and wrapped my arms around my chest. The cold evening air was starting to sink into my bones and turn the tips of my fingertips numb.

"Annie, is everything okay?" Liam's voice shook me back into reality.

I turned to see him approaching me with caution, like he was worried he was interrupting something important.

"It's okay, she's gone."

He took off his jacket and offered it to me. "What's going on? I saw you take off with someone. You've been out here for a while."

I shrugged on his coat and stuffed my hands in the pockets. It was warm and smelled like him—earthy and with a tiny hint of onions and garlic from the pub. "I was talking to Elspeth. She's the writer and psychic who predicted George's death."

"You look a little shaken." He stepped closer to me and followed my eyes down the sidewalk.

Elspeth was gone, but her warning repeated on a loop.

"I'm probably blowing this out of proportion, but she made it sound like she knows about Scarlet and that I'm getting close to solving the case."

"How?" Liam frowned and pulled his attention away from the village square.

"She told me I'm next. At first, I thought it was part of her schtick, and then I thought she was giving me a general warning, maybe trying to throw me off her scent if she killed George."

"That's possible."

"But then, the way she was talking, I don't know…" I trailed off, unsure how to articulate my thoughts.

"What?" Liam pressed. "Annie, what does your gut say?"

"I'm not sure. It couldn't all be connected, could it? George

—Silicon Summit Partners? He did make his money in Silicon Valley."

"Has his name come up in any documents?" He moved to the side to allow a group of happy couples to reach the outdoor tables, where flames flickered in the gas firepit, ready to warm hands and toast marshmallows.

"No." I sighed and wrapped Liam's coat tighter. "I've never seen his name. Not even on their client list."

"He could have asked to remain private," Liam suggested.

I appreciated he was contemplating possible scenarios, but it felt like too much of a stretch.

"True, but Dr. Caldwell gained access to their financials and client records, and one of us would have flagged George's name if he had appeared on any of the documents."

Liam waited for another group to pass. The line to the bar wound all the way to the door now that couples began arriving. "What if he used an alias?"

"Or what if I'm grasping for connections that don't exist?" I met his eyes, which were soft and open. "The more likely scenario is Elspeth is intentionally making a scene and trying to get under my skin to shift suspicion away from herself."

"Either way, I'm not letting you out of my sight." He scooped me into a hug. "Do you want to go back inside or call it a night?"

"Yeah, let's go back in." I leaned into his burly frame, grateful for his insight and instinctive need to want to protect me. I wasn't sure I needed protecting, but knowing Liam was by my side brought me extra peace of mind.

"Where's the resident psychic—or better yet, psycho?" Pri asked when we returned. I shrugged off Liam's coat and handed it back to him. Then I scooted my chair closer to the fire.

"She's running around the village trying to scare our Annie," Liam answered for me.

The phrase "our Annie" made my heart flop.

"What?" Pri puffed out her chest like she was ready to fight. "Where is she? We can take her."

I laughed. Then I filled them in on our strange exchange.

"She's a fake," Pri said, dipping a fry in ranch dressing. "My money's on her. I like your theory that she digs around and finds personal facts to use in her so-called 'psychic visions.' I bet she's the killer, and she's getting desperate because she knows you're closing in on her."

Penny nodded. "I agree."

"The problem is proof. We have no proof at this point. I don't even know how he was killed."

"I thought you said it was an allergic reaction." Pri dabbed her hands on a napkin and went in for another fry.

"Yes, but how did the killer trigger the reaction? Was it in something he ate or drank? Did they stab him with a toxin, or am I missing something?"

Pri winced and crossed her fingers. "I hope it didn't happen at Cryptic."

"I keep returning to the timeline," I said, bringing the image of my rough sketch to mind. "Since he left the coffee shop in seemingly good health, not showing any signs of an adverse reaction to his coffee or pastry, that makes me think the killer must have struck in the garden. Who was the mystery woman? And did she have a syringe or something on hand while they argued in the garden?"

"Elspeth matches the description," Liam said, thanking the server who delivered our food. "Didn't you say she was wearing flowy clothing?"

"Yep." I took my bowl from him. The colorful array of veggies made my stomach rumble. "Flowy clothing, but that's not much to go on. There's this tiny issue of evidence when it comes to making a formal arrest."

"Someone could also have impersonated her," Pri said, munching on a ranch-dipped carrot stick. "They might have dressed in intentionally loose and fluid clothing in hopes that if they were seen, they'd be mistaken for Elspeth."

I poured the avocado dressing over the bowl and mixed everything with my fork. "Yeah, that's also a possibility. If there's truth to George making amends for his past mistakes with his financial generosity, then we have to consider who may have had ties with him and who would benefit from his death. I feel like we can rule out Victoria after her confession. Assuming she's telling the truth, George's death adversely affects her."

"That's good for Fletcher, too." Pri made googly eyes at Penny. "He's crushing on her so hard."

"Oh, that's sweet." Penny swirled her wine glass. "Fletcher deserves love."

"And, given that her business plan is to bring books to underserved communities, I have a hard time wrapping my head around why she would want to kill George." I paused and took a bite of the tender marinated chicken and quinoa. "I was sure she was stealing corporate secrets, but now that I've heard her plans, I'm in full support of her and Fletcher."

"Our first bookstore match." Pri lifted her glass. "That calls for cheers." She clinked her glass with each of us.

"So let's rule Victoria out for the moment. That leaves Aaliyah, Gertrude, Linx, and Elspeth." I took another bite, letting the flavors mingle together in my mouth. The bright, zesty dressing, sauteed veggies, and earthy quinoa were a perfect melody.

"I can vouch for Linx," Pri said. "After our text exchange earlier, I did a little digging of my own. You might have to add me to the Novel Detectives payroll." She winked. "On my break, I reviewed our surveillance camera footage. I watched it at least three times in slow motion and didn't see anything unusual. If Linx slipped him something, props to her. She could land a job as a magician because her sleight of hand would have to be out of this world."

"I agree," I said after finishing the bite. "She was honest about their connection, giving up her scholarship and dropping out of school. It sounds like George was trying to convince her to finish her degree, but she's already made up her mind. I got the impression she was annoyed with him, but why kill him? I looked into the scholarship. There don't appear to be any stipulations about paying back the money if a student opts not to continue their studies. The only thing I could find was language about the money not getting renewed if students didn't maintain a C average."

"She said the same thing to me." Pri nodded. "I realize I'm not as trained as you in the art of decoding body language and whether someone is lying, but she comes across as very sincere and earnest about her goals to work in the industry. I can't deny that she has a gift for coffee. She's a natural and passionate, at least when she's not hungover."

"Was she hungover?" Penny asked, leaning over to grab a fry from the basket.

"Oh yeah. She was wrecked this morning," Pri said, looking at me for confirmation.

"She was in bad shape," I agreed. "I wondered if she could have been up all night, stalking George and scoping out how she could kill him, but that theory fell apart once I had a solid timeline. She can't be the woman in flowy clothing because she was working at Cryptic, so to your point, unless she slipped him something there, she can't be the killer."

"You're crossing off suspects one by one," Penny said with admiration.

"It's great watching a pro at work." Liam shot me a playful wink.

I smiled, trying not to blush. This was where I thrived, systematically eliminating theories and suspects that no longer served me. "That leaves us with Aaliyah, Gertrude, and Elspeth. Gertrude wasn't anywhere near the bookstore this morning, at least not as far as I know. She wasn't on any of the surveillance videos. I can't find a solid thread or point of connection between them short of her freaking out because he strongly resembled her late fiancé."

"Temporary emotional breakdown?" Pri offered.

"Could be." I took another bite of my food. "They're about the same age, so I've also been toying with the possibility she's lying, and maybe they had a past connection. A fling gone wrong? I haven't found a link yet, but I'm not ready to rule her out either."

"I would hate for it to be her; she's so sweet," Pri said, twisting her mouth into a frown.

"Agreed. She's a bookstore favorite, yet her reaction to seeing George was unusual, to say the very least. I've been replaying it because it feels like there's something critical there." I stabbed a tomato with my fork. "Aaliyah and Elspeth showed up shortly after I found him. They both had an opportunity to interact with him in the garden and then could have wandered over after the police arrived and blended in with the rest of the onlookers."

"The casual killer," Liam said, raising an eyebrow.

"Right? It's a good move. Aaliyah knows more than she's telling me. I'm sure of that. And Elspeth, wow, Elspeth, where do we even start?"

"Who do you think it is?" Pri asked. "If you were in Dr. Caldwell's shoes and you had to arrest someone tonight, who would it be?"

"No pressure," I teased.

"None. Not an ounce." Pri pinched her fingers together.

"I'm vacillating," I said truthfully. "But if I had to make an arrest at this minute, it would be Elspeth."

# TWENTY-SIX

"I completely agree," Pri exclaimed, quickly lowering her voice when heads around us turned in her direction. "Sorry, I didn't mean to shout. It has to be her. That explains her theatrics. It's a brilliant strategy if you think about it—warn your victim of their impending doom in front of hundreds of people. No one would automatically suspect her. She tried to intervene, warn him, and keep him safe when, in reality, she was the mastermind the whole time."

Liam cleared his throat. "If that's true, you need to be extra careful, Annie. She's targeting you next."

"Why?" Penny asked what I had been thinking. "Did you do something to make her realize you suspected her?"

I shook my head. "The only thing I can think of is the smudging. I wasn't nice about her being upstairs in our private quarters. I caught her in my office, and she played it off by claiming she was cleansing the space. I'm sure she was going through my desk. That's another reason I keep coming back to Scarlet. Maybe there's a connection. Was she looking for the documents Natalie sent me or evidence linking her to George's murder?"

"The paperwork was still there, wasn't it?" Liam asked, brushing a strand of hair from his eye.

"Yeah." Working through my suspect list had suddenly made me even hungrier. My dinner was vanishing fast. I couldn't stop eating. It was the fuel my brain needed to connect the dots. "I'm stuck on that, too. Unless she took photographs of the documents."

"What could be in your office linking her to George?" Penny asked, popping a cherry tomato in her mouth like it was candy.

I appreciated how invested they were in helping solve the case. It was good to have friends to bounce theories off and ask questions that prompted me to revisit ideas or defend my thought process. "Honestly, your guess is as good as mine. The only thing I've come up with is perhaps George learned she was a fraud. Maybe he had documentation or evidence. She was insistent about wanting to cleanse Hal's rooms. I didn't let her."

"Maybe she was checking your office on the off chance he stashed them there," Pri said, warming to my theory.

"Or looking for the key to Hal's quarters," I said, not even realizing I had considered the thought until this very moment. "That's much more logical than an obscure connection to Natalie or Scarlet. Hal and George were supposed to meet for a drink or a game of chess. George never showed, but maybe she overheard their conversation about getting together and assumed George had been upstairs."

"It seems like you're close to figuring it out," Liam said, looking at me over the rim of his beer.

"Close, but still not quite there." I scowled, wishing I could place the final puzzle pieces.

"Is she potentially dangerous?" Pri asked. "She's on the loose in the village. Should we be worried?"

"She doesn't strike me as the violent type," I said. "Whoever killed George put some serious thought into it. His murder was definitely premeditated. It was a strategic killing made to look like an accident. I can't imagine Elspeth wielding a weapon, but I'll loop Dr. Caldwell in. I promised her an update anyway."

"Good." Liam nodded with approval and reached across me for my empty glass. "Another round?"

"Sure." I wanted to stick around longer and observe Aaliyah in action. "If it means getting to hang with you all, count me in."

"Pri, Penny?" Liam shifted into bar-owner mode, grabbing glasses and picking up our empty plates.

"Since you're already up." Penny handed him her wine glass. "I wouldn't turn down another, and I'd love to hear more specifics from you, Annie."

While Liam waited in line at the bar, I answered Penny's questions, keeping an eye on Aaliyah. She wandered between the tables, chatting with couples, taking notes, and making sure drinks were refreshed. Nothing about her interactions seemed out of the ordinary. If anything, she came across as professional and invested in the romantic success of her clients. Like Liam, she tidied up and signaled for the dessert course to be served.

Tomorrow was the final day of the event—her last chance to successfully match participants. Is that why she was taking notes?

What had George wanted changed?

It was important. I knew that much.

But what was the significance of his last-minute adjustment?

A couple he didn't want to be paired, perhaps?

I needed to get my hands on her master list. Maybe something would jump out at me.

Liam returned with drinks, and the conversation drifted away from the murder and to a happier topic: Penny finally getting approval from the Redwood Grove city council to proceed with upgrades to her organic orchards and vineyard.

"This spring, I'd love to throw a party at the farm," she said to me. "A redo from our botched Halloween dinner."

"Fun. Do you have something specific in mind?" I asked. When Penny purchased the old Wentworth farmhouse, the entire property was in disrepair. She'd poured her savings into restoring the house but had come up short on funds to improve the grounds. Pri and I arranged a murder mystery dinner, complete with local actors, as a fundraiser, but when one of the guests dropped dead, we scrapped our plans.

"No, I'm open to your ideas and suggestions. I've seen some gorgeous orchard and vineyard dinners on social media—the farm-to-table concept. Not that I'm growing anything yet, but we could host it outside, string up lights, put out shared tables; Liam, maybe you'd consider catering again?"

"Count on it. You can pay me in IPA." He ran his finger along the rim of his pint glass.

"This is the first I've heard about a garden party, and I can see it now—orchardcore. Dinner under the stars, pale green gingham linens, wildflowers in Mason jars. We should do it. There's so much planning to do," Pri said, patting Penny's knee and giving her a demure smile.

"Will this be another fundraiser?" Liam asked.

"No. Thanks to the grant that Hal helped me secure through the historic land trust, my costs for renovating the vineyard and orchard are covered. This would be a thank-you dinner for the community," Penny said, and then turned to me. "Annie, while I was scrolling through orchard dinners, I also happened upon book swaps. Have you ever done one at the store?"

"No. What are they?" I asked, grinning. "Let me guess: readers swap books?"

"You nailed it." Penny touched the tip of her nose and smiled. "It's sort of a fresh take on a book club, but instead of everyone reading the same book, people bring a favorite book to share. You go around the table, and the first person gives a one or two-minute pitch on the story and why they loved it. Then the next person can take the book or pass. It's like a white elephant but with books."

"That sounds so fun. I'm happy to be of assistance in any way I can." I was sure Fletcher and Hal would be into the concept, too. If it was a success at Penny's party and I couldn't imagine why it wouldn't be, maybe we could do something similar in the store.

We brainstormed dates and menu ideas. Sketching out party ideas was a welcome distraction from George's murder, but my thoughts returned to his mysterious death when Dr. Caldwell entered the restaurant. She systematically scanned the bar and dining area with her astute eyes. She was looking for someone.

It didn't take long for her to focus on her target—Aaliyah.

She made a beeline for the matchmaker, whispered something in her ear, and ushered her outside.

Had Dr. Caldwell uncovered definitive evidence linking Aaliyah to the crime? Was she here to make an arrest?

I didn't want to get my hopes up, but maybe George's killer was about to be placed behind bars.

# TWENTY-SEVEN

"Did we all see that?" I asked everyone. "Dr. Caldwell didn't hesitate. She either wants a word in private with Aaliyah, or she's about to make an arrest."

"I hope it's the latter," Pri said, gazing toward the patio, her foot bouncing with expectation. "It would be a relief to know that whoever killed him isn't running free in Redwood Grove."

"I'm getting arrest vibes," Liam said, moving his body to the side to try and get a better look out the windows. "Whatever she's saying is serious. They're not swapping scone recipes."

I chuckled at the image of Dr. Caldwell baking a batch of scones, her petite arms up to her elbows in the sticky dough. Not that it was out of the realm of possibilities that she baked. I didn't know much about her personal life or interests outside of criminology, but for some reason, I couldn't picture her as a baker. I'd have to ask her what she enjoyed in her spare time. She must have activities she engaged in to combat the weight and darkness of her investigative work. One of the things she used to stress to us was the importance of finding balance, but after all these years, I'd never asked her about her balance point.

I would have to remedy that later.

Dr. Caldwell quizzed Aaliyah for another twenty minutes. We took turns trying to subtly get a glimpse of their conversation by taking glasses up to the bar or pretending to get up to use the bathroom.

Everything about Dr. Caldwell's rigid and unyielding body language told me she had her guard up. There was no question she was in control.

Aaliyah jerked away from each of Dr. Caldwell's questions like it was painful for her to answer. I watched from the steamy window as she shook her head vehemently at something Dr. Caldwell asked. The question shook her. She waved her arms wildly.

Dr. Caldwell folded her arms across her body and stood her ground.

Aaliyah's gestures became more animated as she protested.

I would do anything to be a fly on the outside walls to hear what they were saying.

Dr. Caldwell showed Aaliyah something on her phone. Aaliyah shrugged and waved her off again.

I was returning to the fireplace from my "bathroom" break when I noticed Aaliyah had left her match spreadsheets on one of the side tables when Dr. Caldwell summoned her outside. I checked around me to make sure no one was looking and pulled out my phone. I didn't have much time, so rather than bothering to scan the papers with dozens of watchful eyes nearby, I snapped photos of them. I could check them later at home.

"Any luck?" Liam asked. His feet were casually propped on the hearth like he was intending to stay for a while. That was fine by me. I wanted to wait until Dr. Caldwell finished interrogating Aaliyah and fill her in on what I'd learned and hopefully see if she could share any other news about the investigation.

"No." I scrunched my cheeks. If only I had a listening device or a convenient and believable excuse to be outside, but Dr. Caldwell would see right through any lie. Sure, technically, she'd asked for my assistance, but I didn't think she'd appreciate me crashing her questioning session and lurking nearby. "No. It's impossible to hear and we fogged the window up so much I could barely see. I will admit I considered grabbing some napkins and wiping the window down, but the odds that Dr. Caldwell would see me trying to spy were way too high."

Penny twirled her hair around her index finger and laughed. "You might have some explaining to do if she caught you doing that."

"I might never be asked to consult on another case if she caught me snooping," I agreed with an impish wince. "Rightfully so. I wouldn't blame her. But I did manage to take pictures of Aaliyah's matchmaking spreadsheets. I'm not sure if there will be anything valuable in them, but I do want to review the matches because that was the last thing George requested before he died. It's potentially significant."

"How did you manage to get pics?" Pri craned her neck in that direction. "There are a bunch of people at the table."

"A bunch of lovestruck new couples," I corrected. "Everyone is so wrapped up making gooey eyes at one another that no one noticed me."

"Are gooey eyes a thing?" Liam curled his lip and brushed a strand of dark hair from his eye. "I need a definition because the first thing that comes to my mind is pink eye."

"Eww." Pri tossed her napkin at him. "Way to kill the vibe."

"I had a friend in high school who was a swimmer, and he used to get it all the time. It looked painful."

"Okay, wrong word choice." I held my arms up in surrender. "I simply meant that no one so much as looked at me. They're in the romance zone. My expectations for the weekend were low in terms of the matchmaking piece, but Aaliyah is good at what she does. I can't believe how many people have clicked."

"Or they're just desperate." Liam shrugged and ducked out of Pri's reach, expecting she might try to take a swipe at him.

"Liam Donovan, do not turn into a cynic now. I've said so many good things about you lately. I don't want to have to take it back. As my mom used to say, I don't want to have to pull this car over, but I will. I will," she scolded.

"Good things. Say more." He rubbed his hands together, caught my eye, and winked.

One of the things that made me start to fall for him was his self-deprecating humor. It had taken me a while to understand that he teases because he loves. At first, I'd found his sarcasm off-putting, but once I realized he wanted the back and forth of a witty exchange, I'd come to appreciate it and crave it.

"My lips are sealed. You're done, sir." Pri zipped her lips shut with her fingers and shot him a challenging stare as if daring him to say more.

Penny rolled her eyes. "What are we going to do with these two?"

"Lock them in a room together for the weekend," I suggested. "Old-school style like the Golden Age mysteries. We'll keep the key and they'll have to figure out a way to get along and get out or they'll be stuck there for good."

"I like it." Penny clapped softly.

Liam patted the spot next to him. "Come sit. It looks like Dr. Caldwell is done with Aaliyah."

I stole a glance outside. He was right. They were both coming inside.

I took a seat next to Liam and tried to look like we'd been discussing anything other than the case.

Dr. Caldwell paused at the bar to get a glass of water before joining us. "May I?" She motioned to the extra chair Pri had conveniently dragged over. "What did you learn from your time at the window?"

"Our time at the window?" Pri asked, intentionally

widening her gaze and clasping her hands together to make her appear innocent.

It didn't work.

Dr. Caldwell concealed a smile. "I saw each and every one of you at the window while I was speaking to Aaliyah. Covert operations are not your skill set."

Nothing got by Dr. Caldwell. I never should have thought otherwise.

"Sorry," I said, biting my bottom lip. I wasn't worried Dr. Caldwell was angry. She was a good sport.

"It gave me a good laugh." She pressed her glasses to the bridge of her nose. "My conversation with Aaliyah was, hmm, how should I put it?" She paused, searching for the right word. "Illuminating."

"You didn't arrest her, though." My attention drifted to the center of the room, where Aaliyah was prepping matches for karaoke.

"Not yet. No." Dr. Caldwell didn't elaborate. "I assume you have intel you'd like to share?"

I nodded and waited for her to get her notebook. Then I proceeded to tell her everything I'd learned, from Linx dropping out of school to Victoria partnering with George for a bookmobile project.

She took copious notes, pausing every so often to ask for clarification.

"This is excellent. Thank you." She shut the notebook and motioned for us to scoot closer. "This will be public information by morning, so I am able to share that George did indeed die of anaphylactic shock."

# TWENTY-EIGHT

"So it was an allergy?" I asked Dr. Caldwell, eager for official confirmation.

"Yes, he died of an allergic reaction. I was grilling Aaliyah because we found mold spores in the book she gave George last night."

I stared at Aaliyah, who flitted about the busy restaurant as if she hadn't a care in the world. Could she have given George a book filled with mold spores—did that mean she knew he had a mold allergy? Did that mean she'd procured the copy of *The Big Sleep* on her own? That's why neither Fletcher nor I remembered wrapping it. Although she had insisted earlier that she didn't remember giving him a book. Was that a lie?

Dr. Caldwell answered my question before I'd had a chance to formulate a complete thought. "George's medical records document a long-standing and severe allergy to mold."

"I did not see that coming." Pri shook her head in disgust. "So, Aaliyah knew about his allergy and used that knowledge to kill him. That's dark."

"The killer used that knowledge to their advantage," Dr. Caldwell replied pointedly.

"How would someone go about acquiring mold spores?" Liam asked.

I was glad he asked. "I've read about this. It was in one of my old textbooks. I've been reviewing them to prepare for my private detective exam. They likely found an item already infected with mold. Perhaps old food, damp clothing, or some sort of decaying organic matter. They would simply need to scrape the mold spores from, let's say, a discarded block of cheese hiding in the fridge. It would be easy enough to scrape off the mold from the surface of the cheese with a sterile knife. Once collected, they could be stored in an air-tight container to keep them dry and ready for use."

"That is diabolic," Pri exclaimed. "Someone grew mold spores and used them to kill George? That must mean they knew about his allergy, right?"

"Assuming my theory is right. Whoever killed him put plenty of thought into this," I said aloud, glancing at Dr. Caldwell. We already knew as much, but this confirmed there was no chance George's murder had been a spontaneous or rash act of violence.

"True. Well done, as always, Annie. I suspect you are more than prepared for your exam." Dr. Caldwell adjusted her glasses. "We've explored other possibilities, such as the killer could have grown mold spores. It's not complicated to create a mold-friendly environment. They would need to seal a damp piece of bread or fruit in a plastic bag and wait for the mold to develop. Additionally, they could have purchased spores online. There are scientific supply companies that sell to labs and education institutions. They're highly regulated, though, so unless our suspect has a connection in the scientific world, I believe that to be the least likely scenario. I'm in agreement with you, Annie. I think it's much more likely that the killer found a simple way to get the spores to bloom in their own home."

"Mold," Pri muttered. "I can't believe it's something as basic as mold. You're right. We have strict protocols in the commercial kitchen to ensure mold doesn't develop."

"Same." Liam nodded.

"I'm curious how the killer knew about his allergy," I said. "It doesn't seem like something that would come up in casual conversation. Not like bee stings or peanuts."

"Another reason we're confident the murder was premeditated." Dr. Caldwell's lips curled into a frown.

"You don't think it's Aaliyah?" Pri asked, stealing a glance at the matchmaker.

"We're waiting on further information." Dr. Caldwell surveyed the restaurant. Couples reviewed song lists, and the disco lighting near the karaoke stage flickered on in streaky flashes. "That's my cue to make my exit. I advise you to be extra cautious around Aaliyah and the other suspects. We haven't released the news about the mold spores, and I trust each of you will keep that in confidence."

I nodded solemnly, as did Pri, Liam, and Penny.

"I'll be in touch tomorrow." Dr. Caldwell left.

"Damn, Annie, I can't believe you put two and two together about mold spores." Pri pretended to bow down to me. "That's like straight out of the pages of an Agatha Christie novel or a film like *Knives Out*. I wouldn't have ever come to that conclusion."

"It helps that I've been refreshing my memory on my old coursework. Just a few weeks ago, I read about a case of an accidental death from mold. The lead detective and coroner couldn't figure out the cause at first—they knew it was an allergic reaction but couldn't find the root cause. The victim was an artist growing mold spores to create art pieces that explored living organisms as a medium. It turned out that the artist was allergic to mold and didn't know it. They inadvertently exposed themselves to the toxin in the process of creating their art."

"Note to self, don't experiment with making our own blue cheese at the restaurant." Liam shook his head, finished his beer, and stood up. "Can I talk you into a walk through the park, Annie?"

"Twist my arm." I reached out my arm. He helped me to my feet. I gave Penny and Pri hugs goodnight and promised to meet at Cryptic before the morning hike. Then I took the flower bouquet and Liam's gift.

Once Liam and I were outside, he pulled me toward his body and cinched a sturdy arm around my waist. "How are you doing? For real, Murray. Hit me with it. I can take it."

"I wasn't lying. I'm okay. I feel better knowing *how* George was killed. That's a breakthrough." Soft, pillowy, pink globe lights hung in storefronts. We passed Valentine's displays with boxes of chocolates and plush teddy bears. "I just wish I could figure out what I'm missing."

"There it is." Liam pulled me tighter as we neared the Pizzeria. I was tempted to peek inside and see if I could spot Victoria and Fletcher, but I resisted the urge.

We continued past the Italian eatery. Liam squeezed my hand. "I can tell when you're in your head."

I tilted my head at him. "Am I? Sorry." I knew he was right.

"It's not a bad thing. It's adorable, almost like I see your brain cells firing at a breakneck pace."

"I have so much on my mind it's like my brain is working overtime to try and keep up. I desperately want to be able to focus on the letter from Natalie and how it ties into Scarlet's case. I can't stop thinking about who might have left it. They vanished. I went outside right after Fletcher gave me the envelope and there was no sign of anyone. And now I'm paranoid that the crows are watching me—I mean, not in a bad way—but like there's something ominous bubbling under the surface that I'm missing." Everything came tumbling out like an avalanche of stones, crashing down uncontrollably. I wasn't even sure I was aware of how much I'd been holding in. "Elspeth is in my head. How did she know everything she nailed about me? How did she predict George's murder? Is she really psychic? I'm struggling to come up with an explanation for any of it. Even the crows. How did they know and why were they watching over me?"

"Breathe." Liam inhaled deeply, filling his chest with air. Then he held his breath for a moment and released it. "This is good. Let it all out and keep breathing."

"There's so much occupying my mind—George's murder, salvaging the rest of the event, Scarlet, Natalie, studying for my private eye exam, getting serious about the next steps for Novel Detectives. You. Us—" I ran out of steam.

Liam pulled me to his chest and kissed the top of my head. "Does that feel better?"

I stopped and looked up at him. "Yeah. Actually. Yeah, it does. Thanks. I guess I needed to get that off my chest."

"Not to sound cliché, but it will all work out. I have faith in you."

I leaned into him as we crossed Cedar Avenue, leaving the village lights behind us. The park was deserted at this hour. Moonlight illuminated our path. Starlight danced on the waxy leaves of the magnolia and oak trees.

If it weren't for George's murder, this would be a perfect night. I hoped he was right. I needed answers. I needed closure.

"Thanks. I appreciate you letting me vent. I really do feel better. You're pretty great, once you get past that gruff history buff exterior," I teased, trying to lighten the mood.

"Gruff? Me? Never." A growl slipped into his voice. "What I recall is that this history buff promised you surprises, and surprises you shall have. How do you feel about a dinner redo tomorrow? My place? I'll cook."

"That sounds wonderful." Heat crept up my cheeks despite the chilly evening breeze. "What can I bring?"

"Yourself." He kissed the top of my head.

We walked in silence the rest of the way to my cottage. I appreciated Liam giving me space. He knew I was stuck in a loop about George and everything vying for attention in my head, but he didn't push it or try to solve it for me.

At my front porch, we paused and enjoyed a leisurely kiss. His touch was soft and tender, searching yet patient. I considered inviting him in, but I had to sleep. The hike was set for nine in the morning. It was going to be another early start.

"Thanks for tonight." I stood on my toes to give him one final kiss.

"Try to give that brain of yours a rest, okay?" He massaged my neck and leaned in to kiss my cheek.

He waited until I was safely inside.

From the window I watched him turn and stroll down the cul-de-sac. Professor Plum latched on my ankles, informing me with his insistent meows that it was long past time for bed. I put the flowers in water, made a cup of tea, put on my favorite soft flannel pajamas, and crawled under the covers.

I propped a pillow behind my head and zoomed in on the photos I'd taken of Aaliyah's spreadsheets. I appreciated her eye for detail. The spreadsheets included everything from participants' favorite desserts to their pastimes, whether or not they have pets, and which side of the bed they prefer to sleep on.

Maybe the minutiae of information was what made her matches successful.

I got a better glimpse of her process by reading through why she opted not to pair particular people and her notes on couples she pegged from the start as being good matches.

I sipped my tea.

If only there were a clear sign. Something unmistakable.

What had George demanded to be changed?

I reviewed the couples. Most of the names were familiar to me. Redwood Grove regulars. Frequent Secret Bookcase customers. Locals, community members, and a handful of out-of-town visitors, but no one with a blatant past or a glaring criminal record.

Aaliyah had done her due diligence on that front. Every participant agreed to a basic background check. It was a smart move from a business perspective. It would be a bad look if she connected a couple only for them to realize that one of them had recently done a stint in the county jail or was on probation.

I sighed as I made it to the last page.

At the very bottom, there were three names highlighted— Linx, Victoria, and Gertrude— along with a note that read Do Not Match.

Was this it?

Did George refuse to let Aaliyah match one of these women? If so, which one of them and why?

# TWENTY-NINE

I finished my tea, considering each of the women. Linx never intended to participate in the matchmaking, at least not as far as I'd heard. She was there purely to help serve refreshments. Victoria was upfront about pulling out when she met Fletcher. What about Gertrude? If I thought about it, I was unclear whether she ever intended to be part of the event. On opening night, she'd been in attendance but taken off quickly when George reminded her of her long-lost love. Then she had shown up but then offered to help wrangle our little readers for story time.

What could have prompted George to ask to have one of these women removed from the match list? Or was I reading too much into it? Maybe Aaliyah had crossed off the names herself.

I turned off the lights and pulled the covers tight as Professor Plum nestled into the crook of my legs. It could wait until tomorrow. I needed sleep. Hopefully, with fresh eyes in the morning, something would come to light.

It must not have taken me long to doze off because the next thing I knew, patchy sunlight tumbled into my bedroom. I stretched and prepped for the hike, dressing in long pants, layered tops, and hiking boots.

After feeding Professor Plum and munching a cranberry orange scone home-baked by my neighbor, I headed for the bookstore. Jekyll and Hyde were waiting for me at the gate. They bobbed their feathered heads, cawing a greeting as they escorted me up the drive, circling high above and greeting the morning with their version of bird song. A thin marine layer hovered in the air like a fog. Hopefully it would burn off in time for our hike.

I did a quick walk-through of the store, turning on lights and making sure everything was ready for the day. In the Study, I found a pair of reading glasses left behind by a customer. I took them to the front to add to the lost and found.

A shiny gold object caught my eye as I set the glasses in the drawer.

*The ring.*

*Oh my God, the ring.*

I picked it up and held it to the light.

I'd seen a ring just like this around Gertrude's neck.

*Exactly like this ring.*

My breath stopped momentarily as I scrunched my eyes to see whether there was an inscription.

There was.

I reached for my phone and used the magnifying app to read the message.

To W, With Love, G

To Walter, with love, Gertrude.

This ring must belong to her fiancé.

*Her fiancé.*

*That's it.*

I dropped the ring and paced from one side of the counter to the other. Images and snippets of conversations flooded my mind. Gertrude's reaction to seeing George, the wedding ring she wore like a talisman around her neck, George forcing Aaliyah to change the spreadsheet.

It all suddenly made sense.

George must be Gertrude's long-lost lover, Walter. Had he lied to her? She mentioned he died in a car accident coming home from his bachelor party. But what if he didn't? What if he'd been alive and well for decades?

My mind swam with possibilities—what if he got cold feet and faked his death?

That would explain his guilt and need to make amends.

And as far as Gertrude was concerned, part of me couldn't blame her. If I had grieved a love for my entire adult life and he showed up alive and well, I might want to murder him, too.

The mold.

Gertrude would have known about his allergy.

It was like I was stacking a block tower, and everything was slotting into place.

I couldn't control the buzzing in my body. I had to move. I had to get out of here and go find Gertrude.

I called Dr. Caldwell. "Sorry to call you so early, but I think I figured it out."

She sounded alert and awake. "No problem. I just finished my morning Qigong and was about to pour a cup of coffee. I'm all ears."

I could barely understand myself as the words spilled out of me. My palms turned sweaty, and my voice was breathless like I couldn't suck in the air fast enough to match the pace of everything I wanted to tell Dr. Caldwell.

"This is good, Annie. Serious detective work, but I'm afraid we're going to need proof."

"What about the mold? Could you get a warrant to search her condo?"

"Yes, but it will take a while."

We didn't have a while.

We didn't have a minute to spare.

Thus far Gertrude had no idea that we knew George's true identity. There could be evidence inside her house—old photos, letters, who knew what else?

"I have an idea," I said to Dr. Caldwell. "What if I drop by her house? I can come up with a story that a new book came in, and I wanted to get it to her. I can at least take a look around."

"A look around? And then what?"

"Maybe she'll open up to me."

"It's a possibility. I need to get to the station. I'll have to check the archives. We didn't get a hit on George's current record, but if he had a criminal past under a different name, we might be able to access it in the archives."

"How do you feel about me dropping by Gertrude's?" I would respect her wishes if she told me not to go, but I desperately wanted to speak with Gertrude.

"I like the idea. Use discretion."

"I will," I promised, feeling a rush of adrenaline pulsing through me.

We hung up, and I left a note for Fletcher and Hal, letting them know I had a quick errand to run and would be back before the meetup at Cryptic. Gertrude was a fan of British cozies, and fortuitously, a new shipment had arrived from one of our UK publishers a few days ago that I hadn't had a chance to unpack and add to inventory yet. I hurried upstairs to grab a copy of her favorite series and locked the bookshop on my way out.

The marine layer still lingered heavy in the sky, veiling the sun in a hazy shroud. I rubbed my arms as my feet crunched along the gravel driveway. Everything felt thick, with a cool, almost foreboding chill.

Gertrude's condo complex was located near the library, but I didn't need to go that far.

I slowed my pace as I raced past the Stag Head and neared

Cryptic. The village square was deserted at this early hour, except for one recognizable person—Gertrude.

She was dressed in a bathrobe and slippers and walking in wobbly circles in front of the coffee shop. Her hair was tied with curlers, and her eyes were glassy, like she was in another world.

She must be freezing.

"Gertrude, are you okay?" I approached her carefully, not wanting to spook her.

She looked past me, unable to focus.

"Gertrude, it's Annie," I said, stepping closer.

Her eyes were like two slits, barely allowing any light in. She rocked from side to side as if swaying to music I couldn't hear.

"I brought you a book." I offered up the cozy as a way to try to bring her back to reality. I recognized the signs of disassociation. "We can go inside, warm up, and get you something hot to drink."

She didn't respond. Instead, she continued to stare past me, down Cedar Avenue, toward the bookstore.

"Gertrude, let me take you inside," I repeated, reaching for her arm.

She snapped it away, clutching it to her chest. "No. I can't go in there. I can't go anywhere. You don't realize what I've done. I've done something terrible." She rocked on her heels as she spoke, dragging her attention to her fuzzy slippers.

"I know about Walter," I said, pressing my lips together and bending my neck to try and meet her eyes.

"You know?" Her mouth hung wide, like a baby bird waiting to be fed. She looked at me with a combination of shock and relief. "You know about my Walter?"

"I do. I figured it out." I pointed to the coffee shop. "Can we talk inside? I'm worried about you. It's cold out here."

"Is it? I didn't notice."

"Let's go sit down." I didn't take no for an answer this

time. I gently reached for the sleeve of her thin bathrobe and led her to the door. A wave of warmth hit me as I ushered her inside the industrial coffee shop with its exposed beam ceilings and epoxy floors. Plants hung from the rafters and lined the walls. It smelled like freshly brewed coffee and banana bread.

The space was sparsely populated, except for a young couple waiting at the end of the espresso drinks. Otherwise the coffee shop was thankfully empty. "Here's a good spot." I helped her to a table in the far corner of the converted garage, surrounded by funky artwork and photos.

She moved in slow motion like she was sleepwalking.

I held out the chair for her and waited for her to sit. "I'll get a warm drink. Stay here."

Gorgeous pastries in the glass cases tempted me—frangipane tarts, apple strudel, and double chocolate muffins. Coffee stickers, temporary tattoos, potted succulents, and reusable mugs were for sale, along with bags of Cryptic's house-roasted coffee beans. Pri was behind the bar, and Linx worked the espresso machine. "Can you make a hot chocolate, extra hot? And call Dr. Caldwell and let her know I'm here with *Gertrude*?" I asked Pri, emphasizing the name and nodding my head in Gertrude's direction.

"Gertrude. It's Gertrude?" Pri shot a glance that way. "Linx just mentioned seeing someone in a bathrobe outside. I was about to go check it out and call the police when you showed up. Is she the killer? You think she did it?"

"I think so." I kept an eye on Gertrude, not wanting her to bolt. "Dr. Caldwell is in the loop, but just let her know we're here and she needs to come. I'll explain everything later."

"Got it." Pri shooed me away. "I'll bring the drinks. You do what you do."

I returned to the table, keeping my tone bright. I didn't want to give Gertrude any indication that I'd alerted the police.

"Okay, hot cocoa is on the way. Hopefully, it will warm you up."

Gertrude tore a napkin into tiny shreds. "It doesn't matter. I don't deserve to be warm. I don't deserve to be alive. I've done a terrible thing."

"Do you want to talk about it?" I tried to keep my voice even and calm. "It must have been a shock to see Walter again after thinking he was dead for all these years."

She tore a strip of the napkin in half and dropped it on the table. Her eyes sharpened as she looked up at me. "What are you talking about? Seeing Walter?"

"Walter. George Richards was really Walter, your fiancé, who supposedly died, right? We found his ring. I have it in the bookshop. I realized it this morning when I saw the inscription."

She used both her hands to gather the napkin pieces into a pile. "You have Walter's ring? Where did you find it?"

"The crows. Our crows—Jekyll and Hyde. Fletcher feeds them peanuts, and they leave him trinkets in exchange. They must have found it outside somewhere."

"I need that ring. It's the only thing I have left of him." Tears spilled down her cheeks.

"I can get it to you." My heart broke for her. She was clearly distraught. Not that I condoned murder, but I could empathize with the pain and shock she must have felt seeing him alive. "Maybe you lost it when you and Walter were fighting in the garden?"

"Why do you keep saying 'Walter'?" She brushed away a tear and squinted at me.

"George was Walter, wasn't he?"

She gaped at me as she fiddled with one of her curlers. "Where did you come up with that theory? Walter is dead. He's been dead for decades because of one person and one person alone—George Richards. George killed my beloved Walter. So I returned the favor."

# THIRTY

It was my turn to react in shock. "Wait, George killed Walter? I thought you said he was killed by a drunk driver."

Gertrude twisted her curler tighter as if she were turning a vice. "Yes. George was the driver. He and Walter were best friends. That's what he said, but he wasn't a friend. He murdered my Walter and has lived a full, wonderful life while ruining mine and cutting Walter's way too short."

This was a twist I hadn't seen coming.

Pri interrupted us by slipping a steaming hot cocoa with a mound of whipping cream and pink sprinkle hearts on top in front of Gertrude and a raspberry mocha in front of me. She backed away from the table but put her hand to her ear to signal me she'd called Dr. Caldwell.

"I'm mistaken, sorry. I assumed George was Walter from your reaction to seeing him the other night and then finding the ring."

Gertrude ignored the drink and cinched a curler tighter. It was like she was trying to inflict pain. "That's because I recognized him immediately. George Richards. I would know him anywhere."

"Can you start from the beginning?" I cradled my mug. Even in the short time we'd been outside, my fingers had started to go numb. I couldn't believe Gertrude wasn't close to hypothermia in her flimsy bathrobe and slippers.

"George arranged the stag party that night. They went drinking at a few different bars in town. This was in Silicon Valley, but before it was the Silicon Valley we know today. Cupertino was a sleepy bedroom town, mainly orchards and small family farms. Walter had a convertible. He drove too fast. I warned him he was going to get in an accident. It was like I knew intuitively. They drank too much and drove home. The car flipped. Walter was tossed out and killed on impact, but George survived with barely a few scrapes and bruises." Her voice was distant and dreamy, almost like she was back in time.

I took a drink of the coffee.

I was confused as to how that translated to killing Walter. Did she blame George?

She continued in a trance, almost like I was in the room with her. "I've always thought there was something odd about that night. Something that George wasn't telling me. He said Walter insisted on driving, but that wasn't like Walter. He wouldn't have gotten behind the wheel if he were drunk. I never believed it, but I never had proof, not until a couple of days ago. George didn't keep in touch. He started his company and moved on. How lucky for him. It must have been nice."

She paused and sighed, looking up at the mustard yellow and teal industrial lights.

"Do you believe George was the one driving that night?" I asked, hoping to keep her talking until Dr. Caldwell arrived.

"Yeah. He confessed everything to me at the bookstore the other night. He told me he swapped seats before the police arrived. He was driving. He flipped the car and killed Walter, but he let Walter take the blame. He had the audacity to ask me to absolve him of his crime. He claimed he'd lived with guilt, that his guilt had prompted him to donate to charities and be benevolent with his funds. He wanted me, *me*, to free him of the burden of killing Walter. Oh, I freed him. Yes, I did."

"You were aware of his mold allergy?" I dipped my pinkie into the foam on my drink.

"Everyone who knew him back in those days was aware. He'd had an issue eating a moldy piece of bread. His throat swelled, and he had to be taken to the emergency room. After that he was always very careful with anything he ate—inspecting it to make sure there was no trace of mold."

"How did you do it?" I asked, savoring the creamy mocha with bright, tangy notes of raspberry. It was warming me up. I wondered how long it would take for Dr. Caldwell to arrive. I couldn't let Gertrude leave until the police showed up.

"A moldy piece of cheese." She almost smiled. "It was easy. I scraped it off with a butter knife, put it in a plastic bag, and coated the pages of the book with the mold. I told George I would meet him in the garden to give him a gift. *The Big Sleep* was Walter's favorite book. He had Walter's ring. That was another lie. The authorities never found Walter's ring because George kept it. He found it near Walter's body and stuffed it in his pocket. He was worried they would figure out he was lying. I don't understand why, but he gave me the ring. I accidentally dropped it when I watched him start to stumble, but I couldn't look for it because I couldn't be seen near him."

Everything about Gertrude's story was tragic. Walter's death, George lying about being the driver and spending the remainder of his days trying to right that wrong, and now Gertrude herself stooping to murder.

It seemed so senseless and unnecessary.

Dr. Caldwell arrived with a team of officers before I could say more. She took over immediately. I listened while Gertrude repeated everything she'd confessed to me. She drifted between states of deep remorse and bitter rage at George.

Once Dr. Caldwell accepted her statement and read Gertrude her rights, one of her police officers escorted her out of Cryptic. It was good timing because couples began arriving for coffee and pastries before we set out on our morning hike.

"Excellent work, Annie," Dr. Caldwell said to me.

"I got it partially right. I'm not sure if I feel better or worse about the real story. It's all sad." I felt terrible for Gertrude. She'd lived with so much pain, as had George. If only they could have connected sooner and let some of the past go.

"It is." She patted my sleeve. "Take some time today if you need it. A case like this can get under your skin."

"Thanks." I smiled. "The hike sounds good, and speaking of cases getting under your skin, I'd love to carve out some time to get together to discuss Scarlet's case once you're done with Gertrude's arrest and subsequent paperwork. I had a chance to review the documents Natalie sent, and everything appears to be pointing to Logan Ashford, the CEO of Silicon Summit Partners."

Dr. Caldwell nodded a hello to a group who passed our table to get in line. Business was perking up. "Is there tangible proof that will hold up in a court of law?"

"I don't think so, but that's why I want your input and for you to go over everything, too."

"I'll be eager to review them." Dr. Caldwell tapped her watch. "I'll reach out once we're done."

I watched the police car pull away from the curb with Gertrude in the back seat. She looked frail and helpless.

While I was glad that we'd solved George's murder, I wished there could have been a different outcome. Gertrude had suffered for too long and now would live out her remaining days behind bars.

Revenge was never the answer.

It made me think about Scarlet. If Logan Ashford had killed

her, I intended to do everything in my power to bring him to justice—but through the proper channels.

## THIRTY-ONE

Pri waited impatiently for details. I tried to fill her in while she rang up orders, steamed milk, and poured espresso shots. I texted Hal and Fletcher to let them know.

> Go on the hike. Hal and I have things under control, and Victoria agreed to jump in if we need an extra set of hands.

I smiled, grateful to have been wrong about my first impression of Victoria and glad that Fletcher had made a match on his own.

The shop buzzed with excitement. Music played on the speakers overhead. People enjoyed savory egg and sausage breakfast sandwiches and oat milk lattes. Pri opened the roll-up garage doors, making more space for people to drift outside to the patio where there were extra tables, chairs, and cozy firepits.

Aaliyah arrived with a new set of instructions for everyone.

Linx leaned on the counter while I listened in on Aaliyah's plan for the day. "I can't believe the sweet, little old lady did it. I never saw that coming."

"Neither did I."

"I was worried you thought I did it. You were so intimidating with your questions. Pri's right, you should be a detective."

"I'm working on it." I chuckled. "What about you? Are you planning to stay for a while?"

She crossed her fingers and glanced at Pri. "As long as I get hired for a permanent position. I promised Pri, no more late nights and band mosh pits. Could you put in a good word for me?"

"I will, but I don't think you need it. I think you've impressed her with your skills, short of the hangover, of course."

Aaliyah caught my eye and waved me toward her. This morning, she was dressed ready to hike in khakis, boots, a Valentine's red thin sweater, and a pink vest.

"I think I'm needed elsewhere," I said to Linx. "Good luck with the job pitch. Keep making coffee like this, and you're solid." I toasted her with my half-empty mug.

"Annie, excellent. Could you give everyone a brief lay of the land in terms of the trail?" Aaliyah asked.

"Sure." I set my coffee on a high-top table and explained that the hike originated from the Secret Bookcase gardens and would wind up into the nearby hills. "We'll take the ditch-creek loop up to the old Wentworth mill. It's about a four-mile hike with just under a thousand feet of elevation gain, so you'll want to be sure to bring water. There's plenty of shade with the redwood trees, and once we get to the top, we'll have stunning views of the Pacific Ocean."

"This will be a perfect opportunity for you to support your partners," Aaliyah continued. "We learn new things about each other when we're tasked with trekking up a cliffside. I'll be eager to observe and hear how this challenge brings you closer."

"Or breaks us up," someone in the back of the room joked.

"Hopefully not. Remember, in partnership, our goal is for both people to succeed." She went over a few more specifics.

When she was done, she turned to me. "Annie, I hear there's been an arrest."

"Yes, it was Gertrude." I gave her a very brief overview. It was still hard for me to process that sweet Gertrude was the mastermind behind George's murder.

Aaliyah rubbed her temples. "I told you, he was distraught about his past mistakes. I feel responsible. Maybe there was something I could have done."

"You had no way of knowing. I only figured out the connection this morning, and even then, my theory wasn't correct."

"The George I knew certainly atoned for his sins." She placed her hand on her chest. "May he rest in peace now."

"Yes, the upside of this morning is that at least we have closure."

She bent down to check the laces on her hiking boots. "Would you mind being the sweeper at the back? I don't want to lose any stragglers."

"Sure."

It took another twenty minutes to get everyone moving. The sun had broken through the cloud cover, highlighting Redwood Grove's charm as we walked along the gravel drive past the Secret Bookcase and toward the trail. Gone was the earlier chill. Maybe the cold had been heightened by my quest to find Gertrude and finally have the many questions about George's murder that had been occupying my head answered.

Knowing that Dr. Caldwell had Gertrude in custody gave me a sense of relief I hadn't felt in days. For some reason, Jekyll and Hyde must not have picked up on the newfound spring in my step. The pair of crows swooped overhead, their dark wings slicing through the air as they cut above me. Their caws rang out sharp and insistent, like an eerie warning that they sensed danger was still lurking, one I hadn't escaped yet.

"I'm fine, you two. It's all good." I waved to them as I encouraged the hiking couples to go in front of me, but the familiar feeling that something was off returned. The briefest flash of fear sent a chill rippling through me. Could they see beyond my outer cheer, tapping into a darker truth I wasn't ready to face?

I shrugged off my anxiety.

Was there such a thing as being too in tune with the crows?

I got lost in my thoughts as I traipsed through the garden and onto the narrow trail through the forest. The investigation into George's death had had some unexpected twists and turns, just like the trail, but overall, I felt satisfied with my performance. I had effectively conducted suspect profiling, systematically ruled out alternatives, and pursued leads with determination. I uncovered the murder method and, through strategic questioning, ultimately secured Gertrude's full confession. It was a solid demonstration of my investigative skills—one that boded well for the future of Novel Detectives.

To start the hike, we passed under a trellis with climbing roses, quickly leaving the manicured gardens of the Secret Bookcase and Jekyll and Hyde behind.

The path gently ascended. Towering trees rose on both sides, creating a shady canopy.

Everything smelled of pine needles and bay leaves.

Sunlight filtered through the leaves in patches, casting an ethereal light on the forest floor.

The mood was slightly more subdued. It could have been because we were in nature, or it could have been because news of Gertrude's arrest had spread, and everyone felt conflicted. The sound of rustling leaves, the occasional birdcall, and couples chatting quietly were the soundtrack for the first mile.

I still found myself turning over the case in my mind. At least I had a clearer picture of each of the suspects. Victoria, Linx, and Aaliyah had been telling the truth about their relationships with George.

But I still had questions about Elspeth. Had it been a lucky guess? Maybe she always claimed that someone near her had dark energy as a strategy to gain clients. Scare people into using her services. But that didn't explain her warning about me and the bookstore or her connection to George. Unless she was an astute researcher. As we had discussed last night, that possibility seemed the most viable—she figured out her "target's" weak points to take advantage of their emotional instability. It wasn't out of the realm of possibility that she'd done her research on me and learned about Scarlet's tragedy in hopes of securing me as a client.

I'd seen her from the other side of the room at Cryptic. She was at the front of the pack. When we got to the summit, I would try to pull her aside and see if I could get some answers.

As I climbed higher, the scent of the ocean mixed in with the earthy aroma of the woods. The hike was strenuous. It got my blood pumping and my heart rate thumping. It felt good to sweat and exert myself. It was like moving all the stagnant—or, to borrow a word from Elspeth—dark energy from my body.

Nature was my happy place. My healing place.

I breathed deeply, inhaling the smells of moss and sea salt.

We passed old, abandoned sheds and followed the creek bed gushing with water from a recent storm.

Being at the back of the pack was exactly what I needed.

I let my mind shut off and sank into the present moment, guided by the sound of ground squirrels scrambling up trees and the gurgle of the creek.

The trees finally began to thin, and the trail widened, revealing glimpses of the brilliant blue sky.

By the time we reached the top, I had torn off my outer layers and was damp with sweat. I emerged onto a cliffside path where the redwoods gave way to an awe-inspiring view of the Pacific Ocean. Below, waves crashed against the rugged shoreline in a dazzling show of turquoise and aquamarine. Standing near the edge, I could feel the breeze, cool and refreshing against my hot skin.

Couples posed near the ledge to take photos, and others collapsed happily on sun-drenched rocks to rehydrate and catch their breath.

Aaliyah gave everyone time to enjoy the view and rehash the experience before turning around and making our descent.

I waited for the last two couples before tying my hoodie around my waist and taking a long sip of water.

Elspeth hung back, too.

"I was hoping I might see you," I said, walking to the edge of the trail to snap a couple of pictures for Liam. We had hiked this loop in December when the trail was thick with mud, and heavy rain clouds had obscured any peek at the Pacific Ocean. "I'm sure you heard about Gertrude."

"I did. I told the police I sensed unstable energy in her aura. I couldn't read her at all, which is usually a bad sign."

"How did you predict George was going to die?" I took out my phone and adjusted the settings in my camera app.

Her eyes darkened as she clenched her jaw and stepped toward me. "You don't get it, do you? I have a gift."

Obviously, I'd made her angry.

Had we made a mistake?

Was the wrong person behind bars?

But Gertrude had confessed.

"You had no idea about George's past?" I asked, firming my footing. I was precariously close to the edge and didn't like Elspeth's menacing stance.

"I didn't need to know about George's past or current situation to see that he had no future. His aura screamed death."

Her tone was almost manic, wild and unhinged.

We were alone at the summit.

Everyone else was a good quarter mile down the trail by now.

"If you were wise, you would listen to me, but you won't. You'll keep digging. You'll keep searching. You'll keep looking. You won't stop until you've uncovered the truth, you little idiot." Spit spewed from her lips as she yelled and took another step toward me.

"I'll listen. I don't know what you want me to do about the warning. Gertrude has been arrested. George's murder is solved. I'm done looking." I flexed my muscles and tried to assess an escape route. Elspeth was blocking my path. I couldn't go backward—that would send me over the ledge, but I could probably take her in a fight. She wasn't much bigger than me, but every muscle in her body was seething with rage. That didn't bode well.

"This isn't about George," she sputtered. "This is about Scarlet."

"Scarlet?" I recoiled.

How did she know about Scarlet?

Had she dug into my past?

Or was she connected somehow?

"You couldn't drop it. You couldn't leave it alone. I'm left with no other options." She enunciated each of her words with precision.

My head began to spin. My hands felt tingly, and tiny spots flashed across my vision.

*Scarlet.*

*What was the connection?*

It didn't make sense.

While I tried to regain my focus, Elspeth swept forward and pushed me with such force it knocked me off my feet.

"This is from Logan Ashford," she whispered as I lost my footing and tumbled off the cliff.

# THIRTY-TWO

Everything happened so fast. It felt like a scene from a bad movie. I fell backward. The drop-off was steep—at least twenty or thirty feet to the ledge below.

*This is it. This is how you die, Annie.*

Visions and memories flashed through my head as my body flailed.

I might have screamed. I couldn't be sure.

At the very last second, I lunged for a branch jutting out from the side of the cliff and caught it with my right hand. The rough, jagged bark sliced my palm, but I clung to it with desperation like superglue.

I dangled in the air, my legs swinging and my mind desperate to figure out how I was going to get back up.

"Help!"

Screaming was probably futile. The rest of the party was likely out of earshot by now, but it was my only chance.

"Help! Someone, help!"

Would anyone notice I was gone?

How long could I hang from the branch? How long would it hold before it snapped and sent me tumbling?

Blood trickled down my wrist.

*Stop swinging your legs, Annie.*

The momentum was making it worse.

I had to stay in control.

My phone was in my pocket.

Should I risk using my free hand to try and get it?

*No, that's not a smart move.*

I could easily slip.

Sweat poured down my neck as more blood dripped from my hand.

*This is bad.*

*It's getting slippery.*

*Hold on, Annie!*

A firmer voice took control.

*Scream.*

*Keep screaming!*

I mustered all my lung capacity and yelled, "Help! Someone, help!"

Was there any way I could claw my way up to the top of the ledge? If I used both my hands on the branch for leverage, I might be able to kick one leg over the side. This is when being short was highly problematic. I wasn't sure my foot could reach.

Plus, there was the issue of using both hands, which might make the branch snap off completely.

My mouth went dry. I couldn't swallow.

*Don't panic, Annie.*

"Help!" I hollered, feeling exhaustion starting to sink in as my arm quivered.

I didn't have much time.

I couldn't just hang here.

I was going to have to make a move—try to get my phone or try to climb to the top.

Climbing won out.

I counted down—one—two—three.

A shadow appeared above me as I was about to clasp my hand on the branch.

"Help! I'm down here!"

Aaliyah leaned over the edge. "Annie? What are you doing?"

"I fell. Can you pull me up?"

She didn't hesitate. She lay on the ground, using one hand as an anchor on the edge of the cliff, and reached her other arm toward me.

Her grasp was solid and firm.

"I've got you. Hold on." She yanked me up.

I clasped her arm as hard as possible and swung my feet onto the cliff face.

She pulled while I got traction with my boots.

It worked.

I collapsed on the ground next to her, saying an internal thanks to the universe.

"Annie, what happened?" She sat up and observed me with concern. "You're covered in blood."

I took a second to steady my breathing before sitting up and assessing my hand. "It's not bad. I split my palm open on that gnarly branch, but I will not complain because that branch saved my life."

"How did you fall?" She reached for her backpack, unzipped it, and handed me an antiseptic wipe.

"Elspeth. Did you see her?" The stringent wipe stung as I dabbed it on my cut and peeled pine needles from my bruised skin.

"The psychic? No? Where is she?" Aaliyah glanced around like she expected to see Elspeth sunbathing on one of the large boulders.

"She pushed me and took off. You didn't see her coming up the trail?" I pressed the wipe into my palm to try and stop the bleeding.

"Why would she push you?" Aaliyah took out bandages and Vaseline.

"I don't know," I lied. I didn't have time to rehash everything. We needed to call the police and find Elspeth immediately. "She must have taken off in the other direction. Otherwise, you would have bumped into her while coming up the trail. Come to think of it, why did you return to the summit? Did you hear me screaming?"

"You should wrap that, so it doesn't get infected." She offered me the bandages. "One of the couples forgot their binoculars. I offered to get them because I was already in the back. I didn't hear any screaming until right before I found you."

She helped me secure the bandage and then get to my feet. "Are you okay to walk down? Should we call the police? An ambulance?"

I was grateful for her concern and attention. "I'm okay. I'll call Dr. Caldwell, but I doubt we have service up here."

My phone confirmed that we didn't. Most of the trail systems in Northern California weren't connected to Wi-Fi. I wasn't going to chase Elspeth alone, so our best bet was to trek back to the bookstore as quickly as possible. As soon as we were in cell range, I would call Dr. Caldwell and let her take it from here.

# THIRTY-THREE

We caught up with the rest of the group quickly. My heart was still thumping wildly, the adrenaline from nearly being killed refusing to loosen its hold. I was highly motivated to return to the village, so I passed everyone and sprinted the rest of the way. My mind worked faster than my feet as I flew past leafy ferns and moss-covered stones. I couldn't believe I'd missed Elspeth's connection to Silicon Summit Partners. It just goes to show I should have trusted my first instinct. The temperature dropped as the redwoods blocked out more of the sun.

Once the chimney and rooftop of the Secret Bookcase came into view, I yanked out my phone and called Dr. Caldwell, not breaking my pace.

"It's Annie," I gasped into the phone. "Elspeth tried to kill me. It's her. She's connected to Silicon Summit Partners. She said, 'This is from Logan Ashford' right before she pushed me off the cliff."

"Slow down, Annie." Dr. Caldwell had me repeat everything.

I explained that I was nearly back to the bookstore and I'd lost Elspeth on the trail.

"Okay, get to the store safely. My team and I will meet you there."

We hung up.

I blew through the last half mile of the trail as fast as my little legs could carry me. Relief flooded my body when the trail finally spilled out into the gardens.

Police lights lit up the entire driveway. It looked like every police car in the county was already on the scene.

Dr. Caldwell was true to her word.

I raced past neatly trimmed hedges and vibrant flower beds and collapsed on a bench on the Terrace.

Fletcher burst from the double glass doors, followed closely by Victoria and Hal. "Annie, are you okay? Dr. Caldwell called us."

He sat next to me while Hal and Victoria huddled.

"You're hurt," Hal noted, pointing at my hand.

"It's not bad," I assured him.

Jekyll and Hyde appeared as if conjured by magic, swooping down onto the Terrace out of thin air. Their claws gripped the railing, and they tilted their heads in perfect synchronicity, their eyes fixing on me with a curious glint. Their feathers ruffled as they bobbed their heads in unison in a gesture that felt like a relieved greeting, as if they were assessing me to make sure I was actually safe.

"I'm okay, thanks," I mouthed.

The sirens grew louder. I took a minute to catch my breath, knowing Dr. Caldwell would want the whole story once she arrived. There was no need to repeat it twice.

She raced to us with a half dozen uniformed officers ready to go. She didn't waste any time with pleasantries. "Give me a condensed version first so I can send the team out to find her."

I explained that Elspeth had pushed me off the summit and that was the last place I'd seen her. "She must have continued up the trail or is hiding out somewhere nearby because Aaliyah didn't see her, and there was no sign of her on the way down. You'll pass everyone on your way up."

That was enough for her to direct her team. They spread out in formation and headed for the trailhead. Elspeth had a head start and the vast network of trails connected with each other. She could be miles away by now.

After Dr. Caldwell was confident her officers were on the hunt, she sat beside me. "Okay, let's hash this out now. Give me all the details."

I told her exactly what Elspeth said word for word and relayed my every movement. "That's why she was in our office," I said, catching Fletcher's eye when I finished. "She wasn't looking for evidence that might have connected her to George's murder; she was looking for the documents Natalie sent or was maybe trying to figure out how much we know."

Fletcher raised a finger while Victoria looked on with admiration. "I can shed some additional light here. After Dr Caldwell rang, I looked online and found more information about our resident psychic." He handed me a stack of printouts—old news articles and social media posts about Elspeth. Except she went by a variety of names. Her appearance was different—sometimes she was blond and other times a deep redhead.

"You found all this?" I asked, leafing through his research and then passing it to Dr. Caldwell. "I'm impressed."

She tapped the stack. "This is so useful; some of this overlaps with similar information we've found. Elspeth has a long track record of scams and questionable business practices. She used the scam she did on George many times—claiming her victims are cursed or have a dark aura and then offering expensive 'removal services' such as cleansing rituals and charms. She preys on people grieving, claiming she can contact the dead and then using generic messages like 'they want you to be happy' or 'she wants you to know she's at peace.'" Dr. Caldwell scowled as she leafed through former complaints about Elspeth. "The list goes on and on—planting a shill to act like other clients and offering soulmate love charms. That may be, in fact, what she was intending to do this weekend, knowing she had a captive audience of people looking for love. Like you, we've been searching for a link with George, never imagining she had ties to Logan Ashford."

"His name didn't appear in anything I found," Fletcher said, sounding disappointed in himself.

"I'm sure that's intentional." Dr. Caldwell straightened the paperwork.

"This means Logan did it," I said with authority I finally felt. "It all adds up. Natalie, my meeting with Mark Vincent, the deal Logan inked with Scarlet to pay for her silence, and Elspeth showing up here. She must have realized we know too much, which is why she tried to kill me. From the beginning, I've felt like someone high up in the company had to be responsible. There's no one higher than the CEO. This proves it: Logan Ashford killed Scarlet."

Dr. Caldwell sighed. "I'm inclined to agree with you, Annie. There's one large issue. We don't have proof."

"What if Elspeth confesses?" Fletcher asked, voicing what I was wondering, too.

Hal spoke up for the first time. "Surely, attempting to kill our Annie is proof enough."

"It gives us what we need to arrest Elspeth," Dr. Caldwell agreed. "But unless she's willing to testify against Logan, we don't have enough to go on. Our first order of business is tracking down Elspeth. Once we have her in custody, we can offer a plea bargain in exchange for her naming Logan."

I inhaled slowly, letting my shoulders sag. My hand throbbed. Dried sweat stuck to my neck and cheeks. I wanted to go home and take a long, hot shower.

Victoria linked her arm through Fletcher's. "I'm so proud of you. Your research goes to show that Novel Detectives is going to be a smashing success."

He beamed. "The same goes for your bookmobile. We're going to get the Book Bus moving."

"Oh, on that note, we were able to confirm George signed the contract. Your funds should be greenlit." Dr. Caldwell addressed Victoria.

Victoria threw a hand over her mouth in disbelief. "Really? That's wonderful news. I had nearly given up hope."

"We need a touch of good news," Hal said, giving me a soft smile. Then he addressed Victoria. "Let me be the first to congratulate you. I know this was a project George was passionate about, and I'll be eager to support your endeavors."

"We have some ideas brewing, don't we?" She looked at Fletcher.

"Yes. Once the dust is settled, let's plan a brainstorming session here at the bookstore, but right now, I feel like, Annie, you should go home and rest. Liam's expecting you whenever you're feeling up to it—we only managed to stop him coming straight here on the promise you were okay and would head over to his place once you're feeling better. He's quite upset and worried—understandably."

I appreciated everyone's concern, and I wasn't about to put up a fight.

"I wouldn't turn down a shower and a cup of tea."

"Or a strong shot of whiskey," Hal said with a wink, trying to lighten the mood.

"That, too." I smiled; this time, I didn't need to force it. I was relieved that I was safe, and hopefully, Elspeth would be in police custody soon. "This is super random, but do you have any hobbies?" I asked Dr. Caldwell.

Her eyes twinkled as she looked at me quizzically. "That's an odd question."

"It came up last night, and I realized we've never discussed it."

A brief flash of amusement crossed her face. "Would you believe it if I told you I SUP on the weekends?"

"SUP?" Victoria asked.

"Stand-up paddleboard," Fletcher answered for her.

I could totally picture Dr. Caldwell cutting through the waters of one of the nearby lakes or reservoirs on a stand-up paddleboard. I was glad I asked because this tidbit made me even more impressed with her.

Dr. Caldwell gathered the papers from Fletcher. "Let's leave it there for now. I'll keep you abreast *when* we arrest Elspeth."

I had no doubt her team would be successful. I wanted them to find her not only because I was furious she had tried to kill me but, more importantly because she was the final link we needed to put Logan Ashford behind bars.

# THIRTY-FOUR

I spent more time than I'd like to admit in a scalding shower. When I finally dragged myself out of the steaming bathroom, my skin was red and happy, and my stress level dropped dramatically. I blew my hair dry, changed into a skirt and comfy sweater for my dinner with Liam later, and curled up on the couch with Professor Plum for some cozy afternoon reading.

I must have drifted off because the vibration of my phone rattling on the coffee table woke me. It was a text from Dr. Caldwell.

> Elspeth is in custody. More soon.

That was a huge relief.

What a day. It started with discovering George's killer and ended with the arrest of someone directly linked to Scarlet.

I knew Dr. Caldwell would press Elspeth for a confession. If she was smart, she would work with law enforcement and the prosecution. Hopefully, she wasn't a martyr willing to take the fall for Logan. It didn't matter because there was no chance he was getting away with Scarlet's murder. I was resolved and determined to spend however long it took to find proof.

I checked the clock. It was time to head to Liam's.

His Spanish-style bungalow was a few blocks off the main village square. As I wound through the park, I felt a new lightness in my step and eagerness to share everything that had happened with Liam. That was a good sign.

He greeted me at the door with a bundle of creamy pink and white roses. "Happy Valentine's Day. Thank God you're okay—come in and tell my what happened."

"For me? You already gave me flowers. But I won't turn down another bunch. Thanks." I stood on my toes to kiss him.

"You deserve flowers every day, Annie." He ushered me inside. A fire burned low in his arched fireplace. Two chairs had been pushed together in front of the fire, and a glass of chardonnay rested on the side table. "Your spot awaits."

"This is so romantic, and it smells incredible." I tried to peek into the kitchen, but he blocked my view.

"No, you sit. Have a sip of wine. I'll bring out the first course because I want to hear everything. The news around the village today has been nonstop. I know the basics about Gertrude and heard a rumor about Elspeth, but I want the real story."

I didn't protest. The earthy smell of the fire and the flickering candles on the mantel gave the room an ethereal glow.

Liam returned with a veggie and cheese plate arranged in the shape of a heart with dips and salami slices rolled to resemble roses.

"Wow, you've outdone yourself." I took in the room. It reflected the many things I'd come to appreciate about Liam—the mission-style furniture, the photography of Redwood Grove, and even the playlist he'd chosen, which was a mix of Coldplay and David Gray.

He gave me a sly smile. "This is just the first course. Pace yourself."

"I don't know; I'm starving after the day I've had."

He sat next to me and reached for my bandaged hand. "Are you okay? Tell me everything."

We sipped wine and watched the logs crackle as I relayed the unbelievable turn of events. This time it already felt more distant, like I was separating myself from the madness of it all.

He let out a low whistle when I was done. "Annie, I don't know what I would do if something happened to you."

I sucked in my cheeks, feeling the raw emotion in his tone. "I'm okay, I promise."

"But you could have died." He massaged my arm with his thumb and got quiet. He paused like he was deciding what to say. "Annie, there's something I have to tell you."

"Okay."

Was it bad?

Why was he suddenly so serious?

"Gertrude's story has me realizing this is long overdue. You've been patient with me, and it's not fair that I haven't been honest with you."

My stomach dropped.

Where was this going?

"It's about my past. It's, well..." He put his glass on the side table next to a stained-glass lamp and wrung his weathered hands like he was trying to work up the courage to say whatever he needed.

I gulped another sip of wine. I didn't like the sound of this or how he wouldn't meet my eyes.

"It's time you should know." He ran his finger along his eyebrow like he was soothing himself. "I was almost engaged once."

"You were?" I breathed a sigh of relief internally. I'd come up with much worse scenarios in my head. Liam having a life and a girlfriend or fiancée before me was something I could live with.

"I don't like to talk about it because it was a rough breakup. Really rough." He cleared his throat. "Her name was—is—Kristy. We met here in Redwood Grove and dated for four and a half years. I was ready to propose. I had the ring and everything when I found out she'd been cheating on me with my brother."

"Your brother?" I couldn't hide my shock. I reached out for his arm. "Oh, Liam, that's terrible. I didn't even know you had a brother. You never talk about your family."

He forced a smile as I massaged his hand. "That's because it's been too painful. I never talk about them because I don't have a relationship with them. You see, my mom was dying of cancer when Kristy and I broke up. Her dying wish was for me to mend things with my brother, but I couldn't. I was too angry. Too embarrassed. Too everything."

I nodded slowly, waiting for him to say more.

"She died two months later." His voice cracked. I squeezed his hand tighter. He cupped his hand over my mine and looked at me with misty eyes. "I haven't spoken to my brother since. He and Kristy moved to LA. I haven't had anything to do with them since."

"That's understandable." I rubbed his arm with my thumb.

He released his grasp on me and dropped my hand.

"What about your dad?"

"He and I never had much of a relationship. My mom was the glue, and when she died, there was nothing to keep us connected. He remarried and moved to Texas a few years ago. We call on holidays and birthdays, but that's the extent of it."

"Liam, that's awful. It's no wonder you closed yourself off. To lose your love, your brother, and your mom all at once. I can't imagine."

His eyes filled with actual tears. He didn't bother to blink or brush them away. Rather, he held my gaze with reverence and intensity, which made my breath catch in my throat. "Yeah, but because of you, I'm coming to realize my mom was right. It's time to let it go. It's time to forgive and move on. Hearing about Gertrude's bitterness and killing George. I don't want that to be me. And ever since we've been together, it feels like a distant memory. It's going to sound strange, but I'm almost grateful because everything that happened led me to you."

His voice caught.

I reached for his hand again.

He leaned closer so his face was only a few inches away from mine, and gently caressed my cheek. "Annie Murray, all that matters to me is that you're safe. And we're together. I love you."

My heart fluttered and skipped in an erratic pattern. I gulped in a quick breath. "I love you, too."

He cupped my face in his hands and kissed me tenderly. I never wanted this moment to end. Liam was right. Our heartbreak and trauma had cracked us open to each other. I wasn't sure what was next for us, but I knew without a shred of doubt that Liam would be by my side as I started my next adventures. There were so many things to look forward to—taking over the bookshop, Novel Detectives, bringing Logan to justice, and maybe, just maybe a next step with him.

## A LETTER FROM THE AUTHOR

My deepest gratitude to you for taking the time to read *A Victim at Valentine's*! I've always been a fan of love in all its forms, and I hope this story provided you with a lovely little escape. If you want to keep up on all the news about future books and bonus content, sign up for my newsletter!

www.stormpublishing.co/ellie-alexander

If you've fallen in love with Annie, Fletcher, Pri, Hal, and the entire crew at the Secret Bookcase, consider sharing a review so other readers can find their way to Redwood Grove!

Well, here we are at book five already. How did that happen, and how are there so many murders in sweet Redwood Grove? I guess it's really time for Annie and Fletcher to launch the Novel Detectives.

In all seriousness, I am grateful for your continued support of the series. It means the world to me to hear that you're enjoying the Secret Bookcase Mysteries and letting Annie and her bookish friends become part of your world.

I can't thank you enough for reading, not just my books, but reading anything and everything. I'm a firm believer that stories connect us, and I'm so happy we're connected!

Ellie Alexander

# KEEP IN TOUCH WITH THE AUTHOR

elliealexander.co

- facebook.com/elliealexanderauthor
- instagram.com/ellie_alexander
- tiktok.com/@elliealexanderauthor

## ACKNOWLEDGEMENTS

I could not write without my amazing brainstorming crew: Tish Bouvier, Lizzie Bailey, Kat Webb, Flo Cho, Jennifer Lewis, Lily Gill, Courtny Bradley, Mary Ann McCoy, and Ericka Turnbull. Writing is a solo endeavor, so it's wonderful to have friends and readers to share the pitfalls and successes along the way.

In addition to everyone above, I also need to extend my thanks for the character inspiration for this book to Kayla Sharee, Beth Cole, Sue Leis Smith, Jennifer Moriarity, Sharon Redgrave, Andrew Skubisz, and Jessica Slavik. It was so much fun to use your suggestions as the inspiration for the nefarious suspect lineup in the book. I can't wait to do it again.

Not to sound like a broken record, but wow, am I ever lucky to have such an incredible partnership with the team at Storm! Everyone who touches this book makes it better, from my editor, Vicky Blunden, to Elke Desanghere and Anna McKerrow, who create such stunning graphics. Alexandra Begley follows the book through every step of copyediting and production, and Oliver Rhodes for his incredible vision and ability to transform publishing in the digital age. I'm so thankful for all of your expertise and enthusiasm for the series.

Last but never least, thank you to my family. You make writing possible.

Made in United States
North Haven, CT
22 January 2025

64809743R00150